PRAISE FOR

HOW WILL I KNOW

"I was completely entranced by this delicious romp of a book."

—Patricia Wood, author of *Lottery*.

"A rollicking good time. *How Will I Know* has Florida echos of Hiaasen and Barry."

—Mandy Miller, author of the Grace Locke series

"Pure magic, a gem. Like finding your own treasure chest."

—Kelly Weaver, author of *Living Your Own Aloha*

How Will I Know

by Marc Renson

ISBN 979-8-88824-274-2

Published by

köehlerbooks™

3705 Shore Drive
Virginia Beach, VA 23455
800-435-4811
www.koehlerbooks.com

Andrea

HOW WILL I KNOW

Where guardian angels go, trouble follows...

Follow your dreams

MARC RENSON

Marc Renson

VIRGINIA BEACH
CAPE CHARLES

Dedicated to
Whitney Elizabeth Houston
and to all the lovers of tropical blue water and palm trees
who seek their solace down in the Florida Keys.
May you all find your own treasures.

CHAPTER 1

THE INSIDE OF Michael's car is sweltering even with all the windows down. It's summer's first hot and sticky day in New York City and his car has started bucking. The engine hesitates; something isn't right when Michael's foot presses down on the accelerator. He pleads with his car as if she could answer. "What's wrong, Gladys?" The motor doesn't react with its normal gusto. He decides to slow down as he continues driving up 5th Avenue. The air conditioner has been broken for almost two years. He's annoyed with this first heat wave and thinks, *Why is there never a breeze in this city?*

His messenger bag lays open on the passenger's seat with his resumes that have fallen out and scattered onto the floor. His shirt is damp from perspiration and sticking to his back. He pinches his shirt and pulls quickly on it, fanning himself. With his arm out the window, the heat coming from the pavement feels hotter than the air. Building after building slowly goes by; he's making every green light as pedestrians are walking parallel in the crosswalks. He slowly passes 38th Street, then 40th. Other cars are whizzing by him, honking their horns. One man screams out a window, "Get the fuck out of the way!"

Michael talks to himself as he's searching the address numbers on the buildings for his next possible place of employment. "Come on, where are you United Food Service?" His eyes glance at every building. The car makes another sudden buck as he looks at the big H logo on his steering wheel and pounds his sweaty palms against it, screaming, "Come on, Gladys!" He hits a pothole and the hula girl that's standing on his dash starts maniacally dancing. Her hips are shaking as she's doing the twist at the same time. He grabs her so she stops shaking. "Whoa chica. I don't want you to break a hip." He thinks the poor thing must be getting whiplash too.

The thermometer light on Gladys, his twelve-year-old silver slightly rusted Civic, *pings* and displays on his dashboard.

"Oh come on . . . Really? Not now, I really don't need this now," Michael begs to himself.

Annie Lennox's song, "Why," is coming through his speakers. He asks himself that same question, "Why, Annie, why?" as he turns the radio down. He makes it just past 48th Street as steam starts coming up from under his hood. Suddenly the sound of water starts hissing and a big cloud of steamy smoke erupts from his front grill. His car makes it a little farther as it spits and sputters, but he's able to steer Gladys as close to the curb as possible. She slows and finally comes to a dramatic stop in a big cloud of steam.

"Shit!" He grabs the steering wheel tightly and he just sits there for a moment thinking what to do next.

He looks around. Rockefeller Center is behind him on his left and Gucci is just up on his right. Just out of instinct, he knows exactly where he is. This spot on 5th Avenue is a place where he spent most of his adolescent life. He turns his head right and sees the beautiful shiny glass facade of the mecca skyscraper that's home to the infamous Double D's Daisy Diamond, the world's leading diamond and fine jewelry store customizing in wedding rings. His eyes scan the brand's tagline that's etched in the glass under the company's name: *Women Want Double D's.*

He screams to himself again from inside the car, "Really . . . here? The car has to break down here!" He closes his eyes and hits his palms to his forehead in disgust. He's as hot as his car. Stressful tears fill his eyes, but he won't let them fall. There are several businessmen, all in expensive suits and carrying messenger bags, walking past him either on their cell phones or using earbuds. A squad of young ladies in little silk dresses and stilettos stroll past, their Louis Vuitton bags hanging off their forearms with their wrists and hands turned up, holding an iced coffee or a cell phone in the other. He sees both Chanel and Versace storefronts. "Is everybody but me rich in this town?"

As if his life wasn't bad enough at this moment, a street dweller walks by and yells out, "Brother, you got yo'self some bad luck!" He laughs a little and slaps his hand on his leg as he continues on his staggered walk.

Michael responds to himself in a frustrated whisper, "Yeah, ten years of bad luck." He looks at the Double D's skyscraper again, wondering if maybe he should go in and ask for help. But before he can even get out of his car, he sees red and blue lights reflecting in his rearview mirror, creating a kaleidoscope effect in his car. Michael's windows are already down as an officer walks up to the passenger side door and bends down to look inside the car.

"The radiator, huh?" The Hispanic officer has brown eyes, sparkling white teeth, and several tattoos going up his chiseled left arm, which now rests on Michael's window's ledge. Michael scans the officer's tattoos until they disappear under his short-sleeved dark-blue uniform. The officer momentarily distracts Michael from his present problem.

The officer looks a little more at Michael and says, "Do I know you? You look familiar."

Michael quickly responds, “No, I’m nobody. Just somebody who’s car broke down in the middle of Manhattan.”

“Huh, you sure do look really familiar. You sure I don’t know you?”

“I’m almost positive you don’t know me.”

“Can I see your license and registration, please?”

Oh shit, Michael thinks as he reaches for his wallet and then into the glove box. He fumbles around for the papers, finally finding the registration and closing the glove box with a slam. He hands them both to the officer.

“I’ll be right back,” the officer says, turning back to his cruiser.

Michael says to himself, “Now he’s gonna know,” as he throws his head back against his headrest. He starts rubbing his forehead, thinking of how he’s going to answer the officer’s questions when he gets back. More perspiration beads around Michael’s neck.

The officer returns, bends down and looks into the car again, “You’re Michael Monroe, *the* Michael Monroe! Olivia Monroe’s son!” He nods his head in the direction of the skyscraper behind him. “Your mom owns that building and she’s the heiress of the diamond business. And your dad was a legend in this city. Sorry about that plane crash, man.” The officer raises his eyebrows and gives Michael a compassionate look. “I thought I recognized you from somewhere.” The officer returns Michael’s license and registration.

Michael nods his head, looking up at the officer from inside his car. “Yep, that’s my mom.” Michael’s hoping that’s all the officer is going to say. Nervous sweat continues to build around his neck.

The officer looks at the condition of the car and asks, “So why are you in this car?” He laughs a little. “You should be in the backseat of a limo, with all her money.” The officer hesitates for a moment before continuing, “My ex had to have one of your mom's Double D's, but I couldn't afford one of those diamonds—not on an officer's salary."

Michael rolls his eyes, sighs, and says, "They are expensive but undeniably noticeable and absolutely beautiful."

"Well, at least your luck had you break down right in front of your mom's place. I'm assuming you'll be all right? You don't need me to call you a tow truck or an Uber or anything?"

"No officer, that won't be necessary. I can take it from here. But thank you." Michael's mind is already racing, trying to figure out exactly how he's going to have the car removed from the front of his mother's building before someone else does it—or his mother finds out.

"Okay then." The officer taps the window sill twice. "Stay safe and cool. Sure is hot out here today." He walks back to his vehicle, shuts the red and blue lights off, guns the motor, and quickly disappears into traffic.

Michael sits there in his car just a little bit longer contemplating. *Should I go in and ask dear ole Mom for some help?* He sighs, shuts his eyes, and shakes his head. His thoughts get interrupted as he hears the rumbling of a diesel truck as it starts to slow down. He sees the cherry-red flatbed pull up alongside him. The diesel fumes fill his car. He hears the driver's door slam, and he recognizes his mechanic, Ted coming around from the front of the truck.

"Jesus! What now, Michael?" Ted's wearing a blue Yeti baseball cap and a gray business T-shirt that reads *Ted's Garage*. The shirt hangs nicely over Ted's broad shoulders, but it pulls tight around his pooching dad-bod stomach. He sees the steam still coming from the hood. "Tell me you didn't blow your radiator?" He glares at Michael with his ice-blue eyes.

"I didn't think it would blow," Michael yells from out his window as he gets defensive. "It's gotten hot before but nothing like this."

Ted walks to the front of the car and puts his hands on the hood but then quickly removes them. He grits his teeth as he rubs his hands on his slightly greasy, tan Carhartt pants to cool them down. "You're lucky I just happened to see your car. It's been such a regular in the shop; I guess I'm just used to looking for her. Come on, let's get it on the truck and get you out of here."

Michael is now standing alongside the tow truck as Ted bends down under the car to hook up a cable winch that will pull the car up onto the flatbed. Ted's pants are hanging a little loose offering Michael a glimpse of his blue Jockey underwear. Ted gets back up and gives his pants a little tug up. Ted pushes down on a hydraulic lever and Michael's car starts rolling up the incline onto the silver tilt bed. The flatbed slowly lowers and finishes with a slam. Ted and Michael jump into the truck's cab.

Ted looks at Michael with a smile on his face and hits Michael's shoulder. "Bro, the car breaks down right in front of your mom's place. Isn't that like some kind of omen?"

Not looking at Ted, Michael quickly responds, "Yeah, it's an omen for I got shit for luck." Michael glances over at Ted who's looking left out his driver's window, watching the road as he starts to pull into traffic. Michael watches Ted as he methodically pushes his left foot down on the clutch, his right arm reaching over as his hand feels for the stick shift. He brings the stick shift down to the left and down again, the motor revs in response and they are both pushed back against their seats. His right foot moves off the gas pedal to the brake. After the downshift while making the turn, Ted removes his foot from the brake pedal and it goes back to the accelerator, and the tow truck begins to pick up speed again. Michael quickly glances at Ted's handsome face and sighs. *So cute, but so straight.*

They pull up to the service station garage and Ted parks the truck, leaving Michael's car on the flatbed. They get out and Ted says, "You need a ride home?"

"No, I'm good. I'll walk. I'm only a few blocks away."

"Okay, bro. I'll call you tomorrow about what's happening with your Barbie sports car," Ted says with a smile. "Don't worry, bro." He slaps his hand on Michael's shoulder. "I'll fix her good as new for you. Promise."

A thousand negative thoughts run through Michael's mind, but instead he says, "Can you fix my life good as new, too, while you're at it?" Michael's all-too-well-known feeling—the sting of defeat—makes his eyes well up. He grabs his man-bag and throws it over his head. It falls onto his shoulder. He turns around and starts walking away, throwing a goodbye wave to Ted. Defeated again, he bows his head and leaves, feeling rejected like a scared and lost puppy.

CHAPTER 2

MICHAEL'S CELL PHONE rings as he's walking home from the garage, and he sees it's his boyfriend Joel. He quickly answers; it makes him feel somewhat happier after his whole car debacle. It's their one-year anniversary. *Well, it was last weekend,* Michael thinks. But they missed celebrating it because Joel had to work. Joel is a model for an online men's underwear company and hasn't been around much lately. Michael hopes Joel is calling to plan some alone time.

"Hey, Michael, wanna meet me out for dinner tonight?"

When Michael doesn't answer right away, Joel adds, "Sorry about last night. You know how it goes. They had us here late redoing all the pictures because somebody didn't put the palm trees in the background. Bunch of idiots."

It's not the first excuse Joel has given this week for why he couldn't meet up for dinner. "So where would you like to go tonight? I swear I will be there."

Michael smiles as he thinks of a restaurant. "How about Bread and Basil? They have the best wood-fired pizza around and their martinis are delicious!"

"Basil sounds good. They have that bartender there—what's

his name, Tony? Yeah, that's it, Tony. He'll be there tonight, and he does make the greatest martinis."

Suspicion flashes in Michael's mind as he wrinkles his forehead with surprise. *How would Joel know about a particular bartender? And he knows his name?* Michael searches memories from his mind; they haven't been to Basil's in over a month. He shrugs it off. He's just happy to finally be able to spend some time with Joel.

"Basil it is. Say, tonight at seven?"

"Seven is perfect." Michael experiences another uneasy gut reaction at Joel's answer.

At seven o'clock, Michael sits alone at a table inside. The cheesy garlic aroma smells delicious. He's looking at the menu but not really reading it. He's just using the menu as an escape. He feels an awkward tension building inside him. Finally, he sees Joel walking in, looking every bit of what a model should look like. He's wearing skinny black designer jeans that are tight in all the right places. His dark shoulder-length hair is pulled back into a slick bun. It makes his dark Romanian eyes pop. He's wearing a form-fitting white T-shirt that flaunts all of the bulging muscles in his shoulders and chest.

Joel has caught the attention of everyone in the restaurant. Their eyes follow him as he weaves through the tables toward Michael, walking behind a young woman holding a menu. He sits and the hostess hands him the menu as she begins to describe the evening specials. When she finishes, she asks Michael and Joel if they would like to start with a drink. They both order the martini special: prickly pear. Michael reaches over the table and grabs Joel's hands and holds them. He's gazing into Joel's beautiful brown eyes as their martinis come and they raise their glasses for a toast.

"Happy one-year anniversary," Michael says.

Joel's whole body seems to tense right up. He gets an ominous expression on his face and casually blurts out, “Michael, this relationship doesn’t work for me anymore. I really don’t want to hurt you. You’re a great guy, but it’s just not working between us. No hard feelings, okay?”

Joel pushes himself up off his chair. He leans one leg against the table as he reaches into his pocket. He throws a crumpled twenty-dollar bill down onto the white linen tablecloth. Joel proceeds to take a long swig of his martini and just walks away from Michael, leaving him alone at the table. Michael is flabbergasted as he watches Joel walk away. He catches his head in his hands as he leans over the table, trying to compose himself in this inconceivable moment. Michael takes a deep breath and sits back up, looking at his watch. His mind is whirling. *Dumped in ten minutes; that’s a new record.* Michael watches Joel walk toward the bar where apparently this Tony person is. This Thor-looking person. This chiseled, hot muscleman from behind the bar. Joel goes right up to him, puts his knee on one of the bar stools, and rests his hands onto the bar, flexing his bulging triceps. He leans over and gives Tony a kiss right on the lips, in front of everyone.

Michael’s heart, not to mention his ego, has been officially crushed. He stands up and puts another twenty-dollar bill down, only his bill isn’t crumpled. He places the half-filled martini glass on top of it. He leaves without finishing his drink. He makes a mental note to finish up the vodka he has at home. As he proceeds to do the walk of shame through the restaurant to the door, he catches several eyes watching him leave.

CHAPTER 3

THE NEXT MORNING, Michael is having a phone conversation. A stern woman's voice is speaking to him. "So again, thank you for your interest in our career opportunity, Michael, but unfortunately you're experience just doesn't match our criteria. Good luck to you and have a good day." The phone line goes dead.

"Just great!" Michael shouts as he ends the early morning call. He's hungover and angry. He just lost out on another job opportunity at a college. He leans back in his office chair and puts his hands behind his head. He closes his eyes as he thinks about what to do next. When no answers come, he screams his frustration out loud. "Just give me a fucking sign!"

He slams his hands down on the arms of his chair. He looks up at his beloved *I Dream of Jeannie* Barbie doll, a gift given to him from his friend Lucy that's perched high up on a shelf in his home office. Lucy told him to pray to Jeannie whenever he needs help.

"Jeannie," Michael begs, "please—I need some help. What am I doing wrong? I have no money." Michael looks around at the bills and all the final disconnect notices on his desk. "Nothing's working out for me. I can't keep a job. I'm dumped by every boyfriend. My mom, well—" he pauses, imagining her luxuriously sitting on a beach chair on some remote tropical isle. "She's a multi-millionaire, and I'm flat broke. What do I keep doing wrong? I need some help and fast!" He falls back into his chair and runs his hands through his hair, sighing as tears well in his eyes.

He looks up with blurry vision and he gives a good sniff. He focuses his sight on his vision board hanging on the wall above his desk. He takes a hard look at the pictures then he takes his hand and dusts it off. Having been hanging for so many years, it's collected a few strands of cobwebs on the turned-up corners of the pictures. He blows away some of the falling dust. "So much for making this vision board." He looks at all the pictures of how he wanted his life to unfold. "Nothing has ever worked out for me."

His eyes are still darting around the images. His vision board is titled, *My Dream Life*. It's written with cut-out letters of different shapes, colors, and font sizes at the top. Below it are several pictures—all scenes of a successful restaurant. One is of a waiter pouring wine for a guest at a table. Another, a charcoal grill with flames that's cooking a T-bone steak that's sizzling to perfection. One of a large red lobster presented on a silver platter with lemon, butter, and a pair of metal lobster crackers. There's a cash register that's overflowing with hundred-dollar bills and a large stack of credit card receipts. A beautiful mahogany bar is shown with multiple shelves filled with many different sizes and shapes of liquor bottles and funky purple background lighting. One is an image of a full dining room, linen-covered tables full of guests eating and drinking. Right smack in the middle of his vision board is written, *Where New York City Eats*, with a commanding photograph of Michael holding tongs with his arms crossed over his chest in his chef's uniform.

Around the culinary pictures are more creative pictures. Palm trees and an ocean scene at sunset. Two men walking hand in hand along a beach. Two silver wedding rings sitting on a satin pillow. A dog catching a Frisbee. A very sporty convertible BMW. Michael shakes his head. "There's not one picture on this board that has materialized," he screams. "Not *one*, Jeannie! What good are these stupid vision boards anyway?"

He looks down at his desk and sees a picture of him and his now ex-boyfriend and thinks about how that one-year relationship had ended last night. *What an epic ending that was.* He shakes his head. *There's nothing like being dumped by your boyfriend as an entire restaurant watches.* Then to top it off, there's Michael's memory of the bartender, who looked like he had muscles where Michael didn't even have parts.

Michael's imagination goes wild as he assumes that the bartender probably drives one of those crotch rocket motorcycles or owns a Maserati. *He's hot as hell, maybe Greek—who the hell knows?* Michael sighs. How could he compete with *that*? Then he catches himself and wonders why he's even thinking about him. Michael accepts that his preordained life hasn't made him into a Ryan Gosling or Bradley Cooper. He looks back at the photo of him and Joel and he begrudgingly lays it face down on the desk.

He blinks his eyes and tries to put last night's events out of his mind. Coming back to the present, he scans his emails and sees an estimate from Ted's Garage. It details three thousand dollars worth of repairs that his car will need in order to pass his next inspection. Reclining back in his chair, his arms are tightly crossed against his chest. Michael thinks about how his New Age friend Lucy is always harping on him about body language.

That's stupid. What does Lucy know about body language? I'm open. I'm listening. Even with my arms tightly crossed over my chest, I'm listening. It's just that nobody is talking. "Hello!" Michael yells into the thin air and waves his arms as if he's trying to be spotted on a desert island.

He focuses his eyes again on his laptop. A notification bubble appears. It reads, "It's been several years since Whitney Houston's passing . . ." The pictures of Whitney capture his attention. He impulsively decides he doesn't really have anything else to do, so he clicks on the notification and reads a bit of the article, which is about Whitney's former friend, Robyn Crawford. She's penned a memoir, *A Song for You*. Among the information about Whitney Houston's career in music and film is an announcement that the estate is presenting a Whitney hologram tour as well as a biopic movie, *I Wanna Dance With Somebody*. The article mentions Kygo's remastered single of "Higher Love" that soared up the charts. He doesn't read the rest of the article but releases a heavy sigh and shuts his laptop. He really liked Whitney's music, and he misses her.

He goes downstairs to the kitchen, and as he's pouring more coffee, his cell phone rings. He answers without looking.

"Hey."

"So, how did it go?"

Michael recognizes the voice right away. It's Lucy Calery, his best friend. They've been together since grade school. Lucy knew Michael had an important job phone interview. She also knows he's been out of work for six weeks. She can hear the disappointment in his voice. "I'm coming over and we're going to get some ice cream."

"I don't want ice cream."

"Who doesn't want ice cream?"

"I'm saying *I* don't want ice cream. I'm not in the mood. And besides, it's only ten o'clock in the morning. I haven't even eaten breakfast yet." He pushes the coffee pot back onto its heating pad.

"So what! Come on, it will do you a world of good to get out of the house. Besides, you can get one of those flavors with nuts in it for your morning protein." She laughs. "Oh, and I want to tell you all about the Theresa Caputo show I went to last night. You know, she's that psychic lady with the big blond hair and those long fingernails who's from Long Island. The things that girl hears, I tell ya. I wish I could've gotten a message from my grandmother." She quickly hangs up.

Before he can even take a sip, a banging at his door commences. Michael rolls his eyes and thinks, why did I move right next door to her? He wrestles with the lock, then opens the door to see Lucy wearing a long, flowing linen dress. Or maybe it's a sarong. The colors are reds and oranges, like a beautiful summer sunset. She has a light-blue scarf tied around her auburn hair and a beaming smile across her face that makes her emerald eyes sparkle.

"Good morning, fancy pants!" Still smiling, she pulls Michael by the arm out of his apartment.

"Hold it, let me at least grab my keys and lock the door!" Michael turns around. He grabs his keys and a hat to hide his bedhead—his favorite pink baseball cap he got last year when on vacation in Key Largo with Lucy.

Lucy sees Michael's baseball cap. "Come back to Key Largo with me this year."

Michael ignores Lucy's comment. He locks his door, and they start walking down the hall.

"I'm serious. It's almost July, my aunt and uncle aren't using their house, and they won't mind if we use it again over Fourth of July week. What do you say? Come on, say yes. A vacation will do you good. We'll have so much fun again . . . *Please*?" she says with sad eyes.

Michael stops and throws his head back as if looking to heaven for an answer. He closes his eyes. *I can't go to Key Largo. I really need to find a job.* He feels defeated and guilty for disappointing Lucy.

Michael grabs the apartment's entrance door and holds it open for Lucy. They start heading in the direction of their favorite bistro. The sun is shining, the temperature is in the mid 70s, and they smell the dirty-cement smell of the city. There are billowy white clouds in the blue sky. As cars zip by, taxi drivers blow their horns. A city bus pulls right up alongside them and slows to a stop. It hisses and lowers for commuters to enter or exit.

Lucy is talking about all the reasons they should go back to Key Largo. Michael is in his own little world, hearing only bits and pieces about the restaurants they liked, the jet skiing, the beautiful blue water, snorkeling at the coral reefs, and how they wanted to go to Christ of the Abyss in John Pennekamp State Park. She mentions something about watching the sunsets and driving down Route 1 over all the bridges and the clear blue waters.

Then Lucy excitedly says, "And café con leche at Sunshine Market!"

A memory flashes in Michael's mind and he smiles. He loves how the Cubans make their coffees. He smiles, thinking of the pulled shots of espresso mixed with warmed frothy milk and how he learned how to ask for sugar in it, "y azucar." All the tropical memories of past visits with Lucy to Key Largo start flooding back to him but he quickly shoves them back down inside. He knows he shouldn't go—at least not now.

"Oh, come on!" She bumps her shoulder up to his. "Live a little. It's practically a free vacation and we can celebrate your birthday."

"I don't know."

Michael looks down at the sidewalk and thinks about being unemployed and how his boyfriend left him for that practically perfect bartender. And now Lucy's just reminded him that his birthday is coming up.

Thirty, he thinks.

Then there's the extra seven pounds he's put on, his car that now needs three thousand dollars worth of repairs—and he hasn't even told Lucy about the breakup last night . . . or the car. He'll save it for when they get to the restaurant. *And now she wants me to go on a vacation with her to Key Largo. Awesome! I'll get right on that,* he almost laughs to himself.

They walk past another bus station near the end of the block that has several people sitting on a bench inside an enclosure, all of whom are looking down at their phones—except one older woman, who's reading a book.

They look up at the glowing white light of the walking person on the street post and cross.

As they walk the next block, there are some colorful flower beds encircling the trees that are enclosed with iron foot-high fences to keep dogs out. The sidewalk itself is sadly littered with several squished plastic water bottles and loose pieces of dirty paper, and apparently someone is moving out. There's a bunch of household garbage stacked at the curb the previous tenants didn't want to take with them. Michael spots an old key on the ground. Made of tarnished brass, it looks like a house key that's been out on the street for a while. It's nothing anybody wants. He keeps walking, Lucy chattering to him, though he's barely listening.

Pick up the key, says a feisty female voice.

Michael stops dead. Lucy keeps walking for a few steps but stops when she sees Michael frozen in place.

"What's wrong?" she asks.

Michael turns around and picks up the key. "Something—or some*one*—just told me to pick up this key. That was weird."

Weirder still, he hears a snippet of someone singing "I'm Your Baby Tonight," a popular Whitney Houston song. He's surprised at how much it sounds exactly like her. He suspiciously looks around to find the car or apartment that's blaring the song but hears nothing. Lucy gives Michael a quick glance as she tilts her head to one side, wondering what's going on.

Baby, that key will unlock all the doors to your future!

Caught off guard again, Michael stops. He looks around but it's just him, Lucy, and the random people walking past them. His eyes dart around, looking for the source of the voice.

Lucy puts her hands on her hips. She's never seen Michael

like this. "What's going on with you?"

She can't hear me. Only you can.

"Nothing!" He glances over his shoulder one final time, still trying to find the body to go with the voice. Michael finally gives up finding an answer, shrugs it off, and they continue to walk.

Well, Michael thinks, *you wanted me to pick up this key, so what do I do with it? Where do I keep it?*

Sha-zam! All you gotta do, baby, is ask, the voice responds. ***We answer wishes just like that!***

Like magic, right there on the ground, Michael spots what looks like a gold necklace.

"Holy crap," he says as he picks it up.

He inspects it. It isn't broken; someone clearly lost it. There's no dirt or debris on the necklace; it's shiny and golden. He slides the key through the chain and fixes it around his neck.

Lucy is surprised. It takes real luck to find a gold necklace. The key is no big deal, but a *gold necklace*. That's a great find. She smiles at his good fortune.

"Maybe your luck is starting to turn around. Here," she says, gesturing to a convenience store as she gives him a healthy push forward. "Go in and buy a lottery ticket." Mimicking the chirpy cadence of New York lottery spokesperson Yolanda Vega, she says, "Hey, you never know!"

Michael walks into the very cramped, cluttered, and overcrowded convenience store that smells like Nag Champa incense and body odor. At the counter, he asks the clerk for a five-dollar Quick Pick for the New York Lotto. The clerk presses some buttons, a ticket prints, and the clerk hands it to Michael.

"Good luck," the smiling clerk says with a thick Middle Eastern accent.

Michael nods, stuffs the ticket into his wallet, and walks out of the store. Lucy, meanwhile, is doing yoga poses in the sunlight on the sidewalk. Michael shakes his head at her and smiles.

They arrive at their favorite restaurant, Ambition Coffee & Eatery. They sit in a booth and a server comes by to take their drink order.

Lucy silently looks at Michael for a few moments as she tries to process his unusual demeanor. Michael is still miles away, absentmindedly stirring cream and sugar into his coffee. He taps his spoon on the rim of the ceramic mug in time with the song coming through the restaurant's speakers. He snaps back to the present when he recognizes it: "How Will I Know," one of Whitney's most famous songs.

"You can't hear that?" Michael asks Lucy. He points his finger upward like something is hanging above them.

Recognition crosses her features. "*How will I know*," she sings along, snapping her fingers, bouncing her shoulders, and swaying her head along to the music. "Of course I can hear this song and who doesn't know it?" It's now Lucy's turn to fix her cup of lavender chai tea; she squeezes in some honey and delicately stirs the cinnamon-sprinkled froth. She sees Michael quickly look up again and around the restaurant, looking for something, anything.

That's right, baby, get some ice cream. I've always loved me a big dish of that mocha moo-moo mint.

Michael hears the woman again talking to him, but she's nowhere to be found. "I think I'm going crazy. I keep hearing a woman."

"What? What's she saying to you?" Lucy gives Michael a look of anticipation.

"Someone just told me to go for the ice cream and that they like the mocha moo-moo mint flavor."

"Are you serious? Mocha moo-moo mint?" Lucy is now captivated. "What else are they saying?

"It's not a 'they,' it's a woman. I think it's . . . well, it's the same voice I've been hearing since we left the apartment."

Lucy asks, "It's *who*? Someone's been talking to you since we left? Do you feel okay? Maybe you just didn't sleep well last night. You know, maybe your mind is just playing games with you."

"Yeah, this key," he grabs it. "This gold chain, and now mocha moo-moo mint. I think it's . . . nah." Images of Whitney swirl through his imagination. "It can't be." He waves his hand as if to erase such a foolish thought.

CHAPTER 4

"YOU THINK IT'S WHO?" Lucy says with a bit of pitch in her voice.

"I think it's Whitney Houston."

"Whitney Houston?" Lucy laughs. "She's dead!"

"I know she's dead."

Lucy squints her eyes and asks, "So, you're saying Whitney Houston is talking to you?"

"I know it sounds crazy, but I'm telling you. I think—"

Lucy sarcastically asks, "Well if you think she's talking to you, and if you think she has the answers, then ask her what color my panties are." She laughs then takes a sip of her tea.

Pink polka-dots!

"Pink polka-dots," Michael says out loud.

Lucy's eyes go wide. She nearly chokes on her foamy chai tea and looks down in her lap to see if her underpants are visible.

"How did you know that?" Lucy suddenly gets a hot flash of embarrassment; she fans her face, wipes her brow, and picks her hair up off the back of her neck for cooler airflow. She slowly blows out a long sigh.

Anything else?

Michael doesn't mention that last comment. They sit in silence. Lucy is the first to break the silence.

"So, what do you think this person—this woman—ahh . . . what do you think *Whitney* wants?" Lucy dramatically drops her jaw and widens her eyes. "Oh my god! This is so weird! I just saw Theresa Caputo. I wonder if this has anything to do with that show last night?"

"I don't know, but something tells me I'm gonna find out."

What do you mean, what do I want? It's not what I want; it's what you want, baby. I am here for you.

Michael quickly moves his stare from Lucy. He looks just slightly to her left and Lucy notices the movement of his eyes. She turns to see whatever he's trying to see but nothing is there. He slightly lowers his head as if to concentrate, squinting his eyes as he stares at something next to Lucy. He starts seeing double. He blinks his eyes to refocus, but the visual disturbance is still there. It's like looking at heat coming off hot pavement. He sees waves of distorted lines. He blinks his eyes even more as he still tries to focus. Now he sees sparkles and small dots of flashing lights and suddenly an explosion erupts. Millions of fiery multicolored glittery lights explode as Michael apprehensively jerks his head back and hits the back of the booth with his arms wide open, as if to catch himself.

"Oh, sweet baby Jesus!" he yells as he quickly slides out of the booth, almost falling to the floor.

"Oh shit, oh shit!" He paces alongside the booth while Lucy just sits there, looking back and forth, trying to see what her friend is staring at. He puts his hands on both sides of his head, as if trying to keep it from exploding. He grabs Lucy by the arm to yank her out of the booth, but she pulls away.

"What are you *doing*?" Lucy swats at Michael's hands and arms as he tries to pull her out of the booth. "You're making a scene! Stop!"

The restaurant has gone silent. Other customers are watching. He calms himself enough to put his hands down on the table. "We need to go. We need to go now!" he says, staring directly at Whitney for the first time.

Now all the diners in the restaurant have begun staring quizzically and whispering to each other, as if waiting to see what the crazy man does next.

Lucy glances toward the space next to her, where Michael's gaze is fixed, then back at him, one eyebrow quirked.

Whitney is sitting next to Lucy, flawless. She appears as she had on her self-titled second album *Whitney*, a big, beautiful smile, brown curly hair, and a white sleeveless shirt.

Whoa, they were right! She steadies herself as she puts her hands on the table. ***That first time through the dimensions.*** She lets out a ***Whooooa . . . baby, I feel dizzy.***

Michael watches as she sort of collects herself. She takes a deep breath and releases it. ***My goodness.*** She looks down at herself as if to see if she's all there and put together. She laughs her big laugh. ***What, baby?*** She crosses her arms and frowns. ***Are you disappointed? Were you really expecting that Barbara Eden doll in her little pink tutu to come popping out of a bottle and grant you your wishes? Here I am. I'm all yours. I'm your guardian angel, and I'm your baby tonight!*** Whitney throws her arms up in the air and as she opens her hands, sparkling silver confetti flutters down on and around her.

Now order your ice cream and then we'll go to work.

And *POOF!* Just like that, she disappears. There are still small silver confetti's falling that only Michael sees.

Michael's still in panic mode, pacing, trying to figure out what to do when he finally realizes it's over. She's gone. He lets out a few deep breaths as he sinks back into the booth. As the other patrons go back to their conversations, the waitress walks back over to take their order. "I'll have butter pecan and chocolate ice cream," Lucy tells her.

"And you, honey?" the waitress asks Michael. When he doesn't answer, she tries again.

Finally, he lowers his eyes and says in a very soft, slightly shaky voice, "I'll take the mocha moo-moo mint."

The waitress shakes her head as she jots down the order.

"What's going on with you?" Lucy sternly asks. "You're here but you're not. You're yelling like a crazy man, we have to leave one minute, then you try yanking me out of the booth and the next, well, the next minute, you sit back down and just order ice cream."

A huge grin appears on his face and Michael looks right at Lucy.

"What? Just say it. What?" Lucy says, agitated.

Michael's stare steadily holds Lucy's attention. "What if I told you Whitney was just sitting right next to you?"

Lucy catches her breath. "You can see her?"

"Yes. I did. She's gone now." He takes a deep breath and releases it. He excitedly says, "She was sitting right next to you. She, well her energy, her vibration, her *something* was right next to you. That's what I was looking at. She exploded out of thin air. She said she's my guardian angel." He looks at Lucy and waits for her reaction.

Lucy's mouth is agape, but she just continues to stare at him. "I don't know what to say, or how to react." Lucy holds her hands up as if they're a scale, balancing truth and fiction. "Jesus Christmas, Michael. I just saw Theresa Caputo last night! I wanted my grandmother to come through. Why is this so hard for me to comprehend?" She shakes her head, "You just saw Whitney Houston next to me, here in this booth, right now? And now she's telling you she's your guardian angel . . . really?"

Michael is beaming, pointing to himself. "How friggin' cool is that?" He lowers his head down close to the table and he's whispering so everyone doesn't hear him. He repeatedly pokes himself in the chest. "Whitney Houston is my guardian angel!"

Their ice cream arrives and Michael digs in; Lucy only stares at hers. She picks up her spoon but only hits it against the ice cream before putting her spoon back down. She leans across the table at Michael, who's now shoving a big spoonful of ice cream into his mouth; she glares and adamantly asks one last time. "Whitney Houston, *the* Whitney Houston, *the* 'I Will Always Love You' Whitney Houston was *here*, sitting next to me, and told you she's your guardian angel?" She folds her arms against her chest and falls back against the booth with a thump. She sucks in her cheek and bites down on the inside. Shaking her head and now restless, she puts her hands flat on the table and starts rapidly tapping her thumbs while staring into oblivion.

Michael patiently puts his spoon down, reaches over, and holds Lucy's hand. "Lucy, look at me." She resists. Again, very patiently and very methodically, Michael softly says, "Lucy, look at me." She looks up at him with water in her eyes. He takes a soft breath. "Lucy . . . " he pauses, "I don't know exactly what's going on today. But what I can say is yes, Whitney Houston was just sitting next to you." He pauses again. "And Whitney did tell me she's my guardian angel."

A tear now rolls down Lucy's cheek; she quickly pulls her hand free and wipes it away. "You, Lucy, are the one who got me into spiritual thinking and talking to the Universe. I mean," he laughs, "I just screamed another prayer to the Jeannie doll you got me just this morning." Lucy laughs as her shoulders bounce and another tear rolls down her cheek. "Did my screaming awaken her? Is that what did it? I don't know, but she's here. And maybe I should be thanking you. The Caribbean-blue-turban-wearing hot mamma that you are!"

Lucy laughs at his comment and with a raspy, exhausted voice, she responds, "It wasn't the Jeannie doll," as she shakes her head with a silly laugh and touches her blue head scarf.

"Well, that's not what Whitney just said." Lucy's eyes excitedly dart directly at him. "She did! Honest! She asked me if I was disappointed it was her and not Jeannie." Michael laughs and throws his head back and claps his hands. Lucy cups both her hands into her chest and sits back in her seat with absolute delight.

They eat their ice cream as Lucy asks questions about the appearance. Lucy pays the bill and they leave.

Each now back at their own apartment door, Lucy walks back over and hugs Michael. "Call me later. I'm working from twelve to six at the center."

Michael smiles and nods, half lost in thoughts of Whitney.

"Yeah, let's meet for dinner. There's something else I have to tell you." Michael's thoughts go to Joel.

"How about seven thirty? I want to hear even more tonight. This whole Whitney thing is a lot to take in," Lucy says. Michael nods again, unlocks his door, smiles, and walks into his apartment.

CHAPTER 5

WHILE INSIDE HIS apartment, Michael gets restless and decides to go for a run to clear his mind. Running is his meditation. He often thinks back to the day years ago when Lucy had first asked him to run a Ragnar with her.

"Ragnar? What's a Ragnar?" he'd asked.

"It's a relay race," Lucy explained. "Twelve people run two hundred miles from one destination to another."

"Two hundred miles!" Michael's voice had risen two octaves. "Are you crazy?"

"No, not two hundred miles by yourself." She smiled back and put her hands on Michael's shoulders. "You share the run with twelve people. Each person runs about five miles and there are three legs. Each person runs their miles and then they ride in a van until the other eleven people finish their runs. Then the second leg begins and then the third leg, and the last runner reaches your destination."

Michael had looked at her with pierced lips. "Lucy," he said, now slowly shaking his head, "I'm not a runner. I don't like to run. You know I get cramps in my sides."

"I'll teach you how to run." Lucy had refused to take no for an answer. “Come on, it will be fun! Plus, Michael, think about it: all those men in little running shorts and spandex. Wha-wha-ba-boom!” She poked him in the stomach and chest a few times. “You never know who you'll meet!” Lucy had pulled out all her begging skills. “Come on, pleeeease?” She'd put her hands in a prayer position and smiled like an innocent child.

Now Michael comes back from his memory just as he's running up the stone steps to the loose gravel of the inner loop that circles around the Jacqueline Kennedy Onassis reservoir. He's breathing in and out through his mouth. He occasionally takes a deep breath in through his nose and releases it through his mouth, calming his heart rate. His pace is about nine minutes per mile. The sun is shining; the temperature is not overly warm at eighty-two degrees. He loves the view of the buildings mixed with the nature of the park. That's the gift of Central Park, nestled in the heart of Manhattan. Finding solace, he runs around the loop twice for a total of three miles and heads back to his apartment.

Back inside, Michael kicks off his running sneakers as he's yanking at his sweaty microfiber running shirt that's stuck to his body, trying to pull it over his head; he undresses as he heads to the bathroom and starts the shower.

While the warm water runs over him, he wonders if he'd imagined his earlier encounter. Did he really see and hear Whitney Houston? Is she really his guardian angel? Why him? What had he done to connect with her?

His hand brushes against the necklace and key.

“Well this much is real,” he thinks. “Lucy saw me find this key and she saw me find the necklace.”

He thinks about all the possibilities the key represents—to be able to unlock all the doors to his future. He smiles at the thought. What does he want first? He wonders if the key will unlock any house, any business, or the lock to someone's heart. He smiles again.

His bathroom is very steamy, as he has stayed in the shower a little longer than usual. He turns the water off and whips the shower curtain open. Sitting there on his bathroom cabinet is Whitney.

CHAPTER 6

HIS WHOLE BODY shakes, he gasps a loud breath, and his eyes widen. "Holy Jesus! Mother of Pearl! Freakin' Christ!"

Michael jumps around in the bathtub, hiding his privates with his legs and his hands. He turns around only to realize that now he's mooning her. He turns back around and pulls the shower curtain over his crotch. Dripping wet, he reaches for the towel Whitney's now handing to him.

Ain't nothing new! We don't care about that physical body stuff after we cross over. The visual part—the attractiveness to the physical body—leaves us, and we only see the soul. I see your soul baby, not your body. And your soul is beautiful inside and out. Don't matter what you think about yourself—none of that will matter in the end. So now, stop wigglin'. We wouldn't want you to fall. We both know what that can lead to. Here, dry off.

Michael takes the towel and awkwardly stands behind the shower curtain just to save his dignity while drying himself off.

When you're done, come see me in your office, where all of this started this morning. You know, with your little hissy-fit, oh, that was hysterical, you screaming in front of that Jeannie doll. Pfft, Girl, please. She laughs, snaps a finger and disappears.

Michael rubs a few circles in the foggy mirror and looks at himself. His dark wet bangs are hanging on his forehead; his hazel eyes are gleaming. They seem to have a little more emerald in them tonight than usual. He smiles. He likes his smile. For the first time in a long time, he isn't focused on what he thinks are his physical flaws. He sees how handsome he is, even if only for a few seconds, before his mind wanders off to things he doesn't like, such as his freckles, narrow shoulders, and that little bit of extra loose skin around his waist.

Echoing off the steamy walls of his bathroom he hears, ***Baby, you gotta learn to shut those voices up! They ain't doin' you no good.***

Michael wraps the towel around his waist and walks to his bedroom, where he puts on his boxer briefs, sweatpants, and a hoodie. Now he's dressed and ready for his appointment with Whitney in his office.

He steps cautiously to the doorframe of the room and pokes his head in and looks around only to see that it's empty. No Whitney.

Cautiously he talks to the empty room, "Hello . . . I'm here." He takes a very slow, soft step into the room. He's nervous. His heart is racing. He breathes out a long sigh. His eyes are darting around the room. His laptop, the Jeannie doll, and the upside-down picture frame are just as he left them this morning. But most of all, it's the anticipation and silence of the room that makes him the most uncomfortable.

Michael waits a few seconds; he takes two more very soft steps, turning himself around. Maybe he's missing something. He speaks again. "Hellloooooo, anybody here?" He feels uneasy, like he's not supposed to be in his own office. He slowly takes a seat at his desk and spins nervously around in the chair. He starts rapidly tapping his fingers on the chair rests, if only to break the silence. His eyes continue to dart around the room, looking for something, anything.

Just 'cause you can't see me doesn't mean I'm not here.

He instantly tightens up; he quickly spins around in his chair like he just heard a ghost. Well, he did. Still, he doesn't see anything.

"Where are you?"

I'm right here.

"Right where?"

I'm right here!

Michael spins back around and finally sees her sitting on his desk. In fear, he quickly pushes his chair back away from her. He then jumps up out of the chair, ready to make a run for it. Whitney is stunning in a full-length red dress with fringe that crisscrosses from her waist down. Her brown hair is shoulder-length and wavy, and she's smiling. Her smile instantly calms him.

"You're beautiful. It looks like you're ready to perform at the Oscars."

Thank you. You're close; I wore this at the Billboard Music Awards in 1993 when I sang "I Have Nothing" from the little movie and album I made called **The Bodyguard.** ***Did you ever see it?***

"Who hasn't seen that movie or heard that soundtrack? But that's kinda how I feel right now . . . like I have nothing."

Well, there's a deeper reason why I'm here today, in front of you, in this dress. She gives him a wink and a smile.

Michael tries to think of a conversation but instead he just dumps his life onto Whitney. "I was just humiliated by my ex, let go from my last job, and I can't seem to find another one. I've put on these extra pounds, and I feel so . . . so fat and unattractive, and now to boot, my car needs a new radiator and inspection. So even if I were to get another job, my car isn't gonna last much longer; even with a new radiator, something else will go wrong. I haven't got the money to get another one. And yes, I can take the subway or a bus, but a lot of my work has been outside the city. Having the car allows me to work longer, not relying on the schedule of public transportation. And let's not forget," Michael's voice gets angry. "Let's not forget to mention that my mother could fix all of this with a quick signature on a check." The animosity in his voice cuts his thoughts. "Okay, so I messed up in college. I was freakin' twenty." He's throwing his hands around as he's speaking, and the anger is rising. "I made some stupid mistakes. I trusted the wrong people. Coming from money the way I did, I didn't have to fight. I didn't have to figure out who I was. I had my mother's money. I should've attended her college, on her references, and then received my degree. I should've come back to work at the family diamond business. That's what I think should've happened."

Michael is furious now. He throws one hand in the air, "But oh no, not my mother! She had other plans for my life. She threw a big monkey wrench in the salad bowl of my life by insisting I go into culinary arts. Only I mess that up too. No one understands how the son of someone so wildly successful could be such a . . . *loser*. Everything just came easy before college. After college, no matter how many people my mother connected me to, I always seemed to mess it up." Embarrassed, Michael sits back down in the chair, leaning on the armrest, holding his forehead up with one hand, looking down at the floor and not at Whitney. "Unfortunately, what I've learned is that drugs and alcohol and the restaurant industry go hand in hand. When things got really bad, all that my mother wanted was for me to go to rehab, hold down a job, and find an honorable partner—a partner who was really single. That's what she said to me as she pushed me out into the hallway and slammed her big wooden door in my face, leaving me to fend for myself." Michael looks to Whitney for sympathy, but she just moves one shoulder, gives a quick nod of her head, and folds her arms.

I'm listening. Keep going.

Sighing and feeling sorry for himself, he continues.

"I'm not sure where I want to go with my life. Okay, yes, Mother is right. I *am* good at culinary arts. I do like it. But I feel so completely lost. I don't know. I'm at my wit's end. I'm ready for my losing streak to end. Ten years, Whitney. I've been at this now for *ten years* and I'm no better off than I was when my mother kicked me out with her ultimatum. I'm ready for some good news. I really thought this last relationship with Joel was the one." He sarcastically adds, "But nope, not Michael; he has shit for luck!"

Michael sighs. "When I was on that phone call this morning, I was so hopeful. I really thought they were gonna offer me the job, but I was turned down, again." He shrugs his shoulders tight and shakes his hands in front of him. "What am I doing wrong? I'm almost thirty friggin'-years old and I still don't have it together!"

Michael finally stops ranting and just sits there, his arms crossed against his chest and a disgusted frown on his face. His eyes well, so he rubs them with his palms to hold back the tears.

Did you ever think that maybe you aren't doing anything wrong? What if I told you right now that you're not doing anything wrong? Would you believe me?

Shrugging his shoulders in disbelief, he looks down. He feels defeated.

Speaking softly and to the floor he says, "I don't know, it just seems like some people don't have to try so hard. Good things just happen to them. I guess they're just lucky and I'm not. I *should* feel lucky. I *should* feel confident. Most people think I have it all. They say things like, 'You're a fucking Monroe, for Christ's sake. What the hell more could you want?' Plus, there's the burden of never having lived up to my parent's reputation. No one I know understands what that pressure is like. Everyone knows who my mother is and most of her peers and business partners look down on me. She's spent the last twenty years being Ms. Double D's in the wake of my dad's death. Mom's been photographed in every magazine and been to fashion shows in Paris, London, and Milan.

Asking "Who's Olivia Monroe?" is like asking "Who's Madonna?" I feel the constant pressure of being the son of two big famous personalities.

Michael, up till now, you haven't found out who you are, how amazingly wonderful you are. And let me tell you, I can see all the great things you're gonna go on to do. Yeah, that's right. She smiles and nods. ***But baby, until you figure out who you are***—Whitney holds her fingers up to create air quotes—***your "purpose," you're gonna keep feelin' like you're in a rut. It's these periods of life we all go through where we all feel like we're stuck, but these really are the magical moments. If we allow our passion to shine through, it will light the way. I want to inspire you. And that's where that key will come in handy. That key will remind you that you are not alone and that I am always with you!***

Michael perks up and says, "Well, I'm ready to make my mark on this big city. How do I learn to find my purpose?"

Baby, you don't have to learn anything. You know what to do. You already have everything you need. You just need to recognize it.

Whitney gets up off the desk and walks over to the doorway. She stops and looks back over her shoulder.

What excites you, Michael? What puts the biggest smile on your face? What would you love to do for the rest of your life? What would you love to be remembered for? As fast as a lightning strike, she disappears, leaving only a few dots of red lights floating in the air.

Michael jumps up and reaches for her. "Wait! Please don't go, not again! Help me figure this out. What do you mean, I know what to do?" But she's gone, and he's alone again, left thinking about what she said.

"Who am I? What do I like? What do I want to do with the rest of my life? How would I like to be remembered?" Michael suddenly realizes he actually feels excited thinking about what he likes. He gets goosebumps on his arms and rubs them as he smiles.

He runs downstairs to the kitchen, grabs his phone, and texts Lucy.

What do I like?

Boys . . . LOL

I'm being serious, what do you think I like?

You like a lot of things; you like to cook.

What else?

Music. Broadway. What's this about?

Whitney was just here again. She said I need to figure out who I am.

You know what works for me.

I pay attention to my dreams.

Dreams tell a lot about what's going on in the subconscious mind.

The phone rings, it's Lucy.

"I've got it! Call your mom. She's always been your biggest supporter, even though she has a very funny way of showing it. I've never met a mother so happy her son was gay. Remember that pool party she threw for your sweet-sixteen-coming-out party?" Lucy laughs. "Between your mom's celebrity friends and the thousands of pink balloons, you'd have thought it was a party for baby Jesus reborn as a girl."

Michael thinks of his mom. In his mind, she's wearing a feathery cheetah-print blouse probably made by Versace, a tight black skirt that falls just above the knee, and magnificent Vera Wang stilettos with rhinestones on the heels, showcasing her toned legs and calves—products of years of aerobic classes.

"I'll give her a call."

"Let me know what she says at dinner," Lucy laughs. "I swear when your mom and Joan Rivers were together in one room, they were unstoppable!"

They hang up and Michael calls his mother.

"Hi, Mother!" Michael says as she picks up the telephone.

"Darling, it is so good to hear from you. Are you going to be watching *Good Morning America* tomorrow? They're going to have the cast of *Kinky Boots* performing as a fundraiser for the AIDS Foundation. It looks fantastic! One of your favorites, that Cyndi Lauper, wrote the musical score. I guess she's going to be there too."

Michael smiles but gets serious, "No, Mom. Actually, I'm having a really rough time right now." He stops himself. He's afraid she'll react negatively to his last comment. He quickly tries to change his tone.

"What do I like, Mom? If you had to put me in a career, what would you think I'm best suited for?"

"Cooking. You have that flair, darling. You always did. Do some catering again. You gave up too soon last time. You didn't even ask me to use you as a caterer."

"I know, Mom, but it's that 'handout' thing. I want to do this on my own."

He feels his resentment building. He didn't ask her? He laughs a cynical laugh to himself. What, is she now going crazy?

The woman who threw him out now wants to give him a catering job? He's getting agitated the more he thinks about it.

"Get yourself involved in theater. Do some plays off-Broadway, like some of your friends. I'm sure one of them could pull some strings for you. It's not what you know; it's who you know, darling."

He can hear her sipping. It's probably a chardonnay. He pictures her swirling the last bit of wine around in the glass.

"Yeah, Mom, but I never got the whole dancing and singing and coordination thing down. For a gay man, I have two left feet."

She gets serious. Michael can feel her whole demeanor change, "Michael, I sent you to culinary school. You love to cook. I don't know why you're fighting me on this. You always throw great house parties. You love to entertain—" She gasps like she does when eyeing the perfect pair of shoes. "I've got it, open that restaurant you always wanted! Open a restaurant here in the city. How fabulous it will be! You'll cater to all the theatergoers, the casts and crews will have parties, and you'll feed Hollywood stars! You can decorate it in your personal style, a mix of Hollywood and Vaudeville. You can paint murals of Marilyn Monroe and Audrey Hepburn. After you open, you can write a book about your restaurant and sell it nationwide and you'll be the next great celebrity chef! I think that's your calling. Everyone will say, 'Who would have thought he would be such a great success?' And I'll tell them, 'I knew it all along!'"

Michael rolls his eyes toward the ceiling and shakes his head. His mother does have a great imagination—a land where nothing is impossible and everything is always a grand scheme.

He opens his mouth to say something when Olivia startles him with another excited gasp.

"You can call it . . . ready? . . . Hello, Dolly! You always did love Dolly Parton, and it ties in perfectly with the whole theater thing."

Oddly, Michael feels as if a chord has just been struck inside him. He's excited but his stomach is turning. He does love Dolly Parton. He does want his own restaurant. He likes the theater, throwing parties, Hollywood, all of it. Goose bumps rise all over his body, and he swoons at the thought of this restaurant coming to life. Then he thinks of his vision board and all of its images and smiles.

"Awesome, Mom! Thanks for the inspiration."

"Oh, I have to call all my friends. Wait till they hear this."

"Mom, Mom, Mom . . . stop. I can't even—" Michael stops himself from saying, "I can't even fix my car, let alone open a restaurant." He feels embarrassed but laughs instead.

"Mwah, darling. I must go." She blows a kiss into her phone before she hangs up.

CHAPTER 7

AFTER THE PHONE call with his mother, Michael quickly gets out of his sweatpants, throws on blue shorts and a gray polo shirt, slips into his Sperry Top-Siders, and goes out the door to have dinner with Lucy. They meet at Island, a tropical-meets-nautical restaurant well-known to locals near 92nd Street and Madison Avenue.

Lucy shows up radiating. Her wavy auburn hair is tightly pulled back in a ponytail resting over her right shoulder. She's wearing a pale yellow linen dress that flows in the breeze with dark brown sandals.

Michael and Lucy grab a table outside. Lucy orders The Buoy—grilled chicken, pesto, fresh mozzarella, and roasted red peppers on focaccia. Michael scans the menu for something inexpensive and tells the server he'll have the baked rigatoni.

"So, you said earlier you have something to tell me?"

As soon as Michael begins to tell Lucy about the breakup, everything comes rushing out. The entrance, the drinks, and how Joel basically made out with the bartender in front of the entire restaurant.

"I was mortified. I swear it felt like I was on an episode

of *Keeping Up With the Kardashians*. I wouldn't have been surprised if Kim had come out and taken a selfie of her and me and posted it to Talk2U, with the title 'Epic Dumping at Basil's!'"

"Well, you know I never really liked him anyway. What a turd he turned out to be."

"Tell me about it. I thought I had actually found a decent boyfriend to bring back to meet Mother. Thankfully, that didn't happen. I guess it was for the best that his schedule always conflicted with family affairs. What a jerk!" Michael says all the right words to convince himself but the bitter pings of hurt and distrust are still very alive in him.

The restaurant outside is now getting full but instead of ordering dessert, they opt to pay the bill and head home.

"What a beautiful night," Lucy says, looking up at the sky. "All those stars!"

They take a detour through Central Park just to enjoy the evening air and each other's company. They stop at a bench during their walk just to look at the stars as they try to pick out which ones are stars and which ones are the planets. Michael yells out, "Shooting star!" But it turns out to be just a plane. Lucy swats him on the arm, calls him Einstein, and laughs.

"I got it," Lucy yells out. She almost forgot she had the Star Walk app. She takes her phone out and opens the app. Star Walk uses the GPS of her phone and it displays all the stars in the night sky. She taps *Visible Tonight* and it displays a beautiful cosmic wonder on her screen. The both of them ooh and aah over all the stars. It illuminates the moon and several zodiac constellations: Sagittarius, Cancer, and Scorpio. They see Mercury, Mars, and Neptune. They keep scrolling the screen as it circles the Earth's night sky highlighting all the stars and they stop at the constellation Cassiopeia. It's named after the vain queen Cassiopeia in Greek Mythology who boasted of her unrivaled beauty. The app tells them this constellation is easily recognizable by its *W* shape formed by five bright stars.

W . . . Michael thinks of Whitney and gets an intuitive ping in his stomach.

Lucy clicks her phone off. They both decide it's better to do this again another night when they both have a little more time. They continue their walk.

Circling the reservoir, they stop at a coffee shop. In addition to their brew, they share a fabulous-looking vanilla cupcake with sprinkles on top and crushed Oreo cookies around the sides. Lucy gushes a little as she pulls her hair away from her mouth. "Oh my god," she coos, enjoying every bite. "This cupcake is so light and fluffy," she says, licking the icing off her fingers. "But, I will say, this cupcake does *not* compare to your boozy muffins. Those are delicious!"

Michael proudly smiles, "My boozy muffins are popular when I cater weddings or bridal showers. I've started making summery flavors—there's strawberry rum and the newest one I've created is raspberry mimosa!"

"Oooh, what's in that one?"

"I use fresh raspberries, of course, and Prosecco. Women are going crazy over them!"

"You'll have to make them for me on our next dinner date night."

After finishing up their coffee and dessert, they walk back to their complex.

"Good night," Michael and Lucy say at the same time. They laugh, hug, and disappear behind their own apartment doors.

Upstairs in his bedroom, Michael changes from his shorts into something comfier, grabbing and pulling on his favorite gray joggers. Coming back down into the living room, he sits on the couch and turns on the TV, but his mind is mulling over all his current stress and anxiety and the show ends up just as background noise. He stares at the TV, but his mind isn't processing the images. So many thoughts of money and debts flow through his mind. He switches his thinking to mostly of his mom and the early success of their Daisy Diamond business. He disappears into his thoughts.

He remembers some of the business engagements that his parents had and how his dad nicknamed the Daisy Diamond business Double D's and coined the slogan, *Women Want Double D's!* Eventually, every woman in the world wanted his father's Daisy Diamond. It was just salacious enough. Whenever customers stepped into jewelry stores, all the salespeople had to say was, "Would you like to see some Double D's?" Sales went through the roof.

He remembers several high-class parties in Manhattan where the men were boasting, "Wanna see my wife's Double D's?" And everyone would laugh. Michael, at the age he was then, couldn't understand why everyone would laugh at that statement. It was a huge marketing ploy that worked, and it worked *very* well. Michael envisions the huge billboards that were all throughout New York, up and down the New Jersey Turnpike, and into Connecticut. Each billboard was just a photo of a buxom model wearing a thin taupe-colored silk blouse, with her hands crossed one over the other pressing into her ample chest, a Double-D's on her ring finger.

Snapping back to the present, Michael's thoughts are interrupted as he hears the TV but he smiles at the happy, successful memories. But as fast as he smiles at the success his family has enjoyed, his current heavy situation rips the joyful memory away.

Frustrated, Michael gets up to make sure his door is locked. He turns off the TV and shuts off all the lights but just falls back down on the couch. As he's lying there, he thinks about what his mother said on the phone.

A restaurant.
Hello, Dolly.
And before he knows it, he's asleep and dreaming.

CHAPTER 8

MICHAEL'S BODY JERKS as he abruptly awakens, his arms and legs jolting into a self-defense position. He forgot he fell asleep on the sofa. Now he tries to recall everything that just happened in his dream. He remembers being in his car and driving on the ocean. It was nighttime. The sky was blackish-gray and there was a bright, full moon shining through the clouds onto the water. He was driving his car up and down over the waves. The car went underwater but quickly came back up. He wasn't frightened. In the dream it seemed perfectly normal to be driving his car on the water.

Suddenly, his car dove straight down into the water, eventually settling on the ocean floor, where his headlights pointed to an old treasure chest. The chest was open, with a golden light emanating that illuminated the ocean floor and everything around it. He could see the sandy bottom, seaweed flowing with the current. There were schools of tropical fish swimming all around and hundreds of seashells. Everything was in full color. In his dream, he tried to look inside the chest but couldn't because of the brightness of the golden glow.

Rubbing his hand through his hair he thinks, *Something*

beautiful and amazing was inside that chest. What was it? as he lies there on his sofa. What *was* in the treasure chest?

Morning breaks and he's awake. He rolls off the couch and goes into the kitchen to make some coffee. As he pours a bowl of cereal, his mind bounces between the dream and his conversation with his mom. A restaurant named Hello, Dolly. He smiles, imagining people sitting at tables, eating and drinking, the chatter of conversations echoing in his mind. He thinks about all the excitement a great restaurant can create.

What if? Michael thinks as he crunches on his cereal and more mental images dance in his mind.

After breakfast, he goes and sits back on the couch and flips on the TV, but after about ten minutes of channel surfing, he decides to get dressed and go for a walk around the city. He thinks maybe he'll stop at some vacant storefronts. *Why not.* He smiles and shrugs his shoulders.

Around eleven in the morning, Michael is casually strolling the sidewalks when an unfamiliar restaurant with a small outdoor patio catches his eye. There are several couples sitting at small bistro tables enjoying quiche, fruit, and French toast. Some guests are enjoying waffles and mimosas. He's admiring the pretty flowers in the entryway when he imagines this place to be his own restaurant. He envisions his sign *Hello, Dolly* hanging in the window when his eyes spot a help-wanted sign.

"I do need a job," Michael thinks. "Waiting tables is fast cash and this will at least give me something to do until I decide what I'm gonna do next."

He reads the name of the restaurant—Fate. He realizes that he's never seen this restaurant before even though he has lived in this neighborhood for almost two years. Michael enters, looks around and immediately has a feeling of déjà vu.

Maybe I've been here before.

Maybe it once was another business but has now changed

ownership. He tilts his head and wonders as his eyes keep scanning the walls. Something feels very familiar to him. He sees all the glowing reviews and awards the restaurant has earned that are hanging in the foyer. He hears the chatter of the guests eating inside. He smells coffee and cinnamon-sugar dough—what he assumes is from the French toast and Belgian waffles he saw the guests outside eating. He approaches the young woman at the hostess stand and asks for an application. Suddenly, out of nowhere a woman with dark hair quickly walks in and stands very close behind Michael. Awkwardly close, Michael thinks.

Thankfully, the perky blond hostess smiles and waves in Michael's direction. "Follow me; right this way!"

They walk into the kitchen through the silver swinging doors and into an office in the back corner where a large man is sitting at a desk.

"Hey Joey," the hostess says. "Here's an applicant."

Michael extends his hand to shake but Joey just slaps an application into it.

"If you fill it out quick enough, I'll be able to interview you today," Joey says.

Oh, goody, Michael thinks. *What a charmer this guy is.*

He's led back to the bar area, where he fills out the application. It takes him about ten minutes, and he walks back through the kitchen to Joey's disheveled office. It has many filing cabinets with several drawers left open. There are a slew of plates, all different sizes, and many different options of glassware all scattered either on his desk or sitting on chairs. *Maybe he's reordering dinnerware,* Michael thinks. And paper, there's paperwork and receipts everywhere. He knocks on the open door before stepping into the room.

"I'm finished. Should I come back later?"

"When can ya start, kid?"

Michael is taken off guard.

"I thought you wanted to interview me first."

"Nah, you'll do. I'm assuming you already have restaurant experience . . . " He grabs the application from Michael. " . . . or you wouldn't be here, right?" He looks up at Michael over his reading glasses with an exaggerated *Am I right?* look. He quickly reads Michael's experience. "Chef, waiter, manager, dishes . . . So, when can you start?"

"I can be here tomorrow."

Michael is relieved Joey didn't say anything about his last name. Most employers have made comments asking him if he was a Monroe.

"Tomorrow it is, kid. Ten o'clock. I'll get you a company T-shirt when you get here," Joey pauses. "Lemme ask ya, kid. Why did you apply here?"

"I'm in need of a job. I was walking around the neighborhood and happened to see your help-wanted sign."

"Ahh," is all Joey says.

"Well, it was nice to meet you, and thank you. I'll see you tomorrow, ten a.m."

Michael leaves the kitchen and walks past the hostess stand, planning to thank the blond hostess, but now an older woman is standing there. Michael continues past her and the hostess stand and walks back out into the sunshine, exhaling a sigh of relief; he has a job. He heads on over toward the park.

Whatchu doing?

Whitney's appearance practically scares him to death. He yells, "Oh my freakin' god!" His body jerks as he throws his arms up to defend himself. "You almost gave me a heart attack!"

I would be a little more careful about the way you're walkin' about, jumping and screaming and talking to yourself like that. People are gonna think you ain't right, she laughs.

"So . . . enlighten me." He angrily puts his hands on his hips, "What's 'right' about talking to Whitney Houston, who's dead but says she's my guardian angel?" He glares at her.

Ain't my fault you choose not to see me, 'cause I'm always here, baby.

"Well, in the future, can you give me a little bit of a notice, you know, maybe a breeze, a white feather? Normal things ghosts do to alert someone that they'll be poppin' in outta nowhere?"

I'll try, she says with a dazzling smile and a wave of her hand. ***Your wish is my command.***

Michael's beginning to think she didn't hear a word he said. They're casually walking along a winding black asphalt path in Central Park. Whitney puts her arm through Michael's as they walk. The sun sporadically shines on them through the leaves on the trees. To everyone else in the park, it looks like Michael is just walking alone. Whitney's wearing a tight, sparkly silvery-blue short dress with a big matching bow tied in her curly brown hair from her "How Will I Know" video.

So, you applied for that job. Whitney says it more like a statement, not a question.

"Oh, you saw that? Yeah, that went real well. Joey, whoever he is, he seems like a real charmer."

Getting you outta the house this morning took a little longer than I expected. That's the thing: even with me guiding, you still have the freedom to do as you please. We almost missed getting you that job. Do you remember seeing that woman who walked into the restaurant after you?

"Yeah, I kinda remember. The brunette, right?"

She was there applying for that same job. But you got it! An older hostess—well let's just say she had to step away from the hostess stand. She asked the little blond girl to seat people until she got back. I just knew that little blondie couldn't resist the possibility of working with you every day. And I knew she would instantly walk you into the office to meet Joey. That's why he was so put off. It had nothing to do with you—he likes you. He was

mad because little blondie shouldn't have brought you back to him. The older hostess is supposed to be doing the interviewing. After you left, Joey came out and told her about you as she was interviewing Miss Brunette, and well, she didn't get the job.

Things aren't always what we perceive them to be. Ya know? First impressions aren't always correct, especially if you ain't paying attention to your body and how you're feeling. If you would've stopped to think about how you were feeling when you saw the outside furniture, the flowers, the restaurant itself, its name, and right down to how reading the help-wanted sign made you feel, you would have known that it was all inviting you. Green light, baby, pass Go and collect three hundred dollars! And by the way, that's how much you'll be making tomorrow. You're gonna be busy, so be ready. Your first day . . . well, ya know, I'm just sayin'. She smiles.

Oh, and I know you ain't thinking of it now, but you'll thank me later. She gives Michael a wink from her left eye and *POOF!* just like that . . . she's gone.

"Why do you keep doing that?" Michael yells into the air.

People gonna think you ain't right! She gives her cackle laugh as a white feather floats down in front of Michael and he hears, ***Like that?***

Michael sees the gently falling feather and smiles. He yells up to the heavens, "Yes, like that!"

The phone buzzing in his pocket distracts Michael's attention from Whitney's latest disappearing act. He looks at the screen. *MOTHER.*

"Hello, Mother! How are you?"

"Darling, I'm in the city, and I just happened to run into Lucy at the department store. We're going to get a late lunch at Belle Bistro. Are you available to join us?"

"Yeah, sure. I'll be there in a couple of minutes."

Michael arrives to see his mother and Lucy sitting at an

outside table under an umbrella. They both have cocktails.

"We ordered you sangria," Olivia says. "I hope it will be as good as the ones you make."

Although she looks effortless, Olivia is done up to the nines. She's sporting a big white brimmed hat with a black ribbon, a silk Chanel scarf is perfectly wrapped around her neck, and she's wearing a crisp white suit with a camel-colored button-down blouse. As always, she's left an extra button undone to show just enough ample bosom. She has big, bulky red bracelets on her wrists and a large sapphire gemstone on her right index finger. And of course, hanging like a monocle from a long, thick gold Gucci necklace, is an unmistakable thirty-carat Double D's diamond. Twenty-five years later, men and women alike stare at Olivia's Double D's.

"So," Michael says as he sits down in the chair, "I took a job today at a restaurant named Fate. I'll be waiting tables until I decide what I'm gonna do next."

Olivia gives him a look of disgust. He can read her face—she's thinking, *my son waiting tables*. Luckily, his sangria comes at that moment, which quickly changes the mood and all three raise their glasses and toast Michael's new job.

Lucy chirps in, "I have some good news of my own. I've just been promoted inside my department to assistant marketing director for the arts center. I'm heading the new nonprofit art program designed to keep inner-city children safe and off the streets by teaching them art. It's now my new duty to get the word out about our after-school programs."

"Well, congratulations to you, Lucy," Olivia says. "I'm always looking for great organizations that are helping our community and please let me be the first sponsor for your new position."

Olivia opens her purse, reaches in for her checkbook, writes a check, and very delicately, in her own Olivia way, gives Michael a curt glare as she hands it to Lucy right there on the spot.

Michael hears Whitney, ***Oh, hell no!***

Michael is relieved knowing Whitney is there but inside he gets angry.

"Hey, what about me," Michael looks at his mother with a playful, maybe sarcastic smile.

"What about you, Michael," she glares at him. "I sent you to culinary college and now you're going to be making your own money waiting tables. You don't need my money." She gives him a dead stare then takes a sip of her sangria. Lucy feels the tension and moves in her chair.

Michael wants to explode, but he doesn't say anymore. His thoughts, however, continue in his mind. *How about writing me a freakin' check? I'm your freakin' son and I'm freakin' broke and struggling!* He quickly decides it's not worth it. As happy as he is for Lucy, it stings him how cold and uncaring his mother can be toward him. He suddenly feels sick to his stomach.

Lucy looks down at the check, "Oh my god, thank you, Ms. Monroe." She gasps a little then out loud as she reads the check, "Three thousand dollars. The gallery will be very pleased tomorrow when I arrive," Lucy squeamishly puts the check right into her small handbag, hoping everyone will just forget it ever happened.

"Oh, it's *Olivia*, darling." She taps Lucy's hand. "*Ms. Monroe* makes me feel like you're talking to Michael's grandmother. And what a goat she was."

Again, that fire of disgust builds up inside Michael; he knows how three thousand dollars would fix his car. He breathes it through again and tries to let the thought go. He thinks, *It's not worth a big fight*. But he's still furious.

Their food arrives and it seems to take the tension off the whole money issue between Michael and his mom. Lucy looks down at her Caesar salad, which has a nicely orange-ginger-glazed salmon resting on the dressed romaine lettuce. The server asks if Lucy would like some fresh ground pepper on top, and she accepts. Olivia has opted for fresh fruit and a marinated chicken breast with a delicate serving of black sesame quinoa. Michael went with the grass-fed burger, with a thin layer of kimchi, aged sharp cheddar and house-made papas fritas. All their food looks amazingly well-dressed, is colorfully garnished, and has been plated with pristine care.

Just as Olivia taps her napkin to her mouth and they all finish eating, a commotion begins on the street. A moving truck is double-parked, its crew loading up chairs, a sofa, several boxes, a mattress, pictures, and lamps. One of the movers is walking out with a big disorganized pile of down comforters and pillows that he's trying to keep wrapped in his arms. He trips on the dangling comforter and loses his grip on all the bedding just as a sudden gust of wind whips it all into the air. The bedding lands on the road and is destroyed by several passing cars, sending white feathers flying everywhere. Another strong gust carries thousands of white feathers over toward the restaurant, where they float down onto all the guests.

Was that the subtle sign you wanted me to use? A breeze and white feathers to let you know I'm here? Whitney laughs and does a little jig as Michael sees her standing next to him.

Take that Olivia! she says with a snap and quickly disappears again.

Michael can't help himself. He bursts out in a fit of hysterical laughter.

Lucy looks at him. She starts giggling herself. "What are you laughing at?"

Olivia looks back and forth between the two of them, getting more annoyed. There are thousands of white feathers everywhere as both Michael and Lucy laugh at something that isn't funny. Olivia stands up and tries wiping the feathers off her outfit. Seemingly getting nowhere, now she starts angrily picking feathers off her outfit, one by one. "What are you two laughing at?" she demands. Then at the absurdity of it, she starts giggling herself. "This is ridiculous!" She shakes her hands in disgust. She looks down at all the feathers all over her and a moment later, she too is roaring. She reaches down into her cleavage and picks out feathers. "Look! They're in my bosom." They all look around at all the other patrons and slowly, one by one, everyone who was angry at the feather storm begins to join in the laughter. It's impossible not to. The scene is like a gay discotheque. Several flamboyant men dance in the feathers. Cars on the streets are coming to a stop, the drivers and passengers are holding their phones up to take pictures and videos. Passersby stop on the street and watch, perhaps wondering if they've walked onto a movie set with a celebrity possibly nearby.

Michael spots a photographer with a big bulky camera taking pictures of the scene. He's watching this man taking pictures of the crowd. Slowly, he starts walking closer to Michael, Olivia, and Lucy. There now seems to be a thousand people who have gathered around, watching the spectacular feathery storm. The photographer is now very close but stands still. Michael can actually hear the rapid sounds of the camera shutter opening and closing with each picture being taken. As the photographer is shooting, something apparently catches his eye as he pulls the camera down from his face as if to see what it is that caught his attention. He sees the photographer looking at his mother. Michael then sees the photographer zoom in on his mother as he snaps more pictures. He pulls the camera down one last time and approaches Michael's table.

"Hello, I'm Ed Turgeon, a photographer with the *Daily Record*," he says with an extended hand. "I've captured a picture of this feathery blizzard for online and tomorrow's paper and was wondering if I can have your names and permission to print the pictures?"

All three willingly give their names. Ed already knows who

Ms. Monroe is, though he's never met her. He makes sure all of the spellings are correct and passes out his business card.

"Thank you for this. I'm gonna title it, *A Feathery Blizzard in Manhattan.*" Ed nods and quickly takes off. He's practically skipping, he is so happy. He jumps into his car knowing that he's got to download these photos fast.

The wind has died down, the feathers have stopped flying around, and all the waitstaff are working feverishly.

Baby, one thing you have to remember is to be careful what you wish for! Because wishes do come true—white feathers and a breeze, Whitney says with a laugh as she appears next to Michael, looking rather proud of herself.

Shoo! Michael thinks to Whitney and waves her away. *No more white feathers.*

Oh no. You did not just 'shoo' me! Oh hell no! Ya better lay low! She glares at Michael.

Go! Michael's thoughts flash to his idol, the disco queen herself, Donna Summer. And how she often said in interviews to be careful what you wish for.

You got that right baby! Be careful what you wish for. Now you got me and Donna following your ass around.

She turns around and looks over her shoulder at Michael. She's in a black sparkly torch dress. She gives one last loud laugh and says, ***Love to love you, baby!*** She winks and disappears, leaving black glitter floating in the air. The black sparkles slowly disappear.

Things fall back into a regular controlled-chaos kind of order. Everyone settles back as they were before the feathery blizzard. There's still a thin layer of feathers covering all the umbrellas over the tables and on the ground like a fresh coating of snow.

Olivia speaks first. "So, what was that all about, darling? You seemed to understand something that nobody else did. Do tell us your secret."

Lucy, once again sits stone still and pierces her lips shut, diverting her eyes away from both Michael and Olivia. She looks down and smoothes the napkin in her lap. She does not want to be the one to explain to Olivia that Whitney Houston is now her son's guardian angel.

Olivia takes one look at Lucy and says, "Spill it!"

It's Michael who answers. "Mother, there are just some things we can't explain. And even when we can explain them, most of the time people aren't going to believe what you just told them."

"Okay darling, is this some kind of riddle? Just explain what happened."

Michael is still looking for a way out, so he pauses and says, "What if I told you a ghost caused that?"

"A ghost?" She looks at him, searching for more of an answer.

"Yes, a ghost."

Michael hears Lucy whisper, "Oh lord," as she twirls a strand of hair around her finger.

Olivia glares at Lucy.

"What are you trying to tell me—that your father is back, flying in on one of those feathers?" She lets out an atrocious laugh, almost sure they're trying to entertain her with some nonsense.

"Not exactly, but yes, something along those lines."

"Is this going to be a guessing game, Michael?" Olivia's attitude switches and now she's annoyed. "Just answer me!"

Michael takes a deep breath and holds it in. He thinks about Whitney's movie, *Waiting to Exhale,* and realizes that's exactly what he's doing. Holding his breath, waiting to exhale, thinking about how he's going to explain this to his mother. And that's when Whitney reappears. She sits like a debutante, straight up in the chair at the table, still in the same black sparkly torch dress. The dress's long slit uncovers her legs as she crosses them. Michael's attention turns to her as both Lucy and his mother see him glance at something in the chair that isn't there.

Go ahead, tell her. She's a big girl. She can handle it.

Michael finally exhales and says, "Mother, I don't know what I did, but somehow I . . . well . . . this will seem very crazy but somehow . . . my um . . . well, oh boy." He shakes his head trying to form a complete sentence. "Okay, so . . . my guardian angel has appeared to me. And she's right there, sitting in that chair next to you." He opens his hand and points toward the empty chair.

Olivia's body lunges forward, "Your guardian angel?" She tilts her head sideways as if she didn't hear him correctly.

"Yes, my guardian angel."

Aren't you gonna tell her who I am? Oh, she'll love that one!

Michael laughs but spills it out real fast, almost in a single word.

"And my guardian angel is Whitney Houston!" He takes another quick deep breath, releases it, and smiles at his mother, preparing himself for what she'll say.

Wait for it, wait for it . . .

"Whitney Houston? Your guardian angel. You're telling me your guardian angel is Whitney Houston?"

Oooh, she's a fast one!

"Yes."

"And she's right there." Olivia points to the empty chair. "Sitting with us in that chair?"

"Yes."

Olivia waves her hand over the chair as if to shoo away a bug.

"And you can see her and talk to her and hear her responses?"

Honey, don't make me knock your hat off!

"Yes." Michael smirks but holds back from laughing at all of Whitney's comments.

"Umm . . . interesting." Olivia forms a tent with her fingertips as she contemplates her next laughable question. "So tell me this: Whitney Houston, your guardian angel . . ." She pauses. "What is she telling you to do?"

"She's not really telling me to do anything. She's just giving me advice . . . kind of pointing me"—Michael uses his fingers to create air quotes—"in the right direction."

"What exactly is she pointing you toward?"

"My purpose in life."

"Your purpose in life?" She lowers her head just slightly and raises her eyebrows; she silently glares her disapproval at him. "I see." She collects more thoughts and says, "Your purpose in life, Michael, should be to learn to work hard." She curtly nods her head up and down, confirming it's something he needs to learn. "I don't know exactly how you view me, Michael, but I'm no stranger to hard work. Before I met your father, I had to put myself through Fordham University on my own. My parents didn't pay for my tuition like I did for you—even after your drug escapades."

Michael is not only shocked by her words, but he feels belittled.

"I hustled my ass off, Michael. I worked the desks of Morgan Stanley by day and was an auctioneer at Sotheby's on weekends. And then I met your father and guess what? he wanted to open a diamond business." She points both her hands at her temples as if to search for some insane answer, "Like how in the hell do we do that?" Another pause, "I worked, Michael; you don't know what work is until the impossible is before you and you have to find the answer. You will never know how I sacrificed after I married your father, helping him get that damn diamond business off the ground. Your purpose, Michael, should be to learn to work hard."

After listening to her and silently taking notes, Michael responds. "Okay, Mother, my purpose; let's start there. Maybe it isn't so obvious to you, but since I was thrown out of the house ten years ago, my life hasn't exactly been all that easy. Don't know if you've ever noticed or not but I haven't exactly been traveling the globe. There have been no Caribbean cruises." Michael's emotional dam finally breaks, and it all comes up as he spews out ten years of resentment.

"In fact, I've been unemployed for six weeks till just today. So, yes, I'm proud to have a job even if it is just waiting tables, which is sooo beneath you, my dear mother. My pathetic excuse for a car? Yeah well, it's broken down and needs three thousand dollars of repairs." Michael sarcastically gives a big laugh.

"And get this, Mother: it broke down right in front of your building. How's that for convenient, eh? You were probably up in the employee break room pointing down, laughing at me." His eyes throw daggers at her. "Maybe convenient for someone else who's parent didn't toss them out." He looks at Olivia with disgust. "And yeah, three thousand dollars worth of repairs that I don't have." He looks at Lucy and it just comes out. "But Lucy over there, she's holding a check for three thousand dollars from you." Michael sees Lucy's unexpected and mortified surprise but he's still strangely relieved to let it all out.

"Thrown out!" Olivia retorts in disgust, "Michael, you were a drug addict! Remember when I had to bail you out of jail after the drug possession charges? Remember your face being splattered on the cover of the *New York Post*." She stretches her arms up in the air and widens them as if displaying a banner. "'Michael Monroe Arrested on Drug Charges!' Or did you just choose to forget that?" She goes silent.

"I WASN'T A DRUG ADDICT!" he screams at her and hits his fists on the table. Lucy flinches and the restaurant goes silent as everyone stares at them.

Through gritted teeth Olivia assertively, slowly, and nonchalantly responds, "I am NOT doing this here Michael!" She grabs the napkin from her lap and touches it to her lips to avoid any more attention, making it seem as if everything is okay. Olivia reaches into her purse and reapplies her mayberry shade lipstick. They sit quietly for a few moments.

Michael knows it's now or never to tell the truth of what really happened that day. "Mom, listen," he says very quickly but softly so she doesn't interrupt him. "The drugs were not mine."

Olivia opens her mouth to speak, but Michael continues before she can. "Mom, please just listen." Olivia's chest rises as she takes a deep breath. "I was young and stupid." He acknowledges her painted picture of the truth. "I was nineteen and until then, I had never left your side growing up." He pauses. "You enrolled me in culinary college. I never understood why you didn't send me to Fordham or NYU for a business degree to help run the diamond business, but off to culinary college I went, and I was a kid in a candy store."

No one is eating at the table but Michael. He dips one of his last remaining papas fritas in ketchup and chews it, trying to resume a normal lunch appearance. He continues, "I was exposed to a world I'd never seen. All the kids around me, they all had drugs. Pot, pills, powder, you name it, I saw it." He swallows knowing the full truth has to come out. "Did I do some drugs, Mother?" He looks her directly in the eyes, "Yes I did. I wanted to fit in and make some friends."

Olivia opens her mouth again to say something snappy, but Michael is quick enough to stop her. "Don't . . . just listen." He sips his water. "Those 'friends' I made stole a car, bought drugs, and then picked me up. We were going out to a beach on Long Island." Michael stops again; this time he throws his head back and grabs his hair with both hands, looking up at the sky for some strength and continues. "I didn't know the car was stolen and I didn't know they had just bought drugs. They stopped at a convenience store. They asked me to sit behind the wheel of the car. Without thinking, I just did. Then they went inside to buy, maybe steal, who knows," he says, shrugging his shoulders. "They said they were grabbing beer, chips, and snacks. But as they were inside, a cop recognized the car I was in as being the one described as stolen. With me there in the car, all my 'friends' saw the cops outside and split and left me and the drugs and the stolen car."

Michael's eyes fill with tears as he remembers the excruciatingly painful memory and he looks down at the table to avoid eye contact. "Because of who I am," he says, hesitating, "your son, the police called you." His eyes are now bloodshot as he looks at his mother. "Then you and your team of lawyers descended so fast on them to have me released, to make all the charges and everything go away, that a blood test was never done, Mother. I wasn't a drug addict. I wasn't using drugs. I was a naive kid who made stupid friends and it cost me . . . EVERYTHING!" He shouts the last word as a tear rolls down his face. He quickly wipes it away.

"Apparently, Mother, . . . apparently this time I screamed loud enough that someone finally heard me. As unbelievable as it may seem, with Whitney appearing, she's helping me understand what it is I'm here to do. So yes, she's helping me find my purpose from being an exiled Monroe." He breathes and takes a large sip of water.

"Michael, did you just watch *It's A Wonderful Life* with that Clarence guy or maybe that movie Whitney remade . . . oh what was it? Oh, yes, *The Preacher's Wife*?"

"No, Mother, I did not."

"I'm trying to accept this, Michael, but I need a little more . . . proof shall I say," she says with a bit of sarcasm and open hands as if Michael can place the proof in her palms.

Oh, goodie, my turn. What does she need to know?

"Whitney just asked 'What do you need to know?'"

"You're really talking to her?" Olivia turns and looks at Lucy. "Do you really believe this?" She twirls her finger in a spiral beside her head. "Lucy, are you okay with this? Are you two listening to yourselves?"

Lucy sighs, "Olivia, I had my share of concerns and I had to push my own skepticism aside. I didn't want to believe it because it doesn't seem plausible or make any sense." She looks at

Michael with concerned eyes. “But I do watch shows like Theresa Caputo’s, where people connect with spirits, and I know what she does is real, but this thing with Michael and Whitney,” she says, taking a big breath in, “I believe something like this is possible. For some odd reason it just seems more possible when it’s a person you don’t know, rather than it happening to someone you do know. Because I just don’t understand how Michael opened that spiritual vortex.” She gives a questioning throw of her eyes and a shoulder shrug. “But Whitney already gave me my proof when I asked. So now I just have to believe.”

“Proof? She’ll give me proof?” Olivia glares at Michael, “Okay, ask your guardian angel, Whitney Houston, to tell you who was the first boy I ever kissed and where?” Feeling confident, Olivia sits straight back regally in her chair.

CHAPTER 9

A DOUBLE QUESTION, ***huh? She's trying to be clever . . . Okay, Olivia! Billy Matthews, fifth grade, on the playground, at the monkey bars!***

Michael repeats what Whitney says word for word and Olivia's face goes pale, her eyes squint trying to figure out how he knew, and her mouth slowly falls agape. She freezes for just a moment.

And by the way, have Olivia tell you the excuse she told her mother when she asked why she missed the bus home!

Michael turns to his mother and relates Whitney's latest comments.

Olivia curtly responds, "Michael, it was a very long time ago; I don't remember."

Tell her, 'liar, liar pants on fire,' Whitney says in a high whiny schoolgirl voice.

Michael repeats that to his mother.

Olivia fidgets in her chair, the truthful discomfort making her uncross her legs as she proceeds to recross them and sit a little more upright. She then leans heavily onto her right arm.

She told her mother she forgot her Girl Scout vest in her classroom, and that was why she missed the bus. But it was

because she was kissing Billy Matthews . . . Oh, and by the way, tell your mother that your father's mother, your grandmother, is now here. 'Ms. Monroe' as Olivia calls her. Your grandmother wants you to tell Olivia that, no, she isn't a goat!

Michael repeats and Olivia falls silent again. There is no room for her to lie anymore. She presses her lips together, taps her index finger to her mouth, and squints. With her other hand, she starts twisting her Double D's necklace in her fingers. It seems as though she's desperately searching for anything to say, any sort of rebuttal, but nothing comes. All three of them just sit in silence.

Finally, Michael speaks up.

"Mother, I'm sorry. I love you. I don't know how I did this but I'm telling you the truth. Whitney Houston is my guardian angel and she's here now and I'm just trying to learn how to deal with all of this and move on and live my best life."

"Michael, it's only human nature to be skeptical." She pauses for a few seconds to find the right words. "I want to believe you, even though I can't comprehend how any of this is possible . . . at all!" She uses her hands to erase an imaginary image in front of her.

Well spoken Olivia, even when new truths shatter perceptions of your own beliefs.

Seconds that seem like minutes pass as the cynical tension begins to lift at the table. Olivia starts asking questions about when it began. Michael retells the story. Lucy just sits there silently, nodding to confirm how it all happened.

The waiter comes back around and interrupts the conversation to ask if anyone wants more cocktails. All three of them look directly at the server and say in unison, "Yes!"

"Make mine a double." Olivia smiles at the waiter, then at Michael and Lucy. Now that there seems to be a sense of calmness in Michael, he thinks his mother is grasping at shreds of truth. Or at least the best she can. He thinks the cat is out of the bag and the worst is over. His secret is out. Now they'll all just need to deal with a new supernatural normal.

Okay, Whitney says to Michael. ***Getting all three of you together has worked. Now the real fun begins—creating what you call a miracle.*** Whitney snaps her fingers and is gone.

"Whitney just left," Michael blurts out. "She said she needed to get all of us together." He inquisitively looks back and forth at them.

Olivia, not shy about wanting to change the subject starts a new conversation.

"So, let's talk about Hello, Dolly."

"What's Hello, Dolly?" Lucy asks as she snaps her head up from taking a sip of water. Michael fills her in on the earlier conversation he'd had with his mother.

"I have to say that I love that idea!" Lucy says.

"I took that job today as a waiter because it's what I'm good at—restaurant hospitality. I enjoy cooking and the artistic expression that comes along with creating new food items. Waiting tables is just fast cash and maybe I can learn a little bit more along the way from working at a small, locally owned restaurant. I believe this is a good starting point. I'm happy and actually glad that the college I applied to work at didn't offer me the position. If I'd gotten it, I would've become content and I might not have even considered the possibility of becoming an entrepreneur."

"Can you see me as the hostess?" His mother touches her hand against her chest and her Double D's, very proud of her new duty.

"Mother, you will make the greatest hostess. I can't think of anyone better, with such an inviting personality. And, needless to say"—he gestures to her power suit and diamond necklace—"style that will make guests feel so welcomed."

His mother smiles and blushes a little.

Lucy chimes in, "Don't forget about me, Miss Newly

Appointed Assistant Director of Marketing. You're gonna need someone who will create a website, advertise, promote your business, and hand out menus." She strikes a pose. "Vogue!" Lucy knows Michael will understand the reference.

"I can't believe how quickly all of this is coming together." Michael is excited, and his mother and Lucy seem thrilled as well.

They all touch their glasses together for a toast. The three of them yell out in unison, "Here's to Hello, Dolly!"

With their late lunch over, Michael and Lucy say goodbye to his mother, and they start their walk home. Michael points out Fate, his new place of employment to Lucy. "I start work there tomorrow," he tells her.

"Huh. I've never noticed that restaurant before," Lucy says.

"Yeah, neither have I. But I'm glad I found it today. I think it was Whitney's doing." He bumps his shoulder into Lucy to knock her off balance and get her attention.

It's half past six by the time they make it back to their complex. Lucy looks at Michael, wide-eyed. "Hey, do you want to watch her movie, *Waiting to Exhale*?"

A smile spreads across Michael's face.

Excitedly, Lucy says, "You make the popcorn; I'll grab the movie and wine and be right over."

When Lucy arrives, Michael has already popped the popcorn and effortlessly created a buttery salted-caramel flavor. He throws a piece in his mouth, smiles, and thinks, *Perfection.* He walks back to where Lucy is sitting on a big cheetah-print pillow on the floor with her back against his sofa sitting cross-legged. She has already poured two glasses of sauvignon blanc.

As the movie starts, Whitney drives a convertible down a long, straight desert highway against a beautiful fiery dusk sky as the four main characters are introduced.

Lucy is in awe. "Wow, Whitney looks amazing. Is this what she looks like when you see her?"

"Yes, sometimes. She's appeared in several different looks from throughout her career so far."

Michael especially connects with this movie because it's all about friendship and all the women in the movie are having difficulties with relationships. He feels so happy to be sitting here with Lucy. His mind, however, races to memories of Joel and he sighs. Michael knows he'll find his Mr. Right someday. He wishes it was sooner rather than later, but he knows it will happen. Michael wonders if Whitney would tell him the same thing.

He starts to look for Whitney but sees nothing. He tries talking to her in his mind, but still no Whitney. He suddenly feels alone. He doesn't know why. Lucy is right next to him. He feels nervous, like Whitney isn't going to come back. In his mind this would be a perfect time for her to show up. So why isn't she? He's thinking way too hard to find answers, to make up answers, maybe even plan out how it should be going. He's thinking of all the reasons why she should be here right now.

Haven't I told you already? I'm always here. I'm always with you. And, anyway, I made that movie! I don't need to watch it. Do you think they'll change the ending? He hears her laugh. ***But seriously, baby, you gotta stop planning how things should go. Dream about how you want things to go and then let your thoughts go.***

Sorry but this ain't Xanadu and I ain't gonna be Olivia Newton-John twirling around here on roller skates. But baby you're magic. Your thoughts create your reality.

Your job is to dream. You know, dream of what you want and then do everything you can to bring it to you. Leave out the how and when. The Universe will make all your dreams come alive and at the right time. It's that simple. It's best to learn this early, baby.

Michael mulls over what she just said, and he wants to agree, but his life these last ten years has taught him that well: he just isn't that lucky. He's chased after dreams that haven't come true. He's tried to obtain the career he wants, but he just can't seem to make it happen. Job after job, boyfriend after boyfriend, year after year, here he is. He wonders why the pictures of his fame and success on his vision board haven't come true.

Michael realizes that he wasn't startled just now when Whitney popped in. He just intuitively turned his head and looked at her when she appeared standing next to the TV.

Whitney is wearing the beautiful brown gown from the movie *Waiting to Exhale* when she enters the restaurant for her New Year's Eve blind date. Her brown hair is pulled up in the back and a few strands of curled hair hang down around her face.

I'm wearing this particular dress for you because you're not the only one who has dreamed, like my character. She was hoping that this date was gonna be the one, only to have another dream of hers not come true. She instinctively puts her hands gently on her hips, running her hands down against her body, pulling any creases out of the dress.

Lucy pauses the movie, but Michael hasn't even noticed. He's too involved with Whitney.

"Ah-hem!" Lucy coughs. That gets Michael's attention. "What's going on?"

"Whitney's here again. She's wearing that brown dress that you like so much from this movie."

"The New Year's Eve brown dress?"

"Yes, that dress."

"I love that dress!"

Tell her I said thank you.

"Whitney says thank you."

"Oh my god, she can hear me?"

"Apparently."

"Where is she?"

Michael points and says, "She's standing to the right of the TV."

"Right there?" Lucy points.

"Yup."

"Can I give her a hug?"

"I mean, I guess you can try."

Lucy gets up and goes to the right of the TV and gives a big open hug to the empty air. She holds her arms wide leaving room not to squeeze Whitney too tight.

What does she think I am, four hundred pounds? Gimme a hug girl!

"I don't feel anything."

Michael laughs at Whitney's comment, "Well, she's smiling and hugging you back."

"This is so cool. And she's really right here?"

"Yes, Lucy, she's right there. I'm not kidding with you."

Well, you two finish the movie. At least I know how it ends, she says, laughing. ***Don't forget, tomorrow is a big day. It's your first day, so be ready. Don't stay up too late.*** She points her finger at Michael as if to warn him, and then she's gone. Michael sees a few sparkles of brown light that quickly fade out.

"Whitney just left," Michael said. "She reminded me not to stay up late tonight. She keeps mentioning that tomorrow is going to be a big day. I'm only working three hours. What can really happen in three hours?"

"I don't know, but if she tells you something, I'd believe it." Lucy throws more popcorn in her mouth. "And did I ever tell you how delicious you made this popcorn? Yum city!"

Out of the clear blue Michael hears, ***Now that's a smart friend!***

Michael looks at Lucy and tells her Whitney's comment, to which Lucy smiles proudly. Together they leave the floor, settle in on the couch, and finish watching the movie. Michael throws a blanket over both their laps. At ten o'clock the movie ends and Lucy leaves to go back next door to her apartment. Michael stays up cleaning until almost eleven. When he finishes, he picks up his phone and opens Talk2U, scrolling through his feed. He sees Lucy made a post:

"Watching *Waiting to Exhale* with @Michael Monroe." There's a picture of the movie cover with Whitney Houston, Angela Bassett, Lela Rochon, and Loretta Devine smiling. Michael smiles and stares at Whitney for a moment. He scrolls some more, reads a few other posts, and watches some videos. Before he knows it, it's almost midnight. He places his phone on the nightstand, turns out the light, and settles into bed.

Michael quickly falls asleep but wakes up at three a.m. from a nightmare. He's breathing fast and beads of sweat line his forehead. His back is sweaty from tossing in the bed sheets. Michael sits up in bed, reminding himself that it was just a dream. But it seemed so real. He was in a very familiar old house that somehow reminded him of his grandmother's house. It was his father's mother's house. Her house had two identical staircases that curved around to the next landing. He remembered the stairs were covered with thick green carpeting. After walking up the stairs, he found several bedrooms, a kitchen, and a library.

In the dream, a doorway to a secret room appeared. Michael walked into the hidden room and walked into a bathroom. He thought that someone must have spent a lot of time in this room. There was clutter all over the counters. He saw a shower stall and as he kept walking on the soft green carpeting, he found himself in a bedroom. Someone was sleeping in the bed. He saw the sheets rise and fall as the person slept. Michael froze, knowing he shouldn't be there. The person sleeping in the bed awoke and jumped out of bed with a sword, swinging it in Michael's direction. Michael realized it was his own father. His father was bare-chested and dressed in an Indian loin cloth with thick leather straps on both his biceps. He swung the sword franticly with the look of a madman on his face.

"Dad, stop! Dad, it's me, Michael!" Michael screamed as his

father swung the sword. He could hear the sound of the blade slicing the air. Michael had put his arms up over his head as the sword was about to come right down on him, and that's when he woke up.

Your dreams are symbolic.

Michael was still catching his breath but was relieved Whitney had shown up. He didn't want to be alone after that dream.

"I have no idea what it means that my father was trying to kill me. I was screaming and he didn't even recognize me. He just kept swinging the sword. I think he would have killed me if I hadn't woken up."

Okay, so you'll have to think a little further. But you gotta still get some more sleep. You'll remember the pieces of the dream you're supposed to when you wake up.

Surprisingly, before he knew it, and with Whitney's comfort, he was falling asleep again. Soon a beam of sunlight comes through his bedroom window, awakening him again. He looks over at his alarm clock. It is five past nine. Jumping out of bed, he complains to himself, wondering why the alarm didn't go off.

He runs into his bathroom, turns on the shower and jumps in. Grabbing his razor, he shaves his face quickly, knowing he'll miss some stubble. He washes all the important parts. Shutting off the water, he quickly towels off, sprays some cologne on his neck, and whirls back to his dresser, where he pulls on socks while jumping in place to keep his balance. He pulls on fresh boxer briefs and adjusts himself. He grabs black pants and realizes he wasn't given a work shirt. Thinking to himself how Joey told him he'll get a company T-shirt when he arrives, he grabs his favorite black Cyndi Lauper concert T-shirt and pulls it over his head. He stuffs his feet into his black sneakers. Giving himself one quick look in the mirror, he runs some gel through his hair and tries to neaten it. "Done!" he says to himself.

Swiping his cell phone off the nightstand and shutting off

the lights, Michael runs down the stairs, picks up his keys, and opens his door. He immediately stops, turns around and runs back in to grab a pen and a pad of paper. He pulls the door shut behind him and turns the key to lock the door. He runs down the hall and through the main entrance doors. Out on the street, he checks his cell phone for the time. 9:36 a.m. "Shit!"

As he weaves through morning pedestrian traffic, he's aware he'll make it, but just barely. He cuts over to 94th Street on a direct path toward Fate. When he arrives at the door at 9:58, he stops, inhales deeply, and then lets the anxiety go. He grabs the handle of the door, opens it, and walks inside.

The entire staff is sitting together for a meeting in the bar area. Stemmed crystal glassware and about forty colorful bottles of liquor, all of different shapes and sizes, decorate the bar. The owner Joey and the older hostess are standing before the staff. Everyone stops and looks at Michael as he enters. The lights are turned up unusually high, allowing Michael to see clearly all the artwork on the walls. Pictures of grapes and cheeses, a Guy Buffet painting of a bartender mixing a drink, some scenes from vineyards, and a mountainside ocean view seemingly from Amalfi.

He can smell the scent of garlic and cheese invitingly floating in the air. There are about a dozen employees. The young blond hostess who'd helped him apply waves, smiles, and pats the chair beside her. He slides onto the seat.

Joey starts talking again. "We also have a new employee starting," he says as his big hand points toward Michael, "Which is only going to add to the confusion. We all have to work together, do our best, and be ready for anything."

Blondie whispers to Michael, "I'll fill you in later."

He nods.

Joey asks, "Are there any questions?"

Everyone silently shakes their heads.

The older hostess takes over. "Okay then, we'll open today

at eleven, not eleven thirty like usual. This will give us just a few more minutes to get into our groove. Today's specials are a creamy tomato soup with fresh basil . . . "

The waitstaff begins writing the specials as she recites them. Michael smiles to himself for being wise enough to remember his pen and paper, which he grabs and joins in.

Just who do you think gave you that thought to grab your pen and paper? Tsk-tsk. You're welcome, baby.

" . . . the sandwich is portabella tapenade panini. A grilled portabella mushroom, smoked Gouda, roasted red pepper tapenade, arugula, and a balsamic glaze swirled on toasted ciabatta. Finally, the dessert is a warm peach cobbler with raspberry gelato, made by Katie." She nods toward Blondie, sitting next to Michael. Katie grins.

The staff disperses to finish their opening side work of rolling silverware, filling salt and pepper shakers, and setting out glasses on the tables. Katie grabs Michael by the arm and brings him to the host station, a podium with a lamp that illuminates the restaurant's seating chart. She points to it and describes how they seat customers, the table numbers, and which servers are in which sections.

"We have three servers for every shift and never seat a server with more than two tables at once." Katie looks at her watch. "We're missing one. Jane isn't here yet, but she's supposed to be in section three." Katie sighs, "Jane usually comes running in about twenty minutes before opening." She shakes her head and rolls her eyes. "Which in today's case, we'll already be open when she gets here." She looks at Michael and says, "So how well can you wait tables?"

"Pretty well. The hardest part will be learning where everything is. Serving really is just common sense. I already know today's specials and I'm assuming the bartender will make my drinks."

"Yeah, I wish Mom and Dad would hire more employees with common sense."

It dawns on Michael for the first time that Katie is the owners' daughter.

"Okay, follow me." Katie smiles. She likes having Michael follow her; she adds a little more boom to her walk. "I'll show you the waitstaff station, but first, the salad station."

She explains how the kitchen staff makes the salads but leaves them in a refrigerated glass case and points to where all the dressings are. She also points at all the labels on the dressings. "Our glasses of water are always served with lemon, and here are the things for hot beverages," she says, pointing to a cabinet for the coffee cups and a box, which she opens and shows him the different flavors of teas.

"All the silverware is here. Always make sure your silverware is wiped down." She taps a cabinet filled with glasses, napkins, straws, crackers, soup cups, and bowls. "Everything else you will need will be in here. Okay?"

They leave that room and go into the dish room.

The dish room feels humid as they walk in. White tiles cover the walls, and it smells like bleach and wet mops. It's warm. There's a big automatic dishwasher, spray hose, and several garbage cans.

"Dirty dishes go here." She puts her hand on a stainless steel rolling cart. "Make sure to scrape the plates before giving them to the dishwashers and make sure not to throw away any silverware or ramekins. That seems to happen a lot here. The dirty glasses go up here in these plastic bins." She lifts her arm and places her hand on the plastic bins above her head. "The silverware goes into this container, which is to always be filled with soapy water."

They walk into the next room, the kitchen.

"Now, this is the window. When you put your order in the point of sale system—or as we say, the POS system—it comes up here. The cooks receive them, and the order is prepared."

Hanging in the food window is a heat lamp to keep foods hot until servers pick them up. Michael sees all the kitchen equipment, the grill, fryolator, oven, and a hanging broiler known as a salamander. He hears the hum of the hood fans that are vacuuming the heat and smoke out of the kitchen. He notes the stainless-steel tables, sharp knives, and several reach-in coolers for the food and prep. He watches the cooks, and the sounds of knives chopping are heard through the kitchen. Another cook comes over and takes the temperature of the soup in the soup warmer. Apparently, he likes the temperature and walks away. All the cooks are doing their last-minute duties, anticipating their first order.

"When your food is ready, your buzzer—which I will give you—will buzz, and the cooks will enter your slip in as done. Now through this door brings you back out to the bar area."

They walk through the door and are back where they started.

"One last thing I need to show you. The most difficult thing is our POS system. When you're at the guest's table, you'll write what they want on your pad. I have to say, I was thrilled to see you brought a pad and pen with you today. That earned you brownie points!" She smiles.

Michael smiles too, thinking, "If she only knew."

"Okay, so the POS system." She taps the screen, and it lights up. "Here are all the entrees. That's the easy part. Now when guests change things like tomatoes for olives or they want shrimp added to their entrée, right here, this square, touch that and it opens up a window where you type what the guest wants changed. The modification prints below the ordered item. If you don't use this window feature the special orders will end up at the bottom of the ticket and the cooks won't know which order gets the special requests. Don't screw that up!" Michael nods.

Katie continues, "Drink orders are here. Again, when a guest wants an extra dry martini, touch that window again, type the special request and on you go. The bartender, Matthew, will have your drinks ready and they'll be sitting right here on the bar." She slides her hand on the bar with an open palm. "And, finally, to get back to what you walked into this morning. Today we're having a movie filmed in the restaurant. The film crew should be here about ten thirty to start setting up. They want to start shooting before noon."

With that, the front door opens, and fourteen film people slowly enter carrying cameras, lights, and endless amounts of cords, all of which invariably bounce off the door frame as they come through.

"And here they are. Let the chaos begin!" Katie takes a deep breath and blows the air upward, ruffling her bangs.

"What's the movie about?" Michael asks.

"I don't know. But they're shooting a scene about a psychic who comes to a restaurant to give her client a reading. They said the scene is about ten minutes long but will probably take about two hours to film. The crew wanted the restaurant to be busy, so they placed an ad in the paper for extras. That's who will be eating here for the next couple of hours. Who knows what will happen today?" Katie laughs. "Like my parents said, be ready for anything."

"And how many tables do you have again?" Michael asks.

"We have nineteen tables plus the eight barstools, which Matthew the bartender handles."

Michael looks around the restaurant. His stomach roils.

He looks at Katie. "The movie crew placed an ad in the paper for extras to come and eat, plus whatever your normal business clientele is on a Tuesday? This place could really become a shit show." He frowns. "Hey, by the way," he adds. "This psychic coming today, are they a real psychic or just an actor?"

"I don't know . . . How fun would it be if they are a real

psychic? Maybe they'll pick up on some of the spirits in the room. This building is very old, and they say old buildings have a lot of spiritual activity." Katie hums the theme to *The Twilight Zone* and waves her fingers.

"Fun times," Michael mumbles but begins to worry. *What will Whitney do?* His stomach drops.

CHAPTER 10

AT ELEVEN O'CLOCK, Fate opens. The camera crews are all in place, crowding over table number seven near the bar. The actors are ready to go, but there's no sign of the psychic. Matthew, the bartender, is delighted to be in the film and is texting his friends about his upcoming movie debut.

The director yells, "Where's the psychic?"

One of the crew members yells back, "I don't know—I'm not psychic!"

Finally the front door bursts open. The psychic enters in a bright haze of light, sunbeams mixing with floating dust, which make it look like thousands of illuminated dancing fairies. She stops, looks around, and puts her arms up as if feeling the air. There's a red scarf wrapped around her hair, edged with fringe and crystal beads. She's short, maybe a little chunky, and is wearing a thick, long black dress that seems to wrap around her, and it's embroidered with feathers, cherubs, and crystal balls. Her feet are clad in socks and Birkenstock sandals.

The director walks over to her. She shoos him away. With her hands still in the air, she walks deeper into the restaurant. "Who's Michael?" she says.

Matthew shouts, "I'm Matthew! Did you mean Matthew?"

"No," says the psychic. "Michael."

The room is silent. Nobody speaks up.

"I'll find you," the psychic says. She begins to sing "Greatest Love of All." Just as abruptly, she stops. "Does anyone connect to that?" The room is silent.

Michael stands poker straight, holding his breath. *Please God,* he thinks. *Please don't, please don't . . .*

One of the servers pipes up, "I sang it in middle school choir."

"Nope, it's not you."

Michael closes his eyes and clamps down on his teeth. *Please don't, please don't.*

A crew member says, "It was the song I danced to with my mother at my wedding."

"It's not you, either."

The fuming director yells, "Can we just film the scene? I don't give a shit about songs, weddings or choir practices. I just want to make my movie!"

Michael exhales, silently thanking the director while adding a blessing to himself, the Father, Son, and Holy Spirit. Everyone gets into position. The psychic sits at a table and is surrounded by makeup artists. The movie crew comes in closer toward them just as the first of the customers are allowed to enter.

Then, like a floodgate opening, forty people walk in. The restaurant is instantly filled with extras.

Several of them go right up to the bar and start ordering drinks. Sangrias, Manhattans, martinis, several shots of Dewer's straight up. Matthew quickly becomes overwhelmed. Michael notices that Matthew is flooded and instinctually goes behind the bar, helping Matthew make the drinks. The older hostess heads into the crowd of people and helps the waitstaff take orders. Katie rushes around the restaurant with silverware and napkins for all the guests who are now sitting at tables.

A male crew member yells out, “Rolling. Scene fifty-four.” He claps the slate down. “Action!”

The camera lights come on and the cameraperson zooms in on the psychic.

“Who is it that you would like me to contact for you?” the psychic asks the young actress across from her.

Her eyes are saddened with grief, and she gives a soft sniff. “My mother, Betty Jane.”

“And did you bring me something of hers that I can draw her energy from? Jewelry is especially good for holding the energy to conjure a spirit.”

“Ah, yes, yes. I brought you her wedding ring.” She hands the white gold and diamond ring to the psychic.

The psychic extends her left hand, palm up, to the young lady. She closes her hand around the ring, shuts her eyes, and starts rocking back and forth.

“Ah yes, your mother . . . did she like Whitney Houston?”

“CUT! Goddammit!” The director hits the side of his leg with his Masonite clipboard. “Just say your damn lines. No improvising.”

The male crew member yells out again, “Rolling. Scene fifty-four.” He claps the slate again. “Take two . . . action!”

This time the psychic gets up from her chair and walks over to the bar.

Michael freezes as the psychic approaches the bar.

“Michael,” she says.

“CUT! What are you *doing*?” The director gets out of his chair and follows the psychic to the bar. “Jesus Christ, lady.” Spit flies out of his mouth as he talks. “It’s simple. Just say the lines. Where in the fucking script does it say to get up from your seat and go over to the bar?”

Michael can see the red light on the top of the camera. The cameraperson hasn’t cut, and the lens is turned on the bar.

The psychic narrows her eyes at the director. “You wanted a

real psychic. I'm a real psychic. What I'm doing is going to make your movie a huge hit. Think of all the buzz and media attention you'll get when this man's destiny comes true right around the release date."

"I don't want a fucking reading of some random bartender! I want my movie the way I wrote it!"

The director's face is red, one large vein bulging in his forehead and two more pulsing in his throat. "And if you won't read the fucking script the way I wrote it, then you're fired. I'll hire an actor instead of a psychic to film the scene. What's it gonna be, lady?"

"I'll tell you what it's gonna be!" The psychic looks at Michael and the film crew keeps rolling. "This man will own a restaurant in less than a year."

She intently looks deeper into Michael's eyes. He sees her shift her head just a little bit as if she's listening now. A confused expression crosses her features, and she says, "I'm hearing Hello, Dolly?"

Michael's eyes widen. He realizes she's talking to Whitney.

The psychic turns back to the director, "And not only that," the psychic continues, "but you're going to need this man when your movie is released. Him and his restaurant."

"I'm gonna need him about as much as I need you! YOU'RE FIRED! Get out!" He throws his clipboard on the floor. Papers spring free and scatter around his feet. "Everybody take five," he groans. "I need a fucking drink and a cigarette." He rams the front door open so violently that the door hinges bounce the door back at him. He's knocked off balance. He tries to rebalance but bumps into the unopened door a second time, wobbles, and falls to one knee on the ground. "For fuck's sake!" He gingerly gets up, walks through the door, and slams it shut.

Meanwhile, the psychic grabs Michael's hand and holds it as the film crew continues filming.

"Honey, you are blessed. You have the beautiful Whitney Houston watching over you. Her energy is really strong around you. And boy is she feisty. She's working with you now, kind of like an angel, umm, no, she just corrected me. Okay then, she insists she's your guardian angel." She rolls her eyes down to the floor, tilts her head back just a little as she curls her lip as if about ready to say some distasteful remark, but then holds back.

She looks up toward the ceiling, listening, and nods. She looks back at Michael and hands him a card.

"Honey, you call me later and we can continue this. I'll tell you what: your reading will be free. Just come by later and see me." With that she walks out of the restaurant, the door closes, and she's gone. Michael looks at the business card she gave him.

PSYCHIC SISTA
MADAME PEARL IVY
PSYCHIC *MEDIUM* TAROT
BY APPOINTMENT ONLY

He turns the card over and sees the phone number on the back.

Matthew, the bartender, bumps into Michael, snapping him out of his little trance. He looks around the chaotic room. Extras are milling all about, most with drinks in their hands. The noise of startled conversation echoes. "Do you think we made it into the scene?" someone whispers.

After several minutes, the director comes back in and tells Joey he's decided to cancel the shoot for the day until he can find another actor to play a psychic.

Michael spies Katie and walks toward her. She sees him but turns and goes into the kitchen. Michael follows.

Katie is taking food out from under the heat lamp in the window when Michael reaches in.

"Let me help you deliver these," he says.

Katie smiles and leads the way to a table of four businesswomen dressed in power suits. They're looking around and laughing at the spectacle around them. One of the women, who's dressed more casually, doesn't seem to be having as good of a time as her colleagues. Her expression is distracted, almost sad.

As Michael puts a plate down in front of her, she looks at him and asks, "So you're going to own your own restaurant?"

Michael smiles and shrugs. "Yeah, I guess I am. Hello, Dolly—or something like that."

"I saw her hand something to you, possibly a business card. You should call her. I mean, who wouldn't want some answers? I know I would. Here, this is my card, contact me. Let me know what happens, promise?"

"I will." Michael reads the business card. *Denise Kinelski, Licensed Insurance Broker.*

"Ladies, you enjoy your lunches. We'll come back to make sure everything is fine."

Michael and Katie walk back to the bar. More people are walking through the restaurant wanting to have lunch. Many of the extras are leaving as the movie crew has stopped filming and has started to pack their equipment up. Katie and Michael greet the new customers and seat them, and Michael falls right into rhythm with the bustling restaurant—taking orders, making and delivering drinks, and turning his tables and before he knows it, noon turns into two o'clock.

Out of the corner of his eye he sees Joey watching him. Joey nods at the older hostess, who Michael now knows is his wife Maria, and then disappears into the kitchen, taking Katie with him. It's not long before Katie emerges and motions to Michael to meet her at the bar. Michael walks over and sits on the barstool next to Katie.

"My parents said to go home. Just make sure all your checks

are cashed out and settled with Matthew and he'll give you your tips from the day."

"How did I do?"

"Yeah, well . . . my parents are going to talk to you about that later," she says as she gets up and walks away.

No "goodbye," he thinks. *No "see you later." She just leaves? That's it?*

Michael is mystified. He did a good job today, considering the commotion. But he cashes out all of his checks at the bar with Matthew, who counts the tips twice and passes a stack of cash over the bar to Michael.

"Wow, I've never given anyone three hundred dollars in tips from a lunch shift before. Congrats, man!"

"Thanks. But it doesn't seem like the owners liked me. They told me to cash out and take off before my shift is even over."

"Don't take it to heart; it's just a job. Besides, you made three hundred bucks! They would be fools not to keep you."

"Well, we'll see about that. Anyway, thanks, Matt. Maybe I'll see you again."

"Yeah, maybe." Matthew gives him a fast smile and then greets another guest at his bar.

Michael leaves Fate and slowly walks home, wondering what could've gone so wrong. He looks at his phone. It's only two thirty. Michael notices an empty park bench and sits down. He closes his eyes, letting the warm sun hit his face.

He becomes aware of a shadow blocking the sun and opens his eyes. The blond businesswoman he waited on earlier stands before him. Wordlessly, she sits down beside him.

Talk to her, Michael. There's no such thing as a coincidence.

He affects a chipper voice, smiles, and says, "So we meet again."

The recognition in her eyes confirms she remembers him. She smiles back, "So did you call that psychic yet?" As she pulls strands of her blond hair back from the slight breeze.

"No, not yet. I need to absorb everything that happened today. It was my first day on the job and I left feeling like they weren't gonna ask me to come back. I think the whole psychic thing scared them. I mean, I can see how. I was supposed to just do my job, but I ended up being pulled right in the middle of all of that, which in itself is another layer of drama. The owners were being paid by the movie producers to shoot that scene in their restaurant the way it was written. But the way it went down with the director was another story." Michael frowns. "I'm not sure if the director will come back to reshoot the scene. I may have lost a great opportunity for the owners, which is probably why when I was told to take off today, I got such a 'warm' goodbye." Michael lets out a chuckle. "The story of my life. I ruin everything before it begins."

"Well, it's funny you feel that way. I saw something completely different. I saw a waiter who—my goodness, you were everywhere! I'm actually a little surprised today was your first day. They would be fools not to bring you back."

"I do love this industry. Foodservice, that is," Michael says. "I've been in it for years. All restaurants are the same really. Waiting tables is all just common sense—reading the guest and intuitively bringing what they need before they ask for it."

"I'm in the middle of a possible merger right now. Those other three ladies I was with today at lunch represent a bigger firm that wants to buy my company. They're a bunch of power-hungry sharks if you ask me," she says with a smirk. "I'm just not sure if I want to sell my company and my client list to them. I truly like to help small-business owners."

Michael perks up. "How do you help business owners?"

"I'm an insurance broker," she tells him. "I sell business policies and renewals. But I only sell exactly what they need at the time."

He looks up to see that her eyes have welled up with worry. She says, "You know what . . . Sitting here with you today I think it gives me my answer. I'm not going sell my company." She slaps her hands down on her lap. "Thank you for crossing my path. When I saw you, something calming came over me. I almost feel like I've been touched by an angel."

Denise stands, scoops up her briefcase and extends her hand to Michael.

"It was truly a pleasure meeting you today. I look forward to doing business with you in the future. Now go get your restaurant!" She smiles.

Michael takes her soft hand in his. "I will. You'll be my first and only call for insurance." He smiles as he lets go of her hand and watches her walk away.

Michael's phone vibrates in his pocket. It's a text from Lucy.

CHAPTER 11

MICHAEL OPENS UP LUCY'S TEXT.

How was your first day?

We NEED to do dinner. What time do you get out?

I'm out at six. Any signs of Whitney?

Oh wait till you hear!

OMG . . . I'm so excited. I'll meet you at your house.

I'll bring the wine!

CHAPTER 12

AT 6:30, LUCY lets herself into Michael's unlocked apartment. Opening the door, she's greeted by scents of roasting garlic and yeast floating through the air. His apartment smells like an Italian market. The pungent aroma of cheese mixed with basil and oregano also wafts through. Barbra Streisand is playing softly from the speakers.

Lucy walks into the kitchen to greet Michael with a bottle of cabernet in each hand when she sees Olivia perched on a stool at Michael's kitchen counter. Olivia looks stunning in her zebra blouse, shiny faux-leather pants, and red stilettos. Olivia spins around on the stool and runs her fingers through her newly styled hair, knowing Lucy will notice the change.

"Olivia!" Lucy gasps. "I love it! Those highlights are amazing." She cheek-kisses Michael's mother. "I didn't know you were going to be here, but it's always great to see you."

"Oh, you know, Lucy," Olivia says, still tossing her new hairstyle around. "A girl's gotta do what a girl's gotta do." She giggles. "I've been waiting for you to get here. Now open that bottle."

Michael smiles at Lucy as he stands at the stove boiling pasta and stirring his homemade sauce. He reaches into the oven and pulls out muffins. The sweet smell of lemon now permeates the kitchen. He holds the muffins up in their tin and proudly says, "White chocolate limoncello boozy muffins. Another new flavor I'm trying out and you two ladies will be the first to sample."

Lucy pulls her hair back as she bends down closer to the muffins for a better whiff. "Michael, these smell amazing! And with you here, Olivia, well now I'm glad I brought two bottles." She holds up the wine.

Lucy gives Michael a fast smooch on the cheek as she walks past him to grab a corkscrew from a drawer. She twists the corkscrew into the cork, and it opens with a loud *pop* Lucy grabs three wine glasses from the cabinet and starts pouring the wine. "Cheers!" she says, passing out the glasses. "To your first day!"

They all clink their glasses together.

"It might have been my last day too," Michael says. "Wait till you hear the story."

Olivia and Lucy are listening as Michael recounts his first day at the restaurant. The room is filled with the sounds of Barbara, wine being poured, and forks clinking on plates. Michael has prepared a delicious Bolognese sauce for the pasta. He mentions how he likes to throw chorizo in his sauce for an extra oomph of spice and flavor.

"So now let's go back to Madame Pearl," Olivia says over Barbra's crooning. "She walks into the restaurant and instantly picks up on Whitney's presence?"

"Mom, it was crazy! She was hearing Whitney and her songs. She gave me her card afterward to come by her office for a free reading."

Lucy eagerly blurts out, "Well I say we make an appointment and meet this Pearl Psychic and hear what she has to say. I know I'm curious."

"Yes, me too," Olivia adds. "Curious in a weird, spooky way." She wiggles her fingers and gives a little body shake.

Lucy quickly responds, "Call her now. Make an appointment, and we'll all go together. This way we can all hear for ourselves. After all, isn't this what Whitney wanted, all of us together?" She makes a curious frowny face.

"Yes, darling," Olivia says. "Call the psychic—but tell Whitney no feathers this time. I was still picking them out of my hair this morning."

All three of them laugh.

Michael grabs his phone and taps in the number from the business card Pearl gave him.

"It's ringing," he says.

"Psychic Sista, this is Ester. How can I help you?"

"Yes, hello, this is Michael Monroe. I was a waiter at the restaurant Fate this afternoon with a movie being filmed that Madame Pearl was hired to—"

"Oh, you!" she says, cutting him off. "Yes, I've already heard all about you. Let me go get Madame Pearl. I know she was hoping you would call her."

Michael pulls the cell phone away from his ear and tells his mom and Lucy that the receptionist is getting Pearl.

"Um, tonight? Like, now?" Michael stutters. He nervously looks at his mom and Lucy with an unsure expression, but both ladies are nodding excitedly.

"Um, okay . . . yes, I guess we can be there tonight. Yes, we can be there at nine. It's okay to bring two people with me, right? Great. Okay, I guess we'll be seeing you shortly. Oh yeah, the address. Fifty-Seventh Street. Got it. Okay, we'll be there. Bye."

Michael taps the phone off.

"Holy shit!" He stands poker straight to collect himself then he shakes his body to release the stress. "What did we just do?" he says, wide-eyed and smiling.

"I need—we all need—another glass of wine before we go," Olivia says. She pours the last of the bottle into all three wine glasses. "Bottoms up! Here's to getting some answers!"

"To answers!"

CHAPTER 13

STANDING AT THE curb in the dark, Michael hails a taxi. A yellow cab pulls up alongside them and they all get in.

"Where to?" says the driver in a thick Middle Eastern accent.

"Fifty-Seventh Street," Michael says, reading the notes he took from his phone conversation.

The driver types the coordinates in his GPS and off they go. The three of them are jerked backward as the driver guns the accelerator and pulls out into traffic. He zips in and out of lanes, accelerating even faster through yellow lights and slamming on the brakes when a light turns red. After jerking forward and backward several times, the cab finally pulls off to the right side of the street.

"Twelve dollar, fifty cent, please," the driver says.

Olivia hands the driver a twenty.

"Thank you for not killing us," she says with an exasperated look on her face. They all get out of the cab and stand on the dark sidewalk next to one another. Looking up at the building in front of them, they see a glowing purple neon sign in the shape of a hand in a circle that reads *Palm Readings.*

There's another red neon sign that says *Tarot and Psychic Readings* and a black sign with white letters above the door that reads *Madame Pearl Ivy. Psychic/Medium.* To the left of the building is a grocery store with bright neon signs advertising Snapple, cigarettes, and the New York Lottery. To the right, a porn shop sign advertises *XXX DVDs, and Adult Toys*. A few people are milling around and smoking outside of the grocery. Although it's getting late, there is plenty of traffic whizzing by them on the city streets. They smell the dank warm air coming up through the subway sidewalk grates. They can feel the ground rumble as the subway passes beneath them.

"Well, here goes nothing." Michael makes the first move toward the front door. There's a single light bulb illuminating the doorway. On the front door is a sign that reads *Please ring bell for assistance.*

Michael presses the button. The inside hallway light flips on with an echo of footsteps and chiming bells. A young, olive-skinned Hispanic woman, probably in her late twenties, is smiling at them.

"You must be Michael," she politely says. She turns to Olivia and Lucy, who introduce themselves.

"I'm Ester. Please come in. Madame Pearl is anticipating your arrival."

As they all walk into the grand foyer, they gasp at how beautiful and tastefully decorated the interior is. The haunting scents of sandalwood and frankincense engulf them. There's a large fireplace at the end of the hallway with a mantle decorated with angel figurines and crystal balls.

The walls are dark mahogany and there's a wide staircase that slowly spirals up with red carpeting and a thick, glossy wooden handrail. To their left is a closed door and on the right is a dimly lit parlor with shelves full of books, Victorian lamps, mismatching loveseats, and throw rugs. This room feels more lived in; the furniture is seemingly chosen for comfort, not appearance.

In the center of the room sits a round table covered with a white lace tablecloth. A crystal vase with freshly cut daisies, roses, and carnations adorns the top of the table and six cushioned chairs surround it.

"Please," Ester's open hand points to the chairs. "Sit comfortably around the table," she tells them. "I will inform Madame Pearl of your arrival. May I bring you a cup of tea?"

All three of them accept and Ester disappears through a doorway at the other side of the room.

"This place is gorgeous," Lucy whispers. "I would have never imagined the inside to be so beautiful from the looks of the outside."

"I guess she takes this very seriously," Michael says.

Olivia quickly quips, "I'm keeping an open mind."

They're listening to the soft sounds of birds chirping and the trickling of water that quietly infiltrates through hidden speakers. Ester now comes back into the room with a silver serving tray holding a pot of tea, honey, sugar, milk, spoons, napkins, and shortbread cookies. She pours each one a cup of tea, asks how they would like it dressed, and then puts a few cookies on each saucer. She passes out the tea and cookies with a napkin and stops when she gets to Michael.

"I've heard about what happened today. It sounds like there was a lot of commotion." She nervously giggles a little.

"That would be an understatement," Michael says. "Total chaos is more accurate." He laughs.

Ester turns to look at all three of them. "Have any of you ever been to a séance before?"

"I have," says Lucy.

"Yeah, me too," says Michael.

Olivia throws her hand up. "Not me. This is my first experience."

"This is not what you see on TV," Ester tells them. "What we do here is for our clients' greatest good. There are no gimmicks.

If the lights do go out, it's more likely because of a power outage." She gives a quick laugh. "I have been working with Madame Pearl for a couple of years now and let me tell you . . . I've never seen someone as accurate, sincere, and respectful when communicating with clients' loved ones who have crossed over."

Madame Pearl now walks in as Ester finishes her sentence. Michael is taken aback. He barely recognizes her. She's dressed nothing like the woman he saw earlier this morning. She is no longer wearing a red fringed turban or a full-length robe. Instead, she's dressed in a simple, flowing, light pink dress. Her long dark hair is twisted into a French braid and hangs over her shoulder.

She walks over and stands in front of them. "What? Were you expecting Whoopi Goldberg?" She gives a laugh at Michael's surprise then says, "When I was cast for the film, they said I should dress how they believed a psychic would dress."

"But playacting quickly turned real. I sensed the spirit of this woman—well Whitney—as I was nearing the restaurant. That's why I was a bit late. She was telling me to find you. Pardon my French, but holy merde! She's very feisty. And she has a message to give to you."

"So, yeah, about that. I have Whitney guiding me." Michael looks at her with a toothy grin; he pauses to let that sink in. "Which is why we're here. To get some answers."

"Well, I don't know if I'll be able to find that out. This is probably one of my most confusing readings ever. As clear as she is to me, she wasn't giving me any specifics of why she's here for you. Seems she wants you to find that out for yourself.

"Hmm." Madame Pearl tilts her head and gives Michael a questioning look. "Well, that does make sense after hearing her song, "Greatest Love of All." It's about self-love."

"Whitney's been appearing to me. All. The. Time! I *hear* her. I *see* her. She's even seen me naked in the bathroom." He laughs.

"She's *everywhere*!"

The room erupts with laughter.

"Yeah, funny, laugh it up," Michael says, growing more embarrassed. He runs his fingers through his hair and lets out an exasperated sigh then says, "She explained to me she's here to guide me. But she won't say to what. She's explained why some things happen as they do. She also told me she can put thoughts into my mind but that I still have total free will to do as I please. She's mentioned how everyone is connected to each other. But basically, she said that there's so much more going on than I could ever imagine."

Madame Pearl looks at him with disappointed eyes, "I don't see how I'm going to be able to help you any more than she is already. Truthfully, I'm in awe and a little jealous that she's this open and honest with you and so easily seen and understood. Do you know what a gift she's giving you? All of my clients would love to have their own guardian angel appear to them."

"I guess maybe because it is coming so easily, I want more. Human nature, huh?"

So now you think I'm gonna be Frankie Valli, your guardian angel from Grease? Do you want me to sing to you a new melody? Whitney starts to croon, ***Cooking school dropout, there's no job waiting for you, cooking school dropout . . .*** Whitney starts laughing, proud of herself.

Excitedly, "Oh my god, she's here!" Michael jumps out of his chair.

"Oh my god!" Lucy's voice is about three octaves higher than normal. "She's here? Can you see her?"

"No, not yet, but I'm sure it won't be long."

CHAPTER 14

SITTING IN THE dimly lit room, all five of them are facing each other in a circle. Their nervousness is palpable. Nobody knows what's going to happen. But they all sit in anticipation. The tension in the room is thick.

Madame Pearl takes the lead.

"Well, shall we begin?" She eyes everyone for their approval.

"Heavenly spirit, we ask you in truth, light, and love to allow Whitney to show herself to us tonight. We ask that Whitney tell Michael why she is here to help him, and we ask for her love and guidance to be used for our greatest good and for our best intentions. We ask this . . . "

With a loud *pop* flashes spark around the room and before Madame Pearl can say anything more, the room plunges into darkness.

Everyone gasps and screams. The nervousness in the air turns into fear. Olivia stands straight up from her chair and accidentally pushes it backward with her legs. It loudly falls to the ground.

Both Michael and Lucy jump up from their chairs to help Olivia.

Suddenly, little lights start glimmering. Lights the size of pin needles are blinking in the darkness. Thousands of tiny red, blue, and yellow lights turn into a beautiful shade of pink and start swirling and circling like a cyclone.

"Spirit lights, Madame Pearl, they're spirit lights!" Ester shouts.

"Yes, Ester, I see them. How beautiful! What a magnificent display of energy."

Madame Pearl speaks to the room. "Everybody, please be calm. What you're witnessing are spirit lights. Spirit lights are produced when the energy of a spirit enters a room." The room starts to fill with a smoke-like fog.

Olivia holds on to Lucy and Michael grabs his mother, all three huddling together.

"Ectoplasm," Madame Pearl says to the room. "The smoky fog is ectoplasm. I've never seen ectoplasm so thick and with so many thousands of spirit lights. This is incredible!" Madame Pearl is feeling the energy again with her arms up in the air as if touching something that isn't there. "This is an absolute miracle. I have never seen something so profoundly beautiful."

The thousands of spirit lights dance and twirl through the fog when a blinding flash of white light explodes in the room. Everyone is bowing their heads and shielding their eyes with their arms as the brightest light they've ever seen illuminates the darkness. Just as quickly as it came, the blinding white light dissolves and Whitney Houston replaces it.

Everyone in the room gasps. Olivia and Lucy scream and hold on tighter to each other. Michael squeezes both of them and reassures them.

"It's okay, it's okay. We're fine. It's okay! Nothing is going to hurt us. Calm down, breathe deep breaths, Lucy. Slowly, in and out. Breathe, Mother, breathe. Trust me, we're fine."

Whitney has appeared as her character, the Fairy Godmother

from *Cinderella*. She is wearing a beautiful, formfitting tan dress that's covered in sequins and charms. Her hair, tight springy curls of brown locks, surrounds her face. She's silently floating in the room about five inches off the floor. Everyone sees her but she's blurry and swaying. Surging and pulsing, she gets brighter and then fades. She moves to the left and then to the right a little. The more she moves the blurrier she gets. There are still thousands of spirit lights blinking all around her. The ectoplasm is flowing through her and around her.

In an apprehensive voice, Madame Pearl says, "Whitney, thank you for appearing to us tonight. If you have something to tell us, we are listening."

"I am here for Michael. I've gotten all of you together because you're all part of his journey. Trust that everything you do will be the right choice." Whitney looks right at Olivia. "Olivia, honey, yes, this is real. I'm real. Well, kind of." She giggles. "And don't you worry, I'm taking good care of your baby. He's gonna make you proud."

Olivia stutters her words a little, but she manages to speak. "He is already—he—he already is making me proud." Olivia's eyes fill with tears.

"Olivia, honey," Whitney crosses her arms and gives Olivia a sideways glance. "I understand why you made Michael leave. But he still doesn't understand. You two will need to come to an agreement."

Olivia is caught by surprise by Whitney's accurate truthfulness of the animosity between herself and Michael. Whitney winks and blows Olivia a kiss. Then, as if someone unplugged a light, the room plunges into total darkness. The bright white light disappears, as does Whitney. Only a few spirit lights are left dancing in the dark room. Moments later, the remaining spirit lights flicker out as the room lights mysteriously flicker and come back on.

Everyone in the room releases the tension they've been holding onto, only for eerie silence to replace it.

Moments, maybe minutes, pass, and Michael finally breaks the silence.

"So, what do we do now?" he says with a laugh.

"Michael," Madame Pearl says "Whatever it is you're doing, just keep doing it. Apparently, you're where you're supposed to be, even if it seems in the middle of chaos. You're very blessed. I have never had a client before who brought forth such a powerful spirit—let alone Whitney Houston—and for her to confirm that what you're doing will all work out and that you're making all the right choices! I wish my guardian angel would tell me"—she points to herself—"that I'm making all the right choices."

Ester, unsure of what to do or say, jumps up and reaches for the teapot.

"Tea . . . cookies . . . anyone?" She smiles nervously. "I don't know about all of you, but my nerves are shot for the night and man, I sure could use something stronger than tea right now!"

Everyone in the room starts to feel a little more relaxed as the tension from the séance lets up. Conversations begin about what they saw and how they interpreted it. No one can seem to get over how beautiful Whitney looked.

As the conversations continue, Michael feels his cell phone vibrate in his pocket. He reaches for it and sees a phone number he doesn't know, but his caller ID recognizes that the line is from Fort Lauderdale. With perplexity, he squints, trying to decipher the number.

He looks at Lucy and says, "Nine-five-four area code? Someone from Fort Lauderdale is calling me, and at ten o'clock? What's up with that?" He lets it go to voicemail.

Finally Michael, his mother, and Lucy all get up and hug Madame Pearl and Ester, thanking them both for an interesting evening.

Madame Pearl gives Michael a quick squeeze on his arm. "Now, you come see me again if you have any questions. You apparently have a great connection to Whitney but sometimes spirits will communicate to us through our dreams. Let me know if you have any dreams you need help deciphering."

"As a matter of fact, I've been having these crazy dreams lately," Michael says. "But I'll save that for another night. I think we've all had enough tonight."

A communal "Amen!" is said.

Madame Pearl and Ester walk all three of them to the door and see them to a cab.

"Thank you. I'll be in touch!" Michael yells back as he closes the taxi door.

CHAPTER 15

FINALLY HOME ALONE, Michael turns the lights on, locks the door and drops his keys in a bowl on the table near the door. He walks into his kitchen, where he grabs yesterday's coffee and pours it into a cup. Michael is reminded of all the people who've asked him, "Coffee so late at night, aren't you afraid of not sleeping?" But coffee is soothing to him, and the effects of caffeine don't seem to prevent him from falling asleep. He microwaves it, smelling the bitter burnt scent that the steam is omitting. He reaches for the cream and adds sugar. The color of his coffee is no longer brown but rather a taupe. He grabs three cookies. *More cookies, just what I need,* he thinks. He carries his snacks to the living room, places them on the coffee table and he practically falls onto the couch.

"What a day!" He gives an exhausted sigh. He doesn't want to think about it anymore. Then he feels the three hundred dollars still wadded up in his front pocket, evidence of the shortest job he's ever had. He flips on the TV; the late evening news is playing. A dark-haired, thick, muscular sportscaster recites the scores of several professional baseball teams.

The camera pans to a brunette anchor. "Next up! Not your

typical day at Fate." She smiles and twists as another camera pans to her from a different angle. "How did a local restaurant, a film crew, and a psychic meet up with . . . Whitney Houston? We'll have it all for you coming up after the break."

Michael's grip on the remote tightens. He watches breathlessly through a commercial for a car dealership, "Hundreds of new and preowned Toyotas are on the lot. Corollas, Camrys, and the highly rated Highlanders—all ready for pick up," a salesman prattles as the 1-800 number flashes on the screen. Then a lawyer who wants to help his clients get the money they deserve from injuries in car accidents or from accidents on the job makes his case for his law firm.

"Come on, come on, come on already." Michael is becoming impatient with the commercials that seem to be slowing time down. A dog goes running across his screen telling the viewers they need to buy Rid-O-Flea shampoo for their pets.

Finally, after what seems like forever, the news music cues. Over the backdrop of the New York City skyline, the brunette reappears.

"Good evening, I'm Tina Roberts. What happens when a local restaurant, a film crew, and a psychic come together? Stacy Robinson was on location this afternoon at Fate. Stacy, tell us all about it."

"Thanks, Tina. I'm standing in front of Fate, a popular uptown restaurant, with owners Joey and Maria Riveria." She points to them standing next to her. "Joey and Maria were approached by the film production company EnterView to use their restaurant for their upcoming movie, *Whatever Happened to Betty Jane?*, about a psychic who helps a detective solve a cold-case murder." She turns to Joey and Maria. "Tell us what happened inside your restaurant today."

Joey steps closer to the extended microphone. "It was sheer mayhem. Total absolute chaos." Joey is a big, eccentric guy and his hands fly every which way as he speaks. "If it could go wrong, it did. The camera crews were everywhere; the waitstaff couldn't get to their tables because so many people came in from that ad they ran in the paper asking for extras." Joey looks from the reporter to the camera. "Hey, great idea!" he adds with a sarcastic thumbs up. He turns back to the reporter and says, "Then the real kicker was when the psychic was supposed to say her lines but instead, she zeroes in on a new employee, Michael Monroe—yeah, the Double D's Monroe. It was his first day." Agitation growing, the whites of his eyes become visible, "That's when the psychic said Whitney Houston was *in* the restaurant."

The camera pans back to Stacy.

"Here's an edited clip from earlier today."

The clip is chaotic, skipping between the packed restaurant, the film crew, and the director shouting "CUT!" We see the camera zooming in on Madame Pearl approaching Michael, telling him Whitney Houston is here for him.

Michael watches himself on TV, his face a combination of confusion and disbelief but above all, he's still in his Cyndi Lauper T-shirt. He smirks, remembering that Joey had forgotten to give him a company shirt.

"Well, at least I look good," he says to himself. "And I'm not making an ass out of myself."

The screen flashes back to Stacy outside the restaurant with Joey and Maria.

"Will the film crew be coming back?"

Maria leans into the microphone. "They haven't confirmed. I guess we'll find out soon enough." She laughs nervously.

"And how did Michael, the diamond heir, handle all of this?" Stacy asks.

Joey looks directly into the camera and grins.

"He's a champ—and a draw. This story caught the attention of every news station and paper all over the state. TMZ has called three times! You can't buy publicity like this." Joey's big arms extend out toward the camera. "So, folks, come eat at Fate and say hello to Michael and the rest of the crew."

Despite the thousands of goosebumps that are now climbing up his arms, making his hair stand on end, Michael feels embarrassed. But he's smiling. He suddenly feels a cool breeze and rubs his arms.

"So, there you have it, Tina. I think we're all curious to know what's going to happen. Will Whitney Houston be a new guest at Fate?" She smiles, looks directly at the camera and says, "Stacy Robinson, reporting live from Manhattan. Back to you, Tina."

The camera zooms in on Tina again.

"Thank you, Stacy. Join us tomorrow when we speak to the psychic, Madame Pearl."

Michael flips the TV off, grabs his phone and texts Lucy.

OMG . . . wait till you hear.

Lucy responds immediately.

I already did!

Then, a text comes in from Michael's mom.

Did you see? You made the news!

I know Mom, I just watched it, and I can't believe this!

How did all this happen?

Talk to you in the morning. Love you.

Love you, darling.

It's almost midnight. Michael heads upstairs to bed. He's just slipping underneath the sheets when he notices another missed call from that same 954 area code. Too tired to deal with it now, he literally falls on his back, pulls the covers up, and drifts off to sleep.

Michael finds himself standing in front of a large floor-to-ceiling tinted window inside a New York City penthouse apartment. Though he's no stranger to money, he knows the owner is rich. He looks behind him at the large, unlit loft apartment. There's nobody around. There's a white glow coming from the moonlight through the large windows that shines onto the white, freshly shined tile floor. The room itself is an open concept. A chic white kitchen, thoughtfully crafted with light-gray granite countertops, white cabinets, and a stainless-steel stove. A large stainless-steel hood fan hangs above the stove. Pots and pans of all different sizes dangle from a circular ceiling rack. On the other side of this room sits a beautiful white sectional that has been arranged in front of a huge flat-screen TV that hangs on the wall.

He turns back around to look out the window. He's about thirty-five stories high, overlooking Central Park. White streetlights twinkle, interspersed with dots of red taillights from passing cars. He can see leaves swaying on trees bordering the park, patches of green grass and the Jackie Onassis Reservoir. All of the skyscrapers encircling the park are illuminated with thousands of scattered white lights from windows. He imagines himself being the one who owns this multimillion-dollar view.

He feels someone approach him from behind and in the reflection he sees an older man.

"This can all be yours," the man says, now standing very close to Michael.

Unfazed and unbothered by the unknown man behind him, Michael continues to stare out at the exceptional view.

All Michael can think to say is, "I can't even imagine having all of this."

The older man gets right behind Michael. He's so close that Michael can feel the warmth of his breath.

"That's your problem. You don't believe this can all be yours!"

Michael turns around to face the man behind him, "Do I know you? Who are you?"

"I'm Vince Lombardi."

Michael snaps out of his dream, sitting upright in his bed. He grabs a scrap of paper from his nightstand and jots the man's name down. Now satisfied that he'll remember the dream and the man's name, he lies back down. Who is the mystery man telling him all of "this" could be his? Michael closes his eyes and sees the penthouse apartment again. In a few minutes, he's fallen back asleep.

CHAPTER 16

THE NEXT MORNING, the first thing on Michael's mind is Vince Lombardi. He gets out of bed, walks into his bathroom, relieves himself from his long night's sleep, goes back into his bedroom, grabs his phone, and looks at it as it illuminates. And there's that freakin' 954 area code number again on his screen.

Michael once again dismisses it and swipes open his phone. He types Vince Lombardi into the browser. On the screen he sees a black-and-white picture of a man in dark-rimmed glasses, a space between his front teeth, wearing a fedora. It's the same man from his dream. Under the picture, Michael reads, "Vince Lombardi, football coach. Died September 3, 1970."

Michael scrolls some more and clicks on his Wikipedia page to see that he was born on June 11, 1913 and died at age fifty-seven.

He died young, Michael thinks.

Michael starts reading all his stats. He was the head coach for the Green Bay Packers and led them to win Super Bowls. Michael's senses pop when he reads that Lombardi was named the best motivational coach in history. That is all Michael needs to read. He has goosebumps.

He runs down the stairs to his living room, excitedly talking aloud. "The best motivational coach in history came to me last night and told me that my problem was I didn't believe I could have everything I was seeing—the apartment, the view . . . So, tell me, Vince. How do I believe?" Then he hears Whitney in his mind.

That's the journey of life, Michael. Believing is a feeling. Believing is faith. Believing is knowing that you CAN have it all. But baby, you need to believe from deep down in the pit of your soul. Most people, ya know, they believe for about ten minutes, and they think that's all they got to do. They think to themselves, okay, I believe. Bring it on.

What Vince told you last night, your problem, is that you don't believe you can have it all, and that's true. You need to feel with purpose, your soul's purpose, and believe that you can do it! You can do anything you put your mind to, baby.

Men have walked on the moon because someone believed it was possible. Your father became a success because he believed everyone would want his diamonds. Vince became an incredible coach because he believed, and he made his athletes believe. Michael, you gotta feel deep down in your soul that you can.

And I'm sorry, baby, but ya know, it ain't gonna happen overnight. But slowly, doors will open. Baby, you're a miracle. You're original. Don't waste your valuable time following someone else. Find your own truths and believe them. Remember what Vince said: 'You don't believe you can.' So believe, baby, believe!

"Believe? Believe what," Michael says, growing agitated. His fists clench as rage builds up inside him. He starts pacing around the room. His mind is now racing as images inside his memory collide. He remembers the wealthy upbringing he had, but those visions are shattered by the images of his current reality. He has thoughts that he wants to say, but they won't come out. He has words forming but they won't make sentences. He's trying to find his truth, but the words he wants to say aren't truthful. How does one think about abundance and prosperity when the words one thinks aren't truthful? He continues to think to himself and then he just finally speaks out loud. "I believe I'm in a relationship with a man who loves me. I'm rich, happy, healthy, successful, and money easily and abundantly comes to me."

"There," his hands grab his waist as his body doubles over as if he's nauseated. "I did it. I said it." His forehead beads with perspiration.

Now, you gotta believe it.

He screams out loud, "It's very hard to believe something that isn't true!"

You gotta make it true in your mind, baby.

"I gotta make it true. Geesh, thanks for the great insight. How do I make it true?"

You gotta fake it till you make it!

"Oh my god, not again!" He throws his arms up into the air and shakes them above his head as his body trembles. "How do I believe?"

A big flash of light bursts like Wonder Woman just spun around. ***Don't you 'oh, my god' me, mister.*** Whitney instantly appears wagging her finger at him. ***Don't you know how frustrating this is for me, too?*** She sternly puts her hands on her hips. She's appeared in a strapless black leather full-length dress. Her hair is a straightened short bob and she's wearing a thick leather neckband with heavy black eyeliner. ***Oh, my god. Listening to you whine. Listen to your body, Michael.*** She shakes her arms at him. ***This morning when you read about Vince, how did you feel?***

"When I read he was the greatest motivational coach in history, something seemed to connect with me. I felt . . . I don't know how to explain but I felt, I felt . . . unstoppable and loved."

You felt loved because you believed it. Maybe it was just a brief moment, but you believed it. That's what your soul knows but you don't. You are loved, Michael. We all get signs and

hunches, those ah-ha moments. Sometimes things, you know, they gotta get ugly before the beauty comes shining through. What does Dolly Parton say? 'You can't have the rainbow without the rain.' Trust it. Believe it, Michael.

"Okay, okay, okay! I'll try my best to believe."

Whitney walks around his living room and then trips on the leg of his coffee table. She falls onto his sofa with an unexpected squeal.

Michael instantly panics but darts over to help her up.

She quickly sits up straight, like a debutante. She smoothes her hair and crosses her long legs, ***Gotcha!*** She points both index fingers at him laughs and says, ***I come and go as I please, can't trip on furniture anymore.*** She laughs as she disappears, leaving nothing but a few black sparkly lights that fade as they fall to the floor.

His cell phone in his sweatpants pocket starts vibrating with an incoming call. He pulls it out; it's that 954 area code number again. On the third buzz, he finally decides to take the call.

Angry and annoyed, he answers with a sharp "Hello! Who's this?"

A chipper voice says, "Good morning. May I speak with Michael Monroe, please? This is Charles Booream from CBN Network."

Michael hesitates as his mind puts together CBN and Charles Booream and how he would know either of them. His mind is racing like a spinning rolodex going through his memory, and then he gets the answer. "Wait, as in *the* Charles Booream of Charles Booream Network?" Michael asks.

"That's the one! Now, is Michael there?"

"Um, yeah, I'm Michael. How can I help you?" He thinks he couldn't possibly be calling for him.

"I'm happy you finally answered. In my industry, you always have to be first with the next hot story. And your story is hot! That's why I decided I would take it on myself."

"Determined to take on my story?" He's confused but smiling. His palms become a little sweaty as he holds the phone.

"Michael, seventy million people watched and shared the news last night on social media and saw you get a personal reading from a psychic who said Whitney Houston is your guardian angel."

"Holy shit."

"Holy shit is right, Michael. I would like you to come down here to our studio for an interview and another reading by that same psychic."

Michael's phone vibrates. He pulls it away from his ear to see his mother is texting him.

"Michael, are you still there?" Charles pauses.

Michael collects himself. "Yeah," he pauses. "Yeah, I'm here." He starts to sweat again.

"A photographer recently took a picture of you with your mother, Olivia Monroe, the Double D's diamond heiress. I know of her because I bought my first wife Double D's. Actually, I bought her *three* Double D's," he says with a laugh. "One diamond and two fake boobs!"

"But anyway, you, your mother and your friend Lucy were in the middle of some wild feather snowstorm. That picture and the news coverage are trending and blowing up social media as we speak! It's on the cover of our paper down here, the *Miami Herald*. With last night's restaurant psychic story, the entire world is going to put these things together, as I have and, well, I want my station to be the first to interview you. So, what do you say?"

Michael's phone vibrates again. This time it's Lucy.

Michael's phone keeps vibrating. "I'm sorry, Mr. Booream—"

"Call me Charles."

"Okay, I'm sorry, Charles. My phone is blowing up as I'm talking with you. This is crazy!"

"This is important, Michael. I'll need you to make a decision."

Michael, confused, falls silent. *What is happening right now?* he thinks. His mind is filled with uncontrollable, wildly rolling thoughts.

Charles inhales deeply and lets out a sharp exhale. "I can even extend the hotel stay so you, your mom, and your companions can enjoy some extra time down here in South Florida. I can have your tickets ready for you to fly this afternoon. We can be ready to shoot as early as tonight. Oh, and Michael, I'll pay you two million dollars for your story. What do you say?"

"TWO MILLION DOLLARS! For *my* story?" Michael repeats and grabs the edge of the counter to steady himself.

"Yes, Michael. Two million dollars plus travel."

Michael panics and hangs up.

CHAPTER 17

MICHAEL GETS ANOTHER incoming call; *Mother* flashes in a black bubble on his screen. He slips his phone open.

She doesn't wait for a greeting. "Michael! Your story broke loose last night. You're famous! You have to see this! My marketing team has already contacted me asking how we want to move forward. I told them it's going to be up to you on how we proceed."

"I know, Mom. Well, I don't know, but I was just on the phone with the owner of CBN, Charles Booream!"

"Wait!" Olivia pauses. "Charles Booream? Oh my god, Michael, he's going to ask you on the show for an interview." Olivia practically squeals with excitement.

"Yes, Mother, that's what he wants. And he wants to pay me two million dollars!"

"Two million dollars for an interview? You have to do it!" Olivia is giddy.

Michael excitedly jumps up and down in his living room, practically screaming. "*I* have to do it? What do you mean *I* have to do it? He wants us *all*, Mother! He wants you, me, Lucy, and Madame Pearl! He wants to give us all plane tickets for today!

Today, Mother! He wants us to fly out this afternoon! He wants to shoot another segment of us with Madame Pearl in a séance tonight! What do I do?" He leans against the wall to keep himself from losing his balance.

"What do you do? You say *yes*, darling. You say yes. And then you'll figure it out!" Olivia's voice is three octaves higher than normal. "Don't worry about everything else, just call him back! Lucy and I can make the other necessary calls and get everything else arranged on this end. Call him back now and say yes!" She ends the call.

Michael closes his eyes, takes a deep breath, and is about to call Charles when Lucy buzzes in.

Lucy is yelling so loudly that Michael has to pull the phone away from his ear.

"Michael, you have got to see this! Your video is streaming on all the socials. You're the number one trending topic! Everybody is sharing the video of you! It's been shared now over eighty million times! This is bigger than the Ellen DeGeneres/Bradley Cooper selfie at the Oscars! Your video has crashed Talk2U!"

Lucy is breathless. "Michael, what is happening here?" Hesitantly, she asks, "Is Whitney doing this?"

"I don't know what's happening right now, but I got a call from CBN. He wants us—you and me, my mom, Madame Pearl, Ester—all of us—to fly to Florida. Fort Lauderdale, actually . . . Today! Lucy, like this afternoon! He wants us to film another segment of Madame Pearl and me—us—in a séance tonight. Lucy, he wants to pay me TWO MILLION DOLLARS!"

"Holy shit! Two million dollars?" Lucy screams. "Oh, my god, I can't believe this!"

There's that word *believe* again. Michael feels tingles in his stomach.

"Lucy, Whitney was talking to me this morning about believing and now every time I hear the word *believe* it gives me crazy goosebumps. I really think—no, I *know* she's behind this. This is crazy!"

Michael is sweating and he hasn't even left the apartment yet. "Okay, so . . . are you in? You coming with us today? Charles said he'll extend our hotel stay so we'll be able to hit Key Largo again! Oh my god, Key Largo! How about it? You in, girl?"

"Yes! Dolly Parton's pom-poms, yes, I'm in! I wouldn't miss this even for a hot steamy date with Chris Hemsworth, and you know I love Thor. Michael. I'm all the way in! Yes, yes, and YES! Woo-hoo, baby! Florida, here we come! Oh, my god. I just realized, what am I doing talking to you on the phone? I'm coming over there right now!"

Michael actually hears her apartment door slam and seconds later she's banging on his door that he is already unlocking.

"Okay, okay, you're making me nervous. Stop pounding on the door." Michael finally opens the door and Lucy throws herself onto Michael, giving him a fierce hug so big that Michael's phone flies out of his hand and lands across the room. They both fall to the floor laughing and rolling around with heart-pounding, nervous, childlike excitement. They both finally lie still on their backs with their arms extended and look up at the ceiling with sheer exhaustion. They turn their heads to look at each other and start giggling again.

"I gotta call Charles back. He's expecting me to give him an answer, like, now." Michael gazes at the ceiling like it's the Milky Way at night. "I'm so freakin' nervous."

"Well, what are you waiting for? You want Whitney to call him?" Lucy laughs.

"What about Madame Pearl? How do we know she'll be available?"

Lucy sternly looks at Michael and says, "Michael. CBN. National news! Trust me, she will make herself available!"

"You're probably right," he says, rolling his eyes with a laugh.

She turns her head again and looks right at Michael.

"I know I'm right. Look how fast she took you yesterday. This is just as good for her as it is for you. The exposure will be amazing. She would be crazy not to take it!"

"Okay, let me call Charles." He takes a big breath and lets it out.

Michael rolls over onto his hands and knees and gets himself up off the floor. He grabs his phone from across the room and sees that Charles had tried to call again four minutes earlier. Michael calls him back.

Charles answers on the first ring. "What time can you be at the airport?"

Michael can hear the excitement in Charles's voice. "Well, it's nine a.m. now. We'll need to pack and—"

"Great! So, I'll have the limo pick all of you up at your place at noon. You'll arrive in Fort Lauderdale at four twenty-five."

Michael has a mini-panic attack. Noon? He hasn't even asked Madame Pearl or told his mom when they're leaving. His mind is racing, knowing she's going to need the most time to get ready. His mom never travels light. Thoughts are flooding his mind with doubt. Should he really be doing this? He almost forgets that he's still on the phone when Charles interrupts his thoughts.

"Hey, kid. You there?"

Michael turns to Lucy with a pleading expression. "I'm still here. You said noon for a limo pick-up?"

"Holy crap!" Lucy squeals. She jumps up off the floor and twirls around Michael's apartment. Lucy then whispers to Michael in a huff of excitement as she points the way to her apartment. "I'm gonna start packing now!" She runs out with a slam of his door, and he hears another slam as she shuts hers.

Michael brings the phone back to his ear.

"Um, okay, Charles. I guess we'll be ready!"

"Atta boy! I'll have another driver waiting for you here at the airport in Lauderdale. He'll be holding a sign with your name on it as you enter the terminal, so just look for him and he'll do everything else. You're in good hands, Michael! I'll just need the names of everyone who will be flying. My staff will take care of the rest."

Michael spells everyone's name for Charles, then says, "Okay, so I guess we'll be seeing you soon, really soon!"

"Yes, see you soon, my man!"

Michael stares at the now-silent phone. He's a little dizzy and his stomach feels like he just got off a rollercoaster.

CHAPTER 18

MICHAEL TALKS OUT loud to himself, "First things first. I need to call Mom and Madame Pearl." Michael looks for Madame Pearl's phone number then hits dial. She picks up and Michael starts in, but Madame Pearl doesn't let him finish. "Michael, we'll be there and ready."

Michael ends that call. "Now Mom." He becomes nervous having to tell her. He dials, she answers. "Hey, Mom . . . Yes, we have to be ready by noon. No, this is not a joke. Yes, we are being put up for free and we're being given an extra week's stay in Florida! No, Mother, no." He shakes his head. "That is correct, Mother. No, Mother. No, he will not be putting us up in some Motel 6 for the week . . . Yes, I'm sure the hotel will offer luxuries like a spa and hair salon. Yes, I'm sure, really! Just pack super fast. Pack light. I know you well enough to know you'll do some shopping while you're down there. Just grab your essentials . . . NO! No, you cannot take your private jet. We have to fly together. You'll just have to slum it like the rest of us . . . Mom! Stop arguing! You'll be fine. No, I'm sorry, Mom, they probably won't have Dom Perignon on the flight. Just deal with what they have . . . I don't know . . . why does that matter . . . Yes, yes, they probably will be using plastic cups and not fine crystal for the champagne . . . Trust me, you're going to live . . . MOM! Just go pack, please! Okay. Yes, I love you too. Bye, Mom." He stares at his phone, shaking his head while he releases a large exacerbated breath through bulging lips.

At eleven forty-five, the limo is idling at the curb in front of Michael and Lucy's apartment complex. Everyone has already loaded their luggage in the trunk and is sitting inside the lobby when Olivia, who's the last to show up, arrives in her own limo. Everyone quickly moves outside. The limo driver opens the door for Olivia and grabs her suitcase. Olivia's Louis Vuitton purse is hanging off her forearm as she leans on one hip and in Olivia-style presents her argument. "I just don't see why we can't take my limo to the airport." Then, as if on cue, the limo driver opens the trunk and unloads five more suitcases. Everyone looks at Olivia, their eyes widen, and their jaws drop.

"Holy crap!" Michael says.

Everyone is clamoring wondering where on earth they're going to fit all of Olivia's luggage.

Olivia justifiably now stands on the sidewalk with a full smile and a big-brimmed straw sun hat like she's dressed for a day of shopping in Boca Raton. She's wearing a white Chanel suit, big bulky silver and turquoise jewelry, and white stilettos.

"Mom, what are you doing?" Michael throws his hands on his head and now deeply concerned says, "Where are we gonna put all of that? You were supposed to pack light." He's getting agitated. "We're going to South Florida for seven days not seven weeks. It isn't a third-world country with no amenities; you don't need all of that."

"Michael, a woman needs things."

"Well, okay, Mom, but *things,*"—Michael makes air quotes—"*things* can fit into one suitcase, not six! Mom, you gotta leave some of this behind."

"I'm not leaving any of it behind," she says curtly, folding her arms, straightening her back, and lifting and turning her head ever so slightly. "If any of my suitcases have to stay behind, then so will I." She dramatically raises her eyebrows just to show her authority.

Michael throws his head back and looks up at the overhead awning while he clenches and shakes his fists. All he can get out is, "Eeeeeeeeeeee!" as he continues shaking his fists in the air.

"Ms. Monroe, can we leave two of them here in my apartment? How about just taking four? " Lucy tries to reason with Olivia but she's holding firm with her six suitcases.

"Four isn't enough," Olivia says. "I need all of them."

Everyone is bickering as they exchange ideas. The conversations get a little heated and their voices are becoming louder when suddenly a piercing whistle rips through the front lobby.

"People!" the limo driver shouts as he lowers his fingers from his mouth. His loud, deep drawl echoes off the buildings. "I don't care what you do with the goddamn suitcases; tie them to the bumper for all I care."

Olivia gasps and presses her hand to her chest, imagining her Louis Vuitton suitcases tied to the bumper, thumping down 5th Avenue and all the way to JFK Airport.

"It's now two minutes past twelve. My job is to get you folks to an airport that's eighteen miles away. We need to be there by twelve thirty and all of you are making my job very difficult. Now, everyone, let's go!" He waves his thick arm in a motion to direct everyone toward the car. "Get in the limo, NOW!"

Everyone stands in silence for a moment, realizing they were all just yelled at like preschoolers.

Madame Pearl speaks up, "Why not just put as much as we can in the trunk and the rest can ride in the limo with us."

"There, that makes perfect sense. Thank you, Pearl, uh, Madame Pearl." Olivia isn't too sure what to call her.

"It's Ivy. My real name is Ivy. Madame Pearl is just a stage name I made up so people won't stalk me."

Olivia smiles at her. "Well, Ivy. I love your name. It's a very beautiful name for a very beautiful woman."

Ivy smiles back.

Michael, still freaking out, says, "Okay, okay! In the trunk and in the car, whatever! But let's go! We have to go now!" Michael pushes everyone toward the direction of the limo. And off they go, barreling toward the airport, five adults and several large suitcases crammed inside the six-seat limo.

With several fast stops, multiple lane changes, a few near misses, and three obscene gestures, they arrive at JFK at twelve forty. The limo driver is only able to get out of his door as all the doors immediately open. He grabs a cart for the luggage. He unloads the luggage in record time and then stands there with his hand out.

Michael smacks his mother's arm, as she has a twenty dollar bill in her hand. Michael raises his eyebrows and wiggles his fingers at her, so she then reaches in and puts a hundred-dollar bill in his hand. Michael hands it to the driver and says, "Thank you."

"It's been a pleasure. You made my whole damn day. It's not every day I get to race through Manhattan like Dale Earnhardt. It's always good to know what this puppy can do." He pats the limo's roof as if to reward it for performing well.

The five of them all disappear into the airport. The security check-in and boarding all go well and before long, they're on the plane, it's taking off, and they're flying thirty-five thousand feet high.

The pilot's voice crackles over the intercom. "Ladies and gentlemen, we're beginning our descent into Fort Lauderdale about ten minutes ahead of schedule. The weather is sunny and hot at ninety-one degrees. It's been our pleasure flying with you today. From myself and the copilot and all the cabin crew, welcome to Fort Lauderdale."

Lucy hits Michael on the arm and says, "I can't believe it. Just a few days ago I mentioned we should go back to Key Largo and now here we are flying into Fort Lauderdale for a séance and two million dollars!" Her smile is bigger than Julia Roberts's.

Michael rolls his eyes as he's trying to make sense of it. "When we're done tonight with this séance and national TV, I'll really be looking forward to some Keys time." Michael tilts his head a little. "Speaking of séances, I haven't seen or felt Whitney at all today." Michael thinks he's probably just so overwhelmed with how today is evolving that he may have just tuned her out.

Oh, don't you worry baby, I'm here. When I saw your Mom packing those six bags, I just tip-toed away. Oh child, that girl can pack like somethin' fierce!

Michael smiles and hits Lucy on the arm. "Whitney's here."

Lucy smiles back and squeezes his arm. "It's all gonna be all right."

Maybe! Whitney laughs.

Michael's heart instantly sinks into his stomach. "Maybe? What's that supposed to mean, maybe?"

Oh, you'll see.

The pilot comes back on over the intercom. "Air Traffic Control in Fort Lauderdale just told us we have to circle for a few minutes before we land. Since we're gonna be up here a few more minutes it's going to be safe to unbuckle your seatbelts and use the lavatories if necessary. The copilot and I are going to do something we have never done before: we're gonna play you a little song to put a smile on your face and welcome you into Fort Lauderdale."

The tapping sound of a drum comes over the speakers, followed by a base guitar with several beats and a triple-clapping segment. "Ah . . . Yeah . . . Woooo!"

Instantly, Michael recognizes the song. "I Wanna Dance with Somebody (Who Loves Me)." Everyone on the plane is swaying, snapping their fingers, and dancing in their seats. Some have even unbuckled their seatbelts and are standing, wiggling their arms in the air. The scene in the airplane is like Dierks Bentley's song "Drunk on the Plane." As the song ends, the pilot comes back on over the intercom informing everyone to buckle back up as they'll be landing soon.

Twenty short minutes later the tires hit the runway and everyone within the plane bounces.

As the five of them step off the jetway and into the airport, they see a man in a black suit holding a white sign with Michael's name on it and they head in his direction. Michael shakes the man's hand, and they're escorted down to the luggage carousel.

The Beach Boys' "Kokomo" is playing over the PA system as everyone collects their luggage. They pile into the limo as Michael gazes through heavily tinted windows. He excitedly watches the palm trees zipping past him on the Florida Turnpike. Off in the distance, he spies a tall building with the large letters *CBN* at the top.

To the strains of Jimmy Buffet's "Margaritaville," the limo slows and exits the highway. They finally come to a stop in front of the CBN building. Standing outside the building is a distinguished gentleman, anxiously rubbing his hands together. *Is this Charles?* Michael wonders.

He's tan with a full smile and reminds Michael very much of George Clooney. Charles's salt-and-pepper hair blows in the Florida breeze as Michael takes in the older man's dark blue polo shirt, tan khakis, designer black sunglasses, and camel-colored leather driving loafers with a matching belt.

Olivia is the first to exit the limo. Not knowing she would have an audience, she causally accepts the hand of the limo driver and steps out, putting her white Jimmy Choo stiletto firmly on the ground and smoothing her Chanel suit. She has her big straw sun hat in her other hand. Charles smiles, perhaps too widely, and nods. *Is he nervous?* Michael thinks.

As they exit the limo, Charles tries to break the tension. "Only five people? I was expecting six."

They give him a quizzical look.

"Where's Whitney?" He flashes a million-dollar smile.

They all burst into laughter. "She likes to keep us on our toes," Michael says and walks up to Charles with one hand extended. "I'm Michael Monroe. It's nice to meet you." As they shake hands, Charles pulls Michael into him for a bro hug. With that Michael turns and says, "Charles, this is my mother, Olivia Monroe."

Charles takes her proffered hand and gives it a soft squeeze, then places his other hand on top of hers and looks her directly in the eye. "It is an absolute pleasure to meet you, Ms. Monroe. I've heard a lot about you from my first wife, who absolutely demanded I buy her your Double D's."

Olivia smiles and with a wave of her hand she says, "We women have a way of getting what we want." She smiles flirtatiously.

Charles holds her gaze and hand for about two seconds longer than protocol dictates, then lets go. Michael introduces Lucy, Madame Pearl, and Ester.

The thick humid South Florida air is already starting to take its toll. "Why don't we all go inside into the air conditioning before we combust," Charles says with an open hand pointing toward the front doors. "Shall we?"

As they enter the large glass atrium, they're swiftly escorted around security because of the VIP treatment from Charles. "I'll give you a quick tour of the studios. I'll show y'all where we'll be taping and then I'll let y'all go so you can check into your hotel and freshen up. Grab some dinner and then be back here again tonight for the taping." Charles looks at Michael. "Michael,"

Charles pats him on the shoulder, "if you would please be here a little earlier than the rest, you'll need to fill out paperwork so we can get you on our payroll." Charles hands Michael an envelope. "This will buy your dinner." Michael nods and Charles hands everyone else envelopes with cash inside.

After their quick tour, Charles walks them back outside to the limo that's still waiting for them. "Let's see," Charles says, looking at his big gold watch. "It's what, quarter to six now? How about having Michael and Madame Pearl back here tonight at nine." It was more of a command than a question. "This way we can get right to the taping, hopefully with a start time at ten. We hope the séance should only take about an hour or two and we can have all of you out of here by midnight or so. Sound good?" Michael and Madame Pearl nod. Charles continues, "Madame Pearl, is there anything else that you will need from us for the séance?"

Madame Pearl looks softly at Charles and says, "My stage name is Madame Pearl, to ward off the crazies of my business." She smiles and laughs. "My name is Ivy. I am a genuine psychic/ medium and I will always try to do my best to offer my clients the most authentic séance experience." She pauses to collect her thoughts. "But you'll need to understand I cannot control Whitney or any other spirit for that matter. Whoever may want to come through in the taping . . ." She pauses again. "I will only be able to read the spirits that allow themselves to come through to me." She raises her hand and points toward Ester. "My assistant, Ester, has everything we need. We will need about half an hour to secure the room."

"Secure the room?" Charles asks.

"Yes, securing the room is to allow only the highest spirit to come through. If proper precautions aren't taken, any spirit can come through and cause havoc." She shakes her head briskly. "You don't want that to happen."

"You mean a dark spirit can come through and haunt us?" Charles wiggles his fingers in the air with a bit of nonchalant disbelief.

Michael can see Ivy concentrating, connecting with Charles's energy and she instantly snaps back.

"Yes, Charles, a dark spirit like your father could come into the room and we wouldn't want that to happen, now would we?" She glares at him.

Taken off guard, Charles's smile vanishes from his face.

Ivy knows she has his full attention. "What a mess he can make if tonight he decides to step into the room. I already felt a heavy energy inside; I'm assuming your father still has quite the hold on this place."

Not one to shy down, Charles replies. "Yeah, well a person like my father doesn't create a multi-million-dollar broadcasting station by being nice." His face suggests that maybe it could've been done better. "It's a ruthless business and he was a tough bird, that one." He's not sure how she received so much information, but he's at least impressed by her ability. "How did you do that—connect with my father?" he says, moving his head to the side. "I've been to a few psychics in my day, and nobody has done that."

"Charles, it's because I'm sensitive. I allow spirits to come to me. I allow all spirits to come to me even when I'm not protected, like now. This is why it's so important for me and Ester to secure that room before the séance."

"Well then, I say we should let you both secure that room before the taping tonight." He claps his hands together. "Okay, I'll let y'all go. See you back here in a bit and let's have a good, safe séance tonight." He looks wearily at Ivy as he says that. She nods as they all get back into the limo and are escorted off to the hotel.

Michael speaks first in the limo, "Mom, what was up with you and Charles?"

"Michael, what are you talking about?"

"Oh, come on Mom, everybody saw you two acting like school kids when you met. All that hand-holding and eye-contact stuff. Somebody has a crush." Michael smiles as he pushes his shoulder up against his mother's body.

She smiles and everyone thinks they see her blush a little. "He happens to be a very attractive gentleman, Michael, that's it."

"Oh, that's it, okay."

They arrive at the hotel and a representative from CBN already has them checked in. Michael and Lucy are sharing one room, Ivy and Ester share another, and Olivia has her own room. Michael and Lucy make their way to their room, grateful as they enter to find the air conditioning already running, cooling the suite. Michael flops down on his queen-size bed and stares up at the ceiling. "Oh my god. I'm already beat, and we still have to do the séance tonight."

"Oh, boo-hoo Mister Two Million Dollars!" Lucy flops down on the bed next to Michael. "I don't know about you or anyone else, but I'm hungry. I say we go to Las Olas Boulevard and find something great to eat. I'm sure we can all agree on a restaurant." She touches her phone and searches *Restaurants, Fort Lauderdale*. "Oh, this looks good. They have a martini bar and a piano bar." Michael grins; she knows him too well. "I'm gonna call them and make reservations for the six of us at six forty-five. That'll give you an hour and a half before you have to be back at the studio. God, I hope your mom can be ready," she says, laughing to herself.

"I'll let her know," Michael says, grabbing his phone to call Olivia.

"Hey, Mom. We're all going to meet downstairs in the lobby

at six-thirty. Lucy found a restaurant on Las Olas that she made reservations for—What? Who? Oh. Okay. Well, have fun. We'll see you at the studio." Michael tosses his phone on the bed.

"Apparently my mother and Charles are having dinner. She's in town for what, twenty minutes and already has a date. Unbelievable!" A thought pops into his mind and he remembers his dream of how Vince Lombardi told him his problem was that he didn't believe. He made a mental note to himself to try and believe anything is possible, even for him.

Atta boy, good job. Maybe I'm finally getting through to you.

Michael just smiles to himself. He doesn't mention to Lucy that Whitney was just in the room. But her popping in gives him hope that she'll show up for the séance tonight. Another scenario pops into his mind that erases all other thoughts. "What is she going to do tonight?" Closing his eyes and clenching his teeth, he puts his hand on his forehead and just holds it there. "Oh, my god. Oh, my god. Oh, my god," he repeats to himself.

Michael sees Lucy staring at him as he seems to be in pain. He's frowning and staring off, lost in the white ceiling.

"What's wrong?" Lucy asks.

"I don't know. Whitney was just here. I instantly got this nausea in the pit of my stomach. I almost feel dizzy." He puts his other hand on his stomach. He looks right at Lucy, hesitates, then lets his worst fear out. "She's up to something. I just know it! I can feel it. I've got this heavy ball of something inside my stomach."

Lucy looks right at Michael and they both fall backward again onto the bed. Lucy smirks and says, "Well, no sense worrying about it now. Let's go eat and then we'll let the games begin."

Not a moment later, Michael's phone rings. He sees it's Madame Pearl.

"Hey, what's up?"

"We're going to have to pass on dinner tonight. We should really get back to the studio. After my encounter with Charles, as lovely as he is, there was that negative energy hovering around the studio, and we really need to make sure that energy stays out tonight."

Michael hesitates. "Okay, you go do what you have to do. I'm sorry you're gonna miss dinner." He hangs up and glances at Lucy. "I guess it's just us and one angry spirit." They both stare at each other but say nothing.

Lucy speaks up, "I better not get slimed in that goo tonight like Carol Anne in *Poltergeist.*" Lucy offers her most convincing smile to Michael. But he isn't buying it.

"Let's just go to dinner. Everything will figure itself out. Charles wants ratings—isn't that what he said? Maybe he should be careful what he wishes for."

Michael finally changes into a slim-fit, black Calvin Klein button-down short-sleeve shirt, tan J Crew khakis, and his Sperry Top Siders. He stands in front of Lucy.

"Shirt tucked or untucked?"

Lucy smiles. "I like it untucked." She grabs a turquoise blouse, white pants, and sandals. She pulls her auburn hair back into a ponytail.

An unspoken anticipation is on both of their minds, looming thickly around them as they finish dressing. As Michael and Lucy are about to leave, Michael grabs the hotel room's doorknob, but it won't open. "Um, that's weird." He gives a few more turns and tries pulling it open. Again, nothing. He pulls on it really fast a few more times, feeling a little anxious. "Come on . . . open." Nothing. He throws his hands down in a huff.

"Here, let me try." Lucy reaches past Michael, grabs the door knob, twists it, and it opens right up. She looks at Michael and says, "You need to calm down."

"I'm telling you . . . you saw it. That door was not opening. I swear it; I'm not going crazy." He stops as the door is about to close. "This . . . tonight, the séance is not going to be good."

CHAPTER 19

ARRIVING AT THE restaurant, they're waiting to be greeted as they look around at all the seated guests. Mostly couples, seemingly on vacation, several with sunglass sunburns on their faces. A man up on a stage plays piano, singing Barry Manilow's "Copacabana." A few TVs are playing at the bar. They can see the beach and the ocean's rolling waves. A hostess finally escorts them to a table and hands them menus. They glance at all the entrees as they await their server. Lucy looks at Michael. "So what's the worst that happens? It's not like *The Exorcist*. I don't see Whitney and this dark spirit dueling it out with glowing swords or anything." She lets out a laugh as her eyes glance over at one of the servers. "Ooh, he looks delicious."

Michael turns around and looks. He smiles; handsome indeed. Lucy has spotted a muscular, dark-haired man with piercing blue eyes. He's about six foot two and on his right arm is a tattoo sleeve filled with tropical images of a bright blue ocean, a sunset sky, flowers, and palm trees. Inked into his forearm is a smiling Buddha, the Om symbol, and Mala beads. His dark hair is firmly slicked down and shaved in a hard part on his left side. He looks fresh from the barber shop and has a smile that lights up the room.

Seconds later that same waiter saunters over to their table. He stops and looks directly at Michael with a smile, then looks at Lucy. His voice is strong and smooth yet friendly.

"Hi there. I'm Andrew, I'll be your server. Tonight, we have South Florida's favorite, the hogfish. It's prepared with a panko breading, fried then smothered with a mango-chili-lime salsa."

Lucy looks at Michael and silently mouths "Meow." Michael smiles; he can tell she'll buy any special Andrew offers.

The server continues. "We also have a filet mignon prepared with a lobster beurre blanc. Both are served with a sea-salted baked potato, and tonight's vegetable is asparagus. Can I start you both with beverages?"

Letting Andrew know they're short on time, Lucy orders the hogfish special and a peach martini. Michael chooses the filet special, but with no lobster and instead he asks for a port demi-glace that he saw listed on another menu item. "I'll take a red sangria, too, please."

Michael turns to watch Andrew walk away in his tight black pants. "I wish *he* was tonight's special!" He smiles at Lucy and lets out a laugh. "Oh lord. If only."

"You know," Lucy says, "I bet he plays on the pink team."

"You think?"

"Michael, he's gay as a two-dollar bill. Weren't you here when he walked up to us and looked right at you? I felt invisible. Hello, yoo-hoo, Andrew, I'm here! Look, Andrew!" She cups her breasts. "Boobs, Andrew." She smiles sarcastically. "Nope, no interest." She waves her hand away. "Yep, he's gay."

"What do you think would be the possibility of me getting his phone number? I mean, we're gonna be down here for a couple of days." Michael smiles devilishly.

"Let me look into my crystal ball." Lucy looks down at the

table and runs her hands around an imaginary ball. "As I see it—all signs point to yes!"

Andrew comes back over to the table with their drinks. He places the martini in front of Lucy and the sangria in front of Michael. His hand lands on Michael's shoulder.

"I'll be back with warm bread for the table." He smiles and walks away.

"Holy shit, he touched me," Michael says in a loud whisper. "I'm starting to swell!"

"Oh, he so wants you. Just go for it."

"Easier said than done."

"Chicken."

"Maybe, but he's exactly the type I always fall for and then get dumped by, just like some epic dramatic Hollywood movie. I don't need another Joel."

Lucy replies without skipping a beat, "Not everyone is like Joel."

"True, but I need to end these patterns. I need someone who's single." The heaviness of the ultimatum his mother made ten years ago quickly pops back into his mind. "One who wants a relationship, has a job, his own place, a car, and the icing on the cake, one that my mother would approve of." He lets out a deflated sigh.

"Well, look on the bright side: we know he has a job." Lucy winks and smiles as she lifts her glass.

Michael lifts his glass to meet Lucy's, "Cheers to step one." He smiles but then his mind drifts off as he looks around the restaurant at all the vacationing happy couples. The smiles on their faces and the way some are holding hands on top of the table. He notices several couples are not even speaking; they're fully consumed by their phones. He thinks perhaps those are the ones who have been together longer. They just slip away into their phones, forgetting where they are, this tropical cultural destination dubbed the Venice of America. Or maybe just how special the person is that's sitting across the table from them that they're ignoring. He ponders why they even went on vacation in the first place if they were just going to do the same things they can do at home.

He looks out at the ocean as he feels the gentle breeze against his face. The sun is still a glowing white ball hanging in the sky that glistens across the water. He faintly hears the crashing ocean waves as he catches the sounds of seagulls flying over the water and the people walking along the solid wet shore.

Michael snaps back as Andrew comes over smiling, this time with warm bread and butter and leaves it on the table. Moments later, he returns with their salads.

"Black pepper, anyone?" Michael accepts. Andrew stands very close as he turns the peppermill. A dusting of crushed black pepper flakes falls gently onto his salad.

"Is that enough?" Andrew asks. Michael nods, not taking his eyes off Andrew. "Is there anything else I can get you two right now?"

Both Michael and Lucy shake their heads. "We're all set for now, thanks, Andrew," Lucy answers with a kind smile.

"Okay, enjoy." Andrew smiles at Michael again then walks away.

"He's toying with you." Lucy smirks at Michael.

"No, he's a waiter and he's doing his job. But he does look great in those pants. His butt is like a perfect half-moon."

Lucy fires back, "I'm sure you can bounce a quarter off of it." They both laugh. "No, but seriously, he's paying way too much attention to you."

"Yeah, okay, maybe he is, but that's okay; I like it." Michael smiles flirtatiously.

Their entrees arrive and they look as delicious as expected. Andrew stops back several times just to make sure they're enjoying their meals.

The sky outside is now starting to turn colors of pink and light orange as Michael looks down at his watch and realizes it's just past eight. He quickly looks up at Lucy and says, "We have to get going. It's getting close to eight-thirty." Instantly he's reminded why he's here. He thinks to himself that he hasn't heard from Whitney in a while. That gnawing feeling begins again in the pit of his stomach.

"Is everything okay?" Lucy asks.

"Yeah, it's just . . . we have to get going."

"You gonna ask for his number?"

"No." Michael knows he's chickening out. "We should just leave and get back a few minutes early to make sure we're ready for who knows what." He throws his hands in the air as a form of expression, but Andrew, who's been circling, thinks the gesture is for him and heads over to their table.

"Did you need me?" Andrew says with a smile.

"Sorry, I was just gesturing with my hands. But, yes, since you're here, we're ready for the check. We've got that appointment at nine and we really need to get going."

Andrew leaves to get the check while Michael and Lucy resume their conversation. When suddenly, they realize the entire conversational hum has gotten quiet. Michael looks up and it seems as if everyone in the restaurant is looking at him and Lucy.

"What's going on? Do we have spots? Why is everyone looking at us?"

They now notice a commotion over in the bar area. People are talking, pointing their fingers at them, and now the same people are taking pictures of them.

A man approaches their table and introduces himself. "Hi, remember me? Both Michael and Lucy connect a vague memory but are still baffled. "Ed Turgeon. The photographer from New

York and that feather storm." Michael's facial expression proves he's made the connection. Ed continues, "I got a tip that CBN paid you to fly down here to the studios and that they're taping a live séance. Now I see on the news," he points to the TV at the bar, "your mom, Olivia, the Double D's heiress and CBN owner Charles Booream are having dinner at Oscar's, here in Lauderdale." A still shot of the film scene from Fate with Michael and Madame Pearl appears on the TV.

"Lauderdale has rich people, but seeing your mom and Charles is like seeing the Royal Family! It's really exciting news."

"Oh Lucy, I don't believe this!" is all Michael can get out before he starts shaking his head. Silence overtakes him while he watches the TV a few seconds.

"Oh my god," is all Lucy can say.

Ed breaks the silence, "I was hoping maybe I could get in and take some pictures of the séance?"

Not looking at Ed, Michael just responds, "I don't think that would be a good idea. Plus, I'm sure Mr. Booream isn't gonna allow anyone to take pictures inside the studios." He now diverts his eyes from the TV back toward the photographer. "I mean you can ask, but that's a pretty unlikely situation." Michael frowns at him.

"Well, I'll meet you two back at the studios and we'll see what happens."

Michael nods at him and he returns to the bar area when Andrew walks over with the check.

"Thanks for dining with us tonight. Hopefully I'll see you again real soon." He smiles one last time at Michael and walks away.

Lucy smiles at Andrew as he's walking away and playfully says, "Oh, Michael would like to see you *real* soon, too. Like tonight, naked, after the séance." She laughs at Michael but he's smiling back for a different reason.

"Look." He hands Lucy the check.

"Oh . . . my . . . god . . . he gave you his number."

Michael pays in cash from the per diem he was given and adds a sizable tip. He takes the receipt with Andrew's phone number on it and pushes it into his pocket. He's smiling as they both leave through all the people who are now snapping pictures of them.

Michael hears Whitney. ***You're welcome.***

Thank you. He smiles. *Oh, my god, thank you,* Michael replies in his head to Whitney.

CHAPTER 20

MICHAEL AND LUCY arrive back at CBN studios at 8:41. As they walk into the atrium, there's a haze in the air and a herbaceous smell of sage engulfs them. They walk to the front desk, where they get signed in and are handed laminated VIP lanyards. Michael is next asked to fill out forms as he signs the last document allowing a direct deposit.

The HR rep helping Michael says, "As soon as I enter these in the system, *zappo*, the wire transfer happens. You should have your funds in about twenty minutes." She smiles at him. Michael is trying to comprehend two million dollars. He nods, trying to act nonchalant. All the while his mind is exploding with excitable images of two-freakin'-million-dollars depositing into his account. He starts counting all the zeros. He does all he can do to keep calm as he and Lucy are escorted from the front desk to the studio by Christie, a charming young receptionist with matching pink lipstick and eye shadow.

"It's pretty smoky in here," Christie mentions in her high-pitched voice as she waves her hand through the haze. "I hope this nasty smoke stink doesn't get trapped in my clothes. I just bought these Donna Karan's!" She lets out a forced cough and continues to wave a hand for fresh air. The sound of her stiletto heels clicking against the marble floors echoes down the hallway in fast little repetitive steps. *Click, click, click, click, click.*

Michael smiles as he thinks of how Christie reminds him of Glinda the Good Witch from the Broadway show *Wicked.*

"For the last two hours I swear they've been having some sort of voodoo sacrifice in there. All I've been hearing are drums beatings and chanting that sounds like the guards from *The Wizard of Oz* defending the castle, 'Oh-wee-oh.'" She moves her arms as if she's marching along with them. "Then"—her face lights up with sudden surprise—"there were wolves howling and birds chirping and the sounds of waterfalls. I thought we were going to be flooded out. And now millions of crickets." She puts her hands on her hips and frowns. "Good luck in there."

Christie opens the door to the studio and a thick wall of smoke engulfs them. "Oh my god, it's like something out of *Hocus Pocus*! Get in, get in, don't let any more of it out." Christie pushes Michael and Lucy into the thick smoke and slams the door behind them.

Michael can hear an "Ugh!" from Christie. She yells through the closed door, "It's all okay out here!" He can hear her clapping her hands as she squeals with delight. Then the sounds of her heels clicking against the marble floor grow fainter and fainter.

As Michael and Lucy make their way through the dense smoke of burning sage, they make out the camera lights. Dozens of thick electrical cords are scattered on the ground. There's the boom, which carries the camera, and the stage, which is where they get a glimpse of Madame Pearl and Ester. Several TV sets are near the cameras. It also looks like there's stadium-style seating for an audience of about two hundred. The crew is there preparing all the equipment. None of them seem to be happy working this late at night, let alone enduring the sounds of thousands of crickets and the robust scent of the sage smoke.

They head toward Madame Pearl and Ester who are both sitting peacefully in the center of the room, eyes shut in some sort of trance. Madame Pearl intuitively welcomes them without opening her eyes.

"You're here." She seems to speak in between long, calming breaths. "We've tried our best with the time we had to secure this room but there's a very strong presence in here. Be ready."

Gingerly, Michael asks, "Do you know who it is?"

"It's Charles's dad. He's been wreaking havoc all night. Just when we think we've done enough and he's gone, he comes back. He's been quiet now for about twenty minutes."

"What did you do to secure the room?" asks Lucy.

"I started by using drums to let the spirits know we are here but mean no harm. I added the howling of wolves and a sacred Indian chant. This grounds the room and brings back nature and peace. Finally, I wash away all disconnected energy by using the sounds of waterfalls and finish with the crickets. Crickets jump and so they're symbolic and allow spirits to jump back through portals. So far,"—Madame Pearl holds up her hands with fingers crossed—"this has worked. But if he comes back again during the séance, I will have to use my iron spikes. They'll work but they're very aggressive and will only irritate the spirit more. But"—she pauses—"if I use them, we'll lose Whitney too. Her energy can't withstand iron spikes."

"So, what do we do now?" Michael grimly asks.

Shrugging her shoulders, she says, "We sit and wait for everyone else to arrive . . . and hope for the best."

Michael and Lucy sit down at two of the three remaining chairs. Michael glances down at the last empty chair. His heart is starting to race. There's a collective nervous anticipation felt by all four of them as they sit quietly in a circle, just as they did back at Madame Pearl's séance parlor. They're readying themselves for quite possibly another spiritual visit.

There's a sudden commotion as they hear the door to the studio open and slam shut again. The footsteps of people entering come through the thick smoke, then Olivia appears, who's being escorted by Charles. All eyes fixate on them—especially on their intertwined hands. They're smiling like two lovebirds. Olivia releases Charles's hand and places her hand on his shoulder, indicating that she's fine now to walk alone. Olivia walks to the center, waving her arm through the smoke. She curtly asks, "Is all this smoke really necessary?" and then begrudgingly sits down. Michael watches her wiggle around in the chair, finding a comfortable placement. When no one responds to her, she blurts out, "Hello, everyone."

Michael smiles to himself and rolls his eyes, thinking she's so unapologetically Mom.

Olivia continues, "Not sure about all of you, but quite frankly, I'm nervous as hell." She giggles.

"I think we're all a little on edge," replies Madame Pearl. She too lets out a silly laugh. "But I promise whatever happens, we will be fine. My only concern is Charles's father. We need to keep him out of the room."

Olivia assertively responds, "I thought you prepared the room so he wouldn't make an appearance."

"I did my best with the time we had. Performing a séance is very tricky, especially if a space is so widely used as this one is. Let's all just take three deep breaths and we'll let go of any discordant energy. Ready? Breathe in through the nose and out through the mouth three times. Here we go. Breathe in, hold on to the breath for a second and release with an *ahh*.

As they finish their three breaths, the filming crew clumsily comes back into the room. Charles is vaguely seen standing alone along the back wall of the studio. At this time, Charles gives a hand motion, and they start letting an audience enter.

"Audience? What is this?" Madame Pearl stands up and

demands an answer. "No one ever mentioned we would have an audience."

At that moment all the peace, tranquility, and silence of the room has disappeared. Among the audience, spectators jockey for seats and snap pictures with their phones. A woman shouts, "Where's Whitney?" and starts a barrage of cheers.

"We want Whitney!" The entire crowd chants, clapping and stomping in unison.

Michael glares at Charles as he furiously walks over to him. "We can't do this with an audience."

"Yes, you can." Charles curtly smiles. "You did it at Fate." He deadpans Michael.

"But that wasn't staged like this is. Whitney wasn't a prop like she's being used tonight," he says, clearly agitated. "I also didn't agree to do this in front of an audience. Nothing was ever mentioned about us doing this in front of an audience."

"Michael," Charles says, becoming very stern, "this is a live studio and I told you we are taping a live séance. That meant there would be a live audience."

"Did my mother know you were going to invite an audience? Did you mention that to her while you took her to dinner? That you had TV crews following you to the restaurant? Was all that staged too?"

Charles cleverly smiles. "Marketing, Michael. In this business it's called marketing."

"You mean that's why my mother and I are on every news station in South Florida tonight?" Michael is furious and at a loss for words. He's just about to walk out of the studio when his mother walks into the conversation. Michael wants to be sure he gets proof of everything, so he opens his phone's video camera, presses *Record* and leans the phone up against his chair to use the video as evidence that he was conned by Charles.

"What's this all about, Charles?" Olivia asks. She's standing with her arms crossed and staring at him with narrowed eyes.

"This is business, Olivia," Charles says in a very condescending tone. "This is a live taping of a séance. This is what your son agreed to do when he accepted my offer of two million dollars."

"Well, if that's the case, I can just write you a check for your two million dollars and we'll be leaving! After all, Charles, as you said, this is business, and it looks like our business here is over." Olivia pulls Michael by the arm like she would've done when he was a child as they start stepping away from Charles.

Michael glares back. "I was lied to. You took total advantage of me and my mother!"

"No! Olivia, Michael, wait!" Charles holds both his hands up to stop them.

"What? What is this . . . you're asking us to *wait*?" Olivia's words become sharp as a scalpel. "Charles, you mustn't know me as well as you think you do. Because I don't wait. My waiting days are over. Michael, grab the others; we're leaving."

Charles points at Olivia and spit sprays out of his mouth. "I'll sue you and your son!"

With eyes like Medusa, Olivia glares at Charles. "And I'll sue you right back. Who has more to lose, me or you, Charles? It's not my business that will be dragged through the news and social media being sued and discredited for breach of contract." Olivia composes herself. "I've gone up against far worse men than you and won. If you think you're going to scare me with your legal tactics, you've picked the wrong woman to scare." She points her finger at Charles. "I have a team of lawyers in New York just waiting to take this case on. They're hungry and ready to rip you apart." Olivia stands still, arms folded against her chest, fearless, a beacon of strength.

Charles stands seething as he considers the various scenarios. Then, without warning, his body seems to deflate. Defeated he asks, "What if I get rid of the audience?"

"We're done here, Charles." Olivia walks back over to the chair she was just sitting in and grabs her purse. All of them are about to leave when they hear a woman hysterically screaming. Like a thundering storm, the studio doors fly open and Christie the receptionist comes running in, still screaming, her heels clicking. She turns around quickly and pushes the doors shut then runs over to Charles.

"There's a man out there in the building on a motorcycle!" Christie is screaming, practically jumping up and down, her curly blond hair wildly bouncing. She's trying to talk while gasping for air. "He's out there, Charles, riding his motorcycle through the building! He was coming after me and that's when I came running in here! He's out there and he's coming this way!"

The loud rev of a motor rips through the studio and there's a heavy crash against the double doors Christie just closed. Christie screams. The motorcycle hits the doors with a loud *bam*! and they shake again. The motor revs even louder and the doors are hit even harder this time.

Christie is hysterical, almost in tears. "He's trying to get in! What does he want?"

The audience clearly has no idea what they signed up for. There's confusion, fear, and chaos in the air as the audience starts getting panicky.

Like a strike of lightning, a huge flash pops, causing everyone to cover their eyes. They open them to darkness. Everything is out, even the red emergency exit lights. Over one hundred audience members scream and begin to panic, tripping over each other as they try to find the exit.

The motor revs again with the throttle wide open, and the motorcycle blasts through the studio doors with a deafening roar. The single headlight pierces the blackness, and a purple haze of smoke engulfs the room. Behind the motorcycle and mysterious rider, the studio doors have fallen to the floor. The smell of exhaust fills the room. The tires squeal as the driver keeps revving the motor and circling the room, driving through the purple haze to where Michael and the others are in the center of the room, all huddling together trying to protect each other from the motorcycle and its mysterious driver.

CHAPTER 21

AS THE MOTORCYCLE glides through the purple smoke, loud music begins blasting. Oddly, it isn't coming through the studio speakers. It is as if it were traveling through the air. There's the sound of a synthesizer, bass guitar, and snare drums. As the rhythms all come together, it fuses into the song "1999." At this moment, people finally understand what is happening. Prince has made his way into the séance. Still revving and circling, he finally stops, gets off and stands next to his bike in his purple outfit with his white poet's shirt decorated with large frills and flowing cuffs. He begins to say the wedding prayer.

"Dearly beloved," His brown eyes circle the room, and he stands there with his flirty smile. "We are gathered here . . . tonight—" *POOF!* He disappears, leaving only little purple twinkle lights floating in the air. The room is still in total darkness. No headlight. No motorcycle. No music. No Prince. The room falls into absolute silence. The hazy purple smoke still floats around the room when they hear another voice break through the walls.

Another apparition appears. This time a man with long, kinky black hair stands in tight red leather pants. "What's with the purple smoke, you crazy funkers? That's right! I'm Rick James, bitch!" Another explosion of red light flashes like a light bulb shattering and Rick James disappears into the ether.

The room is silent until the audience goes crazy, screaming, yelling, and roaring with cheers. "Prince! Prince! Prince! Superfreak!" Everyone stomps their feet and chants with excitement. The audience starts swaying and singing "Purple Rain."

Seconds later, another thunderous rattle shakes the building. Everyone feels a vibration that feels like an earthquake. Sparkling lights start to appear and seem to be forming a glove.

A soft, high-pitched voice echoes, "You may be a Superfreak, but I'm the King of Pop! *HEE-HOO*!" A sparkling glove hangs suspended in midair. As light shines down from the glove, a man, wearing his fedora, white shirt, black pants, sparkly white socks, and penny loafers appears. The glove explodes into millions of tiny sparkling lights, taking the figure with them and instantly disappearing. The audience goes ballistic.

"MICHAEL JACKSON!" Absolute pandemonium breaks out as the audience screams, some crying and holding each other.

Meanwhile, Michael and his gang are still in the center of the room as Charles and Christie run to them. Christie screams, "Oh My god! I love Prince! I love Michael Jackson!" She jumps up and down. "Oh, my god, Oh my god! This is so amazing! Wait till I tell everyone about this!"

Even in the pitch-black darkness, the audience is screaming and yelling with excitement.

The excitement is broken, followed by surprised curiosity when all of a sudden they hear an incredibly loud single drum beat followed by a second of silence. Then a voice rings throughout the room. "And Iiiiiii . . ."

"WHITNEY!" The audience erupts screaming again, professing their love for Whitney Houston. Women are crying, babbling, and begging for Whitney. Michael hears the screams of the crowd as they chant in unison.

"Whitney! Whitney! Whitney!" As audience members are screaming for Whitney, a sudden explosion of raging, fiery lights, like demonic fireworks light up the room. Shades of reds, yellows, grays, and blacks swirl, bursting and flickering on and off. The swirling lights make a cyclone and spin like a tornado. The angry cyclone starts floating around the room, moving from floor to ceiling, bouncing wildly off walls and into corners. People duck to avoid being hit. Some people stay down, others keep jumping up and down, not wanting to miss a thing.

Like a pinball machine, the fiery, flickering cyclone bounces off the walls. It starts to slow down and becomes less erratic. Inside the twinkling lights of the cyclone, an image begins to form.

"I see a figure!" screams someone in the audience. Split seconds of darkness are replaced by bursting split seconds as millions of devilish flickering lights appear and disappear. As the lights bounce and flicker, Ivy begins a prayer of light and love, and Ester repeats her words.

"Hear us, divine spirit. Offer us love and light. Keep us safe in your loving light." Ivy grabs Michael and tells everyone to hold hands and make a circle.

The angry lights are still flickering but seem to be fading as Ivy keeps her prayers going and Ester repeats her words.

Meanwhile, the film crew's equipment is still out. Nothing is working. The set crew is plugging and unplugging outlets and checking all the electrical cords. They turn the power buttons on and off over and over again, but nothing is working. All the equipment remains dormant without electrical power.

Lucy now joins in and starts repeating and reciting the words she hears. "Love. Light. Truth. Divine."

Michael and Olivia are next to join. Reluctantly, Charles finally joins in. All of them chant together. "Love. Light. Truth. Divine."

The glowing cyclone orb is now floating right above Michael and the group. Little crystal sparks break away from the cyclone and fall, fading as they land on the floor. Sparkling crystals shimmer like boiling lava cascading in an array of lights.

Down from the ceiling comes an invisible sinister *BOOM!* The noise is deafening as the sound rips from ceiling to floor, bounces off the floor and evaporates through the walls. The audience is thrown to the ground. Panicked screams and cries pierce the air. A few groups of people are able to get up and run out the door that Prince had previously destroyed. Seconds later, another invisible demonic *BOOM!* travels from the ceiling to the floor and again evaporates through the walls. Most of the audience members flee for their lives, running out of the studio.

The seven still in the center of the room in a circle are still unharmed, even as the vexed cyclone floats above them. There are about fifty people still in the studio when a monstrous voice from the cyclone screams, "GET OUT!"

Charles recoils. " Dad?" he whispers.

As fast as the cyclone spins, it explodes and disappears. Inexplicably the lights flash, flicker, and illuminate once again. The recording equipment starts to light up and begins working again. All the red emergency *EXIT* signs come back on, and the sparkling glitter, cyclone, and purple smoke are all gone as if they were never there.

All seven of them look at each other and sigh in relief. Ivy sharply exhales as she smooths strands of her hair back. A strained smile is plastered across Ester's face.

Charles looks dumbfounded, Michael and Lucy stand quietly, and Olivia's face seems as if she's scheming a million ways to bring repercussions to Charles and CBN. Finally, Christie speaks up.

"Well, after that, Momma needs a drink." She pauses. "And I'm going *out* tonight!" Her heels *click, click, click* as she leaves.

She grunts as she steps over the broken doors lying on the ground. She's about to walk through the doorway with the last of the audience when Michael yells over. "Hey, wait for us; we need a drink too!"

Everyone starts walking toward Christie when Michael realizes he left his phone on his chair. He goes back, picks it up, and realizes it had been filming the entire time—a ten-minute video. He grins, presses the stop button on the camera, closes his phone, and shoves it in his front pocket.

CHAPTER 22

ALL OF THE remaining audience members are escorted out of the studio and now it's just Christie applying more of her pink lipstick, looking at herself, and fixing her hair in a mirror hanging near the front reception desk. Michael thinks about asking Christie where they're going to meet and with that, a thought pops into his mind: *maybe Andrew, the waiter, can meet us out.*

So Michael asks, "What bar are we going to meet at?"

Christie snaps out of her make-up trance and says, "Hunter's. It's my favorite gay bar," then immediately turns back to adding her finishing touches.

Lucy and Michael look at each other with matching smiles.

Olivia adds, "Well, I, for one, can't wait to taste one of their gayest martinis!"

Ivy and Ester both decline, admitting to being too tired.

"Oh, but you must come out," Michael says. "What fun would it be if we weren't all going out together on our first night?"

Christie chimes in. "Yeah, come on you two. Lighten up. Anyway, you know how all those gay boys love their psychics. You can tell them their futures and they'll buy you both drinks!" She laughs. "They'll love you." She turns and wiggles her body with open arms for a hug.

Ivy snaps, "One. I'll come out for *one* drink." She holds up her index finger to make it clear she means business, although her stern face soon turns into a smile.

Ester follows and says, "One drink won't hurt. You know . . ." She bashfully looks to the ground. "I used to be a pole dancer." She smiles, lowers her head again and drops her eyes to avoid making eye contact. Her long brown hair falls over her face. She scoops it back up and provocatively puts her hand on her hip. "But that was years ago." She rolls her eyes again and looks at Ivy.

Charles paces in the background, feeling like an outcast at his own business. Michael knows Charles overstepped by inviting the audience, but he admits to himself that perhaps he could have handled their altercation better and not just flown off the handle. Now he's wondering if he should include Charles to come out with them tonight. His mom had seemed smitten with him.

Mustering up the courage but also not being one to shy away, Charles is also hoping they can let bygones be bygones. He walks up with his masculine swagger and in his best bravado says, "Well, since I didn't get my séance, Michael, how about y'all buy me the gayest two-million-dollar whiskey drink a man could want?" He winks and flashes his million-dollar smile as he puts his hands up and shrugs his shoulders. "Whaddya say?"

Olivia responds for Michael. "I think Michael will be just fine with that. It's a great compromise." Olivia's hard feelings seem to melt away. "Plus, I personally would love to see how you defend yourself against all those gay men." She laughs thinking of him being chased and pinched around the bar.

Lucy pipes in, "Yeah, if I were you, I would probably avoid the bathrooms or make a beeline for one of the stalls!" They all laugh.

Charles pulls his shoulders back and stands up straight. "Let me just tell y'all one thing. I may be a straight man, but hey . . . twenty bucks is twenty bucks." He smiles flirtatiously and they all walk out of the studio. Charles lightly touches Olivia's hand and whispers close to her, "We good?"

Olivia smiles and gently lays her head on his shoulder. "We are. You've redeemed yourself, Mr. Booream, a true man of honor." She gives him a kiss on the cheek. Charles makes arrangements to have his limo drive all of them to Hunter's.

CHAPTER 23

THE LIMO MAKES its way down Wilton Drive and pulls into a strip mall. Everyone exits and hears the *boom-boom-boom* from the music inside the bar. There are a few men outside smoking. As they're about to walk in, Michael says, "I'm gonna text someone real quick."

Lucy looks at him and smiles. She knows who he's texting. Michael pulls the restaurant receipt out of his pocket, punches in the phone number and creates a new text message.

**Michael from the restaurant tonight.
You served us. We're at Hunters now.
Wanna stop in?**

He adds a smiley face emoji and hits send. Three dots in a bubble let Michael know that Andrew is responding.

**OMG! I'm here now. Outside. Where
are you?**

He sends a smiley face emoji and a heart.

Michael smiles and starts to look around. He spots Andrew and sends him another text.

Turn around.

Andrew quickly spins around, and his eyes search to find Michael. He smiles a big toothy grin and walks up to Michael. They properly shake hands and greet each other. Michael thinks Andrew looks even more amazing than he did at the restaurant—if that's even possible. Andrew is wearing a blue formfitting microfiber Salt Life T-shirt that accents his muscular upper body. He thinks Andrew might be wearing the same black pants as earlier, but flip-flops have replaced his work shoes.

Michael doesn't hesitate to say, "Wow, you look great!" He smiles and gets a closer look at Andrew's tattooed arm. "Nice artwork."

Andrew smiles back. "You look great, yourself. I'm so happy you texted. So how was your meeting that you had to run out for?"

"Don't even ask. It's a long story and I'd rather put it behind me for the rest of the night. But on that note, I came with everyone that was at that meeting. You remember my friend Lucy, who was with me tonight at dinner? She's inside with my mother, a psychic, her assistant, and Charles Booream."

"Charles Booream, *the* Charles Booream? CBN Charles Booream?"

"That's the one." Michael smiles. "I'm gonna go inside and find them. Did you come alone?"

"Yes, I came alone. Well, I'm waiting for a friend, but I'm not seeing anyone." Andrew leans his head to the side and smiles. "Actually, I was just dumped a few weeks ago. He told me waiting tables isn't a real job. I said, 'Well, I guess we can't all be real estate agents!' Screw him."

Michael smiles and thinks, *Two for two so far. Employed and single.* "You were just dumped too?" Michael acts surprised but smiles. "I was just dumped a few days ago, myself. I apparently wasn't good enough either because I'm not a smokin' hot bartender."

Andrew turns around one last time to look for his friend. "Well, maybe she's already inside. Shall we?" Andrew smiles and gestures toward the bar. Andrew pulls the door open as the music blasts at them and Michael steps inside.

A disc jockey's remix of Donna Summer's "Bad Girls" is playing as they walk in. The bar is dimly lit with flashing colored strobe lights and smoke decorating the large dance floor filled with men dancing with their hands in the air, bumping and grinding on each other. Michael notices that there are actually three bars. They walk up to the closest one and Andrew puts his arm in front of Michael. "I'm paying first round. Thanks for that great tip tonight."

Michael smiles. "You're welcome. Your tip was well deserved."

A bartender approaches and Andrew leans over the bar to order two drinks without asking Michael what he'd like.

"I got you a sangria since you liked yours at dinner, and I know they make good ones here."

Michael smiles and thinks maybe Andrew is too good to be true.

There you go again. Ain't you learning?

Michael quickly jerks his head to one side after he hears Whitney's whisper, but Andrew catches his reaction and looks at him with concern.

"Everything all right? Seems like something just happened."

The crowded bar is very loud so Michael leans in closer to say, "Yeah, no. Everything is fine." Michael plays it cool. "I've always liked Donna Summer and I was listening maybe a little too intently to this remix. I've never heard this version before."

"Oh, yeah, the DJ tonight is really good." Andrew smiles and looks at Michael. "Wanna walk around, maybe head out back to the patio?"

Michael smiles and nods. "Sure. We can look for my mom and friends, too. They're in here somewhere."

As they walk around, they hear an excited crowd cheering and hollering. It sounds like quite the commotion. They take a few more steps and turn a corner.

Michael stops dead in his tracks, causing Andrew to bump into him. Michael is too preoccupied with what he sees that he doesn't see his mom or Charles, but oh man, he sees Ester.

She's twirling around a pole. Her long dark hair is tossed around as she whips her head back and forth like Beyoncé. Up and down she goes, one arm above her as she twirls around and spirals down again to the floor. She places her feet firmly on the ground, grabs the pole with her hands, and bends over halfway. She straightens her legs out and her booty jiggles as she shakes her hips and twerks for the crowd. She slowly stands back up and does a little catwalk in a circle as she holds onto the pole. Then she turns and grabs the pole tightly with both hands, sliding down it like a fireman. She snaps around and does the same with her booty, this time grabbing the pole with both hands above her head and stretching out her torso while sliding up and down. The crowd is going absolutely wild. All the gay men are cheering and throwing money at her.

Andrew smiles and cheers her on. "Atta girl, look at her go! Make that money, honey!" He turns to see that Michael is wide-eyed and totally shocked. He taps Michael and then points to Ester. "She's pretty good, huh?"

Michael fumbles for the words. "Uhhh, yeah . . . " He can't take his eyes off of Ester. "I'll admit, she's pretty good. Oh, and by the way," he puts his hand on Andrew's shoulder, "that's my friend, Ester. She's part of my group." Michael grabs Andrew's wrist and pulls him toward her. "Oh, dear God, we have to save her before the ping-pong balls start flying."

Andrew throws his head back and lets out a big laugh as he claps. "Ha! Can she really do that?"

Hesitantly, Michael says, "I don't think I want to find out."

Andrew looks at Michael, laughs, and gives him a little shove. "Go save her!"

As the song ends, Ester stops dancing. The crowd is still cheering. She picks up all the dollar bills and takes a very low bow. She flips her hair back as she stands up and flicks it over one shoulder with a quick twist of her head, just like Cher would. As the crowd around Ester starts to disperse, Michael spots Lucy and his mother. Michael sees his mother and Lucy both smile as they take in the very handsome man with his arm around Michael's shoulder. Michael puts his arm around Andrew's lower back and he walks toward them.

Andrew suddenly stops, which jerks Michael to a halt as well. "Oh, my god." He's looking right at Olivia. "Oh my god, that—that's Olivia Monroe. The freakin' Double D's heiress. With freakin' Charles Booream!"

With a smile on his face and his arm still around Andrew, Michael walks up to his mom. "Mom, this is Andrew . . . " Michael looks at Andrew, realizing he doesn't know his last name.

"Collins. Andrew Collins."

"Andrew, this is my mom, Olivia." He turns to Charles, who has his arm around Olivia. "Andrew Collins . . . Charles Booream. Charles . . . Andrew."

Andrew is star-struck. Nervous, he shakes hands and bows to Olivia and Charles like they're royalty. Olivia laughs and swats him with her clutch. "I'm a New Yorker not the queen of England!" She steps closer to the boys and says, "By the way, Michael, I already approve. He's certainly easy on the eyes." She purses her lips and tilts her head to make a better assessment as if she's Meryl Streep in *The Devil Wears Prada*.

Andrew smiles, pulls Michael in tightly, and whispers in his ear. "You didn't tell me Olivia Monroe was your *mom*." He smiles then jokingly says, "I'll get you back for this!"

Michael realizes Andrew is now three for three: employed, single, and mother-approved. He smiles proudly.

Lucy swoops in and formally introduces herself to Andrew. "See, I told you, Michael. He's on *your* team." She hits Michael on the shoulder.

Christie bounces over in her stilettos and goes right up to Andrew. "Andrew, honey!" She jumps up and down with her hands in the air like a teenager who's getting a present. "You did come out tonight!" She gives him a big hug while still bouncing up and down. "Sorry I didn't wait outside," she says with a pout. "We all came together in Charles's limo, and we just walked in. I was hoping I would find you inside with some *cutie*"—she looks and smiles at Michael—"and look . . . I was right."

Michael looks at Christie and smiles. "This is so weird. So you two know each other?"

"Know each other? Are you silly?" Christie is practically screaming. "We went to high school together. I've known Andrew for years!" She rests her head on Andrew's chest. Even in her stilettos she stands below Andrew's shoulders. "He's my bestie."

As everyone is introducing themselves and talking, none of them notice another crowd forming—this time around them. Everyone in Hunter's has gotten the alert from social media that the Double D's heiress Olivia Monroe, Charles Booream, Michael, and a psychic are in the club. Everyone is holding up their phones trying to get the perfect angle to snap pictures and videos.

When they notice everyone staring, they all make their way back through the crowd. As they're walking toward the front door and across the dance floor, "Native New Yorker" by Odyssey begins.

Olivia stops and says, "Charles, I love this song."

Charles shrugs and extends his hand. "May I?" He pulls her in close, raises his one hand with her hand in his up to his shoulder and Olivia places her other hand on his chest. They begin to spin around in the center of the room. The crowd parts and it's just the two of them twirling around and around. It's like watching John Travolta and Princess Diana dancing at the White House. The crowd around them claps and snaps pictures as they dance. Olivia is stunning while Charles is debonair. At one point, Charles picks Olivia up and rests her body on his hip; she wraps one arm around his broad shoulders as he spins around.

Olivia is still rocking her white Chanel pantsuit and Jimmy Choo stilettos. Her Double D's pendant is sparkling in the flashing lights and swings as she dances. As the song ends, Olivia and Charles take their bows and walk off the dance floor, hand in hand. People are cheering and hooting while holding their phones up high.

Michael and the rest of the crowd fall in line behind Olivia and Charles as they all make their way back to the entrance and out the front door. The limo is waiting for them, and the driver is holding the door open. They jump in, one after another, and head back to the hotel.

"Mom, you and Charles were awesome in there."

"I still have all the moves," Olivia responds.

"You're absolutely captivating and enthralling," Charles says. He grabs her hand and brings it up to his lips. He makes direct eye contact and kisses her hand and then her cheek.

"I think I'm blushing!" Olivia says. "I feel like a sixteen-year-old schoolgirl."

As they're being driven, Lucy asks, "Any word from Whitney?"

"Yeah, she showed up really fast in the club. But nothing else since."

Confused, Andrew asks, "Who's Whitney?"

The limo goes silent for a moment. All eyes turn to Michael, then everyone starts laughing.

"Who's Whitney?" Olivia blurts out. "Honey, she's the reason all of us are here right now."

"Yeah, but Whitney who?"

The entire group says in unison, "Whitney Houston!"

"Whitney Houston? She's dead." Andrew says, looking at everyone as if they've gone crazy.

Christie smiles, "Oh, Andrew, sweetie, not anymore," shaking her head. "No, honey, she is alive and well . . . kinda." She laughs and gestures to everyone in the limo. "That's why there's a psychic here." She points to Ivy. "Charles paid them to come and have a séance on live TV . . . although he didn't get what he was expecting, that's for sure." She laughs but suddenly stops when she notices Charles is throwing daggers at her with his eyes. She points to Michael. "And he's the reason all of this is happening. Whitney is his guardian angel."

Andrew just sits there looking at everyone. "So, you're the ones all over the news from that restaurant in New York with Whitney Houston and a psychic . . ." he says, unsure what to make of what he just heard. Everyone stays silent, allowing him time to process.

A few more moments pass, and Michael breaks the silence. "Well . . . *Charles* may not have gotten his séance on video . . . but I did." He smiles and his eyes dart over to Charles. "When we found out about the audience and I was about to walk out," Michael says, throwing Charles a pointed look. "I turned my phone camera on and pressed record to protect myself from a possible lawsuit. But my phone for some reason was the only thing that was working in the room. I. Got. EVERYTHING!"

Charles adjusts himself and sits straight up. He coolly looks Michael in the eyes and says, "Everything?"

"Yes, everything." Michael pulls his phone out, opens up to the video, and presses play. The whole séance plays back for everyone to watch. They're sitting in the limo not realizing they've been parked outside their hotel for almost ten minutes as the video ends.

Ivy speaks up. "Does it make sense now, Andrew?"

Lucy notices they've parked and quickly swings the door open. "I, for one, want to go to bed. It's two in the morning, bitches, and I'm officially on vacation!" She steps out of the limo, putting an extra strut in her walk.

Everyone starts exiting the limo when they realize they have more people than they have rooms.

"Christie and Andrew, just stay with us in our room tonight," Lucy says. "You and me, Christie, can share one bed and Michael and Andrew can share the other. BUT NO NOISES." She points and laughs, looking right at the boys and then walks toward the entrance of the front lobby. Olivia and Charles know the limo is meant to take Charles home but they both ignore it.

"Pick me up tomorrow, well I guess, later today, maybe one o'clock," Charles tells the driver. The driver silently nods, shuts the door, gets back behind the wheel and drives away.

Lucy is the first to wake up. The hotel's digital clock reads 8:20. The hotel room is dark. A relative stranger is lying next to her in bed. She looks over at Michael and he's still sleeping soundly cuddled next to Andrew. She gets out of bed, grabs her pillow, and whacks Michael with it. "Wake up, bitches!"

Michael is startled awake and puts his arms over his head to defend himself. Andrew pops awake. "What the hell?" he moans.

"Wake up, bitches. Don't make me whack you a third time. We've got a sunset to catch in Key Largo. Come on, move it!" She's standing over them like a drill sergeant, except her uniform is a light pink sleeveless shirt and little blue panties.

Michael rolls over and sits up with his legs hanging off the edge of the bed. He turns and reaches over and gives Andrew a nudge. "You better get up. She means business."

Andrew looks over his shoulder at them through one squinted eye, smiles, and says, "Well, good morning and a fine how-do-you-do!" He drops his head back on the pillow with a grunt.

Lucy says in a threatening tone, "It won't be long. Any minute now your phone is going to ring." Not a second later, Michael's phone lights up and starts vibrating with an incoming call. It's his mother. "I told you." Lucy shrugs and walks off to the bathroom.

"Morning, Mother. Yes, we're getting up." He looks over at Andrew and mouths "I'm sorry," as he stands. "Yes, we'll meet you downstairs in the breakfast lobby. Just give us a few minutes. Maybe half an hour. Okay, see you in a bit."

He puts the phone back on the nightstand as Lucy walks out of the bathroom. She's already dressed in a turquoise sleeveless button-down shirt and comfy-looking coral lounge pants. Her hair is tied up in a bun to hide her bedhead.

Michael is next to use the bathroom. He's in and out in a couple of minutes. Lucy looks at Michael, gives him a big smile, and raises her eyebrows, trying to draw attention to the fact that Andrew is standing in nothing but his underwear.

He's wearing thin Abercrombie and Fitch boxer shorts. Very thin. He's lean, muscular, and very defined. He's got five Japanese symbol tattoos going down his ribcage. He reaches for his pants and starts putting them on. His belt jingles as he pulls his black pants over one leg and then the other. He slips the button through the hole then pulls his zipper up and fastens his belt. He looks up and smiles. "I usually don't get dressed with an audience."

Michael's fast to respond. "I didn't mind at all." He smiles, as Andrew is still shirtless. "So, tell me, what do those tattoos mean?"

Andrew slides his hand over his ribs and points to one at a time. "Faith. Life. Wisdom. Happiness. And Love."

"What about your sleeve?" He slides his hand up and down Andrew's arm.

"These tattoos are what the Florida Keys mean to me. Peaceful nature and beauty. This Buddha here represents my church. That's what the Florida Keys are to me: my church." Andrew steps closer to Michael and his hands gently cradle Michael's head. He gives him a light kiss on the forehead and then heads into the bathroom. Michael looks over at Lucy, gives her a big Cheshire Cat smile, and hugs his pillow.

Christie's now finally getting up. She stretches her arms in the air and yawns loudly. She looks at the time on her phone and practically screams, "I gotta go! Shit, my boyfriend is gonna kill me . . . having brunch with his mom and I gotta play Pretty Miss Perfect. Ha! Ain't that a lie. Wait till I tell her I slept in bed last night with another woman. Oh, that'll get her panties in a pinch!" She laughs loudly to herself as she reaches for her clothes from last night.

Andrew walks out of the bathroom as Christie hops toward him while trying to put her foot in her shoe. "Mwah," she says out loud and kisses Andrew on the cheek. "I'll call you later. Happy you came out last night. You needed to come out of hibernation and get your feet wet again. And maybe . . . something else." She smiles and pokes Andrew a few times. "Love you, sweetie. Bye, everyone! Thanks for a fun night and the bed," she shouts over her shoulder as she walks out the door. Andrew pulls on his tight blue shirt from last night and the three of them head for the breakfast lobby.

When they arrive, they find Olivia sitting in a corner facing the window. Charles is sitting next to her. They approach slowly and Michael taps her on the shoulder. "Morning, Mother."

Olivia swats at him. "*Shh!*" she whispers. "We have to leave. Now. Charles's limo is coming for us. We're all over the news. Every station. Every social media platform. Talk2U is going crazy again. Millions of views and shares. At the restaurant, the séance, and Hunter's. Grab a coffee to go and we'll eat somewhere else that's safe and quieter. We've already had the manager and several others come up to us."

As she says that, none other than Ed Turgeon walks up to them all chipper.

"Good morning! The morning after, what a great picture. I knew it wouldn't be long before you two—uh, three showed up. So, what's on the agenda today?" He has a sly look on his face. "Maybe another séance?"

Olivia curtly stands and Michael knows this stance all too well.

"Edward," she says, "you can have your picture. But you can't afford my lawyers when they come after you. Please, before a scene breaks out, just show us respect and let us leave." He stands there biting his lip, deciding what to do. He snaps a few pictures and steps aside to let them leave.

"This is a once-in-a-lifetime story, Ms. Monroe. Not many people have Whitney Houston as a guardian angel and feathers and séances and CBN and gay bars. I've followed you around since the restaurant last night. Can I at least call you for a story and I promise I won't bother you anymore after that?"

"Just one story. One!" She is adamant. "Give me one of your cards and I'll call you. No more following. No more sneaking pictures. No more nothing!"

Ed smiles. "Deal." He hands her a card.

Everything is going as planned.

Michael says out loud, "How can everything be going as planned?"

"What did you say, darling?" Olivia asks.

"Whitney's here." Everyone looks at Michael and Ed's eyes light up. Charles checks his phone and jerks his chin toward a door marked *Fire Exit*. "Let's go," he says. They run through the door, not even stopping when deafening sirens start blaring through the hotel.

They all make a beeline for the limo. The driver closes the door and pulls away as the police and fire trucks are approaching, lights and sirens blaring. The driver pulls the limo out the front entrance and just misses a cop car. He punches the accelerator as the hotel gets smaller behind them.

The safest place Charles can think to go is his home. He tells the driver to take them there. As they're driving, Michael watches Charles on his phone sending text messages. They reach Charles's house and pass through the security gate. The driver pulls the limo up to the garage, parks, and opens the door for everyone to step into the safety and privacy of Charles's six-car garage. Suddenly they realize they are two people short. Ivy and Ester are still at the hotel.

Michael quickly grabs his phone and sees that Ivy has already texted him.

Alarm going off. Where are you?

Are you safe?

Alarm just shut off. I guess all is good.

Hope you're safe.

Michael texts her back.

Long story. We are safe. No longer at the hotel. We'll have someone come

back to pick you both up.

No need. We're fine.

Séance is over. We're gonna enjoy the extra days down here.

Have fun. See you back in NY. ♡

PS The most fun we've had in a long time.

Tell Whitney we said thanks!

Michael smiles and sends her one last text.

Thank you. It was nothing short of a miracle.♡😇

CHAPTER 24

CHARLES'S WATERFRONT BEACH home is breathtaking. It sits right on the Atlantic Ocean in South Beach. White sandy beaches are marked with swaying palm trees as the tide crashes on the shore. Seagulls soar over the water. Sailboats and yachts drift on the horizon.

The housekeeper Charles had texted from the limo serves them scrambled eggs, bacon, biscuits, fresh fruit, coffee, and orange juice out on the patio. Charles makes a few calls as they eat. Everyone is watching the sun climb higher in the sky. Charles hangs up the phone and lets everyone know that their luggage has just been dropped off.

You in Miami baby. Look at you! Where to next . . . Key Largo, hmmm?

Whitney appears only to Michael. She's wearing a cabernet-red silk evening gown with a full-length white faux-fur coat. Apparently she doesn't realize how warm it is.

I was here in Miami for the shooting of my video for "Heartbreak Hotel." Look at that sand and blue water, mm-mmm, sure is beautiful. I've always loved Caribbean vacations and the Tropics, and this is the closest thing we have to it in

America. She disappears, leaving behind little white lights that spin around in circles until they all fade away in the bright sunlight.

"So, Michael," Charles says as he leans back into his chair and folds his hands into his lap. "That video on your phone. Exactly what are you going to do with it?"

All eyes are on Michael.

"Haven't decided yet." He wipes his mouth with a napkin and pauses. "I know that since I'm the only one who got a recording that it recorded for a reason." He sips his coffee. "I'm just gonna wait to see what Whitney wants me to do with it." He looks Charles right in the eyes. "I know it's not the answer you want, but it's the right answer right now."

Michael hears Whitney again.

Maybe it's not just about the séance?

Michael absent-mindedly responds to Whitney out loud.

"What do you mean?"

Charles throws Michael a look. "Mean about what? He seems a little agitated. "I didn't say anything."

"No, not you." Michael waves an apology to Charles. "Whitney is here again. She told me maybe it's not just about the séance." He quickly looks at everyone around the table.

Michael is looking at Andrew, who sits quietly at the table next to him, but Michael doesn't know what Andrew thinks of all this Whitney Houston stuff. He's trying to make sense of it. He thinks maybe Andrew feels he's stumbled upon a bunch of crazies. Now he's alone with them, trapped in a house, and he doesn't even know where he is. He's without Christie, who's the only one he knew, but now she's gone too. Michael wonders if maybe Andrew didn't think fast enough to leave with her.

Michael watches Andrew pull his phone out only to find it's dead. "Great," he mutters, turning the phone upside down on the table. "Absolutely stuck." As he breathes out tension, he slouches down in his chair.

Michael grabs Andrew's hand. "You are safe." Michael gently lets go of his hand and Andrew just sits there, not making eye contact, staring around at Charles's house. He slowly nods his head up and down, acknowledging what Michael said then puts his hands on his thighs and nervously rubs them back and forth.

Lucy looks over at Andrew. "It's a lot to take in." She looks at him with sympathy. "We all felt the same way you're feeling right now. You should've seen Olivia when she found out," Lucy says with a chuckle. Olivia and Michael laugh too, and it eases the tension. "It takes a lot of trust, Andrew." She smiles genuinely at him. "Anyway, do you really think Double D's over here is gonna do anything to hurt you?" Andrew lets out a chuckle. "We're all in this together. That's what Whitney said in our first séance. Apparently, she wants you and Charles to be with us. Take that as a huge compliment."

Lucy's phone dings. She looks at it then looks back up in excitement and says, "Our rental car is ready!" She smiles at Michael. "Florida Keys here we come!" She throws her hands in the air as if her team just scored a touchdown. "I rented us a Jeep Wrangler. Remember last year, we said we would rent a Jeep so we could take the top down and the doors off to ride through the Keys over all the bridges? The wide open blue water on both sides . . . " She smiles. "It's gonna be amazing."

Olivia looks at Michael and Lucy. "I'm going to stay here in Miami for a few more days. Charles said he would like to show me some of the area neighborhoods like Coconut Grove and Coral Gables." She gives her approval by tapping her hand on Charles's and looking at him. "He's taking me to Fairchild Tropical Botanic Garden, which sounds absolutely wonderful!" Olivia smiles pleasantly.

Michael looks at Andrew and says, "Well, this is it. The rest is up to you." He smiles nervously. "Would you like to come with us to the Keys? Or we can call you a cab to take you home."

Andrew seems to think about it and answers, "I would like to go with you. I love the Keys, but there are a few things I need to clean up first. Like myself for starters. I have no other clothes. I would need to tell my boss I'm gonna need a few days off, and then there are a few bills I need to pay, water my plants . . . I'm not sure if I can make it work." There's still a familiar uneasiness in Andrew's stare of accepting all this Whitney Houston stuff.

Michael's face shows his disappointment and he knows it, but he smiles through it. "I understand. This has been quick. I'm sorry to have sprung this on you like that."

"Don't be sorry. I'll try to catch up to you two. But if I can't, go have fun." He smiles. "Can one of you call me a cab?" He waves his phone in the air. "Mine is dead."

"I'll have my driver take you home," Charles says. He smiles at Andrew as Andrew nods in acceptance of his offer.

"Well, I guess this is goodbye. Or maybe see you later." Michael looks at Andrew and thinks, *Well, that's another one gone.* There's a heaviness in his heart, but he keeps smiling. He reaches out to shake Andrew's hand but Andrew steps closer and comes in with a big strong hug. Michael feels chills as their bodies make contact. Andrew rubs his hands on Michael's back and whispers in his ear, "I'll do my best to meet up with you two. You already know from my tattoos that I love the Florida Keys. I want to go, but it's just not that easy to pick up and leave."

Michael's eyes start to well up, but he holds it back. They look at each other and then Charles tells Andrew that the car is ready. Andrew turns and walks out of the kitchen, his feet thumping down the stairs.

Lucy and Michael say their goodbyes to Olivia and Charles. They both thank Charles for the breakfast and his hospitality. Michael adds, "Take good care of my mom." He smiles and shakes Charles's hand and turns to hug his mom. "Be nice to him, Mother! He doesn't know what he's in for." Both Michael and Lucy laugh.

Lucy chimes in. "Yeah, once she starts shopping, watch out!"

Olivia giggles. "Shush, I'm not that bad," she says, rolling her eyes as if to admit that she knows it's true.

Lucy and Michael give one last final wave, and they walk out to the street where an Uber waits to take them to the car rental company.

CHAPTER 25

HAVING BACKTRACKED TO Fort Lauderdale to pick up the rental car, they're now cruising south down the Florida Turnpike in their white Jeep Wrangler with the doors off and the top down. The sun is hot, but the wind feels amazing. The sky couldn't be any bluer with only a few scattered fluffy white clouds. Palm trees whizz by as they zoom down the six-lane highway. The radio blasts Madonna's "Holiday" as Michael and Lucy sing along.

They cruise past the Seminole Hard Rock Hotel and Casino with its colossal guitar-shaped hotel. Driving near the North Miami Beach area, the highway expands to an unbelievable ten lanes. Cars aggressively speed by, and motorcycles scream past them. The motorcyclists quickly weave from lane to lane through the traffic. Lucy yells to Michael over the noise of the wind, "Holy crap, I thought New Yorkers drove crazy. These people are making me seem like I'm standing still and I'm going seventy-eight!" Her knuckles are white as she grips the wheel, and her eyes don't leave the road as she talks to Michael.

They zip past signs for the Miami Dolphins Stadium. They take an exit on the right for Homestead, which eventually brings them past Florida International University, an IKEA, and Cutler

Bay until a little bit farther down the turnpike a big green highway sign reads *FLORIDA CITY/KEY WEST*. They take a jug-handle exit ramp for Route 1. At the end of the exit, they stop at a red light. Signs for the Everglades point to the right, premium outlets to the left and Key West forward.

Half a mile ahead they reach another green highway sign that reads *Card Sound Road/Upper Key Largo*. Lucy yells over the highway sounds, "Here's where the magic really begins. 'The Stretch' as the locals call it."

The stretch is the last piece of mainland Florida before reaching the forty-four coral rock islands, or the archipelago known as The Keys. Passing the entrance to Card Sound Road on their left, they continue straight and pass an old relic, The Last Chance Saloon on their right, which seems like an end-of-the-world dive bar. The water views are hidden from the highway by the tall, thick, and overgrown mangrove trees.

Mangroves are important ecological resources to the Keys, as they hold back or slow down the surge of seawater caused by storms or hurricanes. Boat owners will tie their vessels to the thickly rooted trees since they are practically unmovable in a storm and little or no damage is caused to boats that are moored to them.

As they drive, periodically the mangroves are low enough for Michael and Lucy to see "Bikini Beach." There are dozens of beautiful boats anchored in the water and drivers will slow down and gawk, causing traffic to thicken and congest as they stare at the boats as if it's a beach full of women sunbathing in bikinis, hence the nickname of Bikini Beach. The smell of seaweed and salty air is thick as the humidity makes it more pronounced.

Michael has his phone out snapping pictures and motioning to one sign that reads, *Caution Crocodile Crossing*. He gives Lucy a *Yikes!* look while she continues to drive. They start to ascend a large bridge with light-blue jersey barriers. Nearing the top, overlooking the miles of tropical blue water and boats, they see the famous Gilbert's Resort below them on the right. The bridge they're climbing is the highest bridge on the Keys, sitting at sixty-five feet high, named Jewfish Bridge, as it crosses both Jewfish Creek and Lake Surprise. They crest the bridge and cruise down, winding around a bend as a big blue wooden sign appears on their left in the median.

Welcome to Key Largo.

They smile at each other and high-five. Any stress they were holding onto is gone. Driving a little over the forty-five-mile-an-hour speed limit, Lucy remembers that the highway is aggressively patrolled by police.

Driving south down Overseas Highway, they pass familiar sights. Lucy swats Michael's arm, "Remember when we watched *Beachfront Bargains* on HGTV and people were buying a condo there in Moon Bay?" They see the taupe-colored five-story solid concrete building as they drive by it.

The Overseas Highway lanes are divided by a median with mangroves dotted in the center. Palms of many species, tall and short, are waving in the breeze. John Pennekamp Coral Reef State Park comes up next on their left. They pass restaurants, diving shops, and several touristy shops that sell a slew of pink flamingos, colorful outdoor hanging nautical sea animals, and black skull-and-crossbones flags, which wave in the breeze. The sun is baking them as they stop at a red light. They see a CVS on their left that sits in the median with Guy Fieri from Diners, Drive-In's and Dives up on a billboard along with a restaurant owner, inviting tourists to dine at Café Largo, an Italian cuisine restaurant. They both agree to save their appetite for lunch at Snappers. They continue their drive and turn right onto Paradise Boulevard.

Paradise Boulevard is a long private road that's tunneled with overgrown tropical hardwood hammocks and has a small blue dot at the end. The dot gets bigger and bigger as they approach the end of the boulevard until it completely surrounds them, and they see where the sky meets the water. The view is breathtaking. There's a little sandy beach and a few palm trees swaying from the breeze. A few small boats are docked in the inlet. Paradise Boulevard is a small, privately owned community where Lucy's aunt and uncle own a home right on the water. They turn into the driveway and hop effortlessly out of the doorless Jeep.

The house is a modest three bedroom and three bathroom, 1,800-square-foot ground-level ranch. Inside, the floors are made of Mexican terra-cotta tile. The beige walls are tastefully decorated with tropical pictures and ocean scenes. There's a large white sectional sofa and several armchairs scattered around the living room. A wall of windows and sliding glass doors gives views of the tropical decorations fenced inside the backyard that has several species of palms and flowering bushes.

Lucy takes the master bedroom—she'd called dibs way before they left Miami. She pulls the blinds open on the large bedroom window and she sees the view of the bay. Michael hears Lucy yell with excitement, thanking out loud her aunt and uncle for letting her use their house.

Michael settles into the bedroom across the hall. It's a cute room with yellow walls, several pictures of seashells and a silent picture of a lone fisherman on a boat who's cast his line, entitled *Early Morning Lullaby*. His room has a dresser and two twin beds with matching end tables. He looks at both of the beds and immediately thinks of Andrew. He gets a little melancholy, but he shakes it off and turns around to open the blinds on the window in his room, which also looks right out over Florida Bay.

Not too bad, he thinks and smiles. He turns on his ceiling fan and listens to the soft sound of air whooshing around the blades.

After settling in and taking fast showers, they leave for lunch. They arrive at Snappers around one thirty. The host greets them and asks if they want to eat inside or outside on the water. They opt to eat outside. They're seated at a table on the deck underneath a tiki umbrella overlooking the Florida Straits, which lead to the ocean. Jet skies available to rent for sixty dollars an hour sit in the water. There's live music and the singer is softly crooning an acoustic version of James Taylor's song, "Sweet Baby James."

Their waiter comes over to take their drink order and returns promptly with two sangrias.

"To Key Largo!" They tap their glasses together. They order lunch and it comes rather quickly. Lucy orders a fried Mahi sandwich and Michael just gets a cheeseburger. They talk about what they want to do and which sights they want to see. They decide to watch the sunset tonight at the house and do some snorkeling tomorrow. Lucy pulls out a brochure from John Pennekamp Coral Reef State Park and says she wants to snorkel at Christ of the Abyss, a concrete statue of Christ that was lowered fifteen feet into the water for scuba divers or snorkelers to enjoy. It's surrounded by the only living coral reef in the continental United States, home to thousands of colorful tropical fish, seagrass beds, turtles, manatees, stingrays, sand sharks, and a mass of other sea life.

When they finish, they sit just a little longer to take in the view and breathe in the ocean air.

After Snappers they head down to the Winn Dixie plaza. They purchase breakfast foods, coffee, cheese, and crackers for sunset, along with three bottles of wine—two pinot grigio and one moscato. "It's very convenient having wine in the grocery store," Lucy says to Michael. "I wish New York would allow it." They pay for their groceries and head back to the house.

Returning to the house, they put away the groceries and

start settling in. There are two Adirondack chairs that Lucy places outside the house. Then there's a table and umbrella with matching chairs in the garage which they lug out to the water's edge. The water's edge is about fifty feet from the house.

"This is where we'll watch the sunset," Michael says. There's a little firepit someone built—they don't think they'll use it, but it's cute. The neighbor, Joe, whose name they remembered from their previous visit, has a long dock and doesn't mind if people use it. His only request is if they jump off the dock, "Just put all the water back." They remember Joe's humorous laugh.

It's about four thirty now. Lucy goes back inside for the moscato. Michael decides to sit outside in the Adirondack chairs next to the house and read his new book, *Is the Coffee Fresh*? A slight breeze is blowing. He reads a few lines when . . .

Whatcha reading?

Whitney sits down in the other Adirondack chair. She crosses her long legs. She's wearing faded blue jeans that are ripped at the knees, cheetah-print half boots and a white shirt. She looks at Michael with playful but loving eyes and a big smile. Her hair is styled in a soft bouncy bob.

"I picked up this book, *Is the Coffee Fresh*? It's about a man who owns a restaurant in upstate New York—more of a coffeehouse maybe—but he writes about his daily experiences dealing with customers. What they do, what they say, and what they steal. It's actually pretty funny." Michael gives a little laugh. "He writes about his day-to-day business dealings, employee challenges, food waste, equipment failures, health inspections, and all that goes into operating a successful restaurant."

Um, sounds like something that could be useful for you. She gives Michael a wink and a big smile.

"Right? You're not kidding."

It's beautiful here. This view. The breeze. The palm trees. The boats. The serenity. I bet if a person gets quiet enough, they could

hear God in the breeze. But then I guess you wouldn't need me. Whitney frowns and turns her head, skillfully looking at Michael from the corners of her brown eyes.

"I would always want you around." He looks at her and he means every word.

Well, you got that wish, because I'm always with you. This is your life, baby, and you have to live it and make your own decisions. Sometimes, you know, decisions feel like failures. But they teach you what not to do again. People, you know—she pauses and thinks—***they want the easy way out. They want the waterfront property.*** She opens her hand and turns her palm up as her fingers point at the Florida Bay, as if to offer it as a gift. ***But they don't want to do the work. Lucy's aunt and uncle worked very hard for many years to purchase this house. Nobody gave it to them. I'm certainly not gonna give you anything. I will, however, give you my love. Like that key, that worthless key you found on the ground. I bet you wouldn't sell that key for any amount of money.*** She gives him a questionable look.

Michael grabs hold of the key around his neck and smiles. He closes his eyes and holds it in his fingers as if he is praying.

Whitney can feel his love emanating. ***I want to inspire you, Michael. Those feelings of love, joy, and bliss are what I want you to know. What's real and what's not. And the wisdom to know the difference is important. That's what I offer. And these feelings are all you'll need, baby, to accomplish all your dreams. A feeling creates desire and desire is what pushes you to believe it's possible. Remember that, Michael—a feeling is all you will need. Remember what Vince Lombardi told you: this can all be yours. Yes, baby, I was there. I'm even with you in your dreams.***

Michael opens his eyes and wipes away a tear that is rolling down his cheek as he looks over, but Whitney is gone. The chair sits empty, though he hears, ***Still here baby.***

The front door opens, and Lucy comes out with two glasses

of moscato. She sits down next to Michael, where Whitney was. Lucy notices his eyes are a little red.

"I know who was just here." She rubs his arm and hands him his glass of wine. Michael nods. He squints his eyes and tries to hold back more tears but another one rolls down his cheek anyway. He wipes it away with the back of his hand, smiles, and then laughs a little and takes a sip.

Michael and Lucy both get lost in the moment looking at the water. They're watching boats speed by, a few jet skis, and a kayaker slowly paddling along. They hear a *whoosh* and both look up but see nothing. A few moments later, they hear the *whoosh* again and see a fin plunge into the water.

They look at each other and yell, "Dolphin!" They quickly get up and run onto the neighbor's dock and all the way out, about thirty feet, to the end of the pier where the water is about four feet deep. They see the dolphin fin come up again. The fin starts moving very fast through the water. It's chasing a fish, its dinner, they presume. The dolphin swims left, then right, then speeds up and swims right under the dock they're standing on. Michael and Lucy take pictures. "Oh, my god!" they both keep yelling.

They're as excited as little children playing on a playground. God's playground. The dolphin keeps circling and swims back under the dock again. They continue yelling and screaming. The dolphin finally accelerates at a great speed and goes straight out to their left, out deeper into the bay, and the water goes still. Apparently, it either caught its meal or gave up, but the dolphin goes back to lazily swimming farther out into the bay before they can no longer see its fin.

"That was awesome!" Michael excitedly says. "And right under the dock!"

Lucy pulls her hair back and she too has a big smile on her face. They walk off the neighbor's dock and back to their chairs by the house, where they sit for what seems like a few minutes only to realize how close the sun is getting to the water.

"It's almost time for our first sunset in Key Largo," Lucy says. "Let's sit out at the table by the water. But first, let me run inside for the moscato and fill up our glasses." Lucy comes back out in a few seconds, wine in hand. They both grab their glasses and walk the fifty steps over the white pebbled pier leading out to the water's edge and they sit at the table and chairs they put out earlier.

"Absolutely beautiful," Michael says. The horizon is starting to take on a yellow-orange glow as the sun gets closer to the water. There are a few scattered clouds in the sky and a single sailboat cruises past. As the moments pass, the sky gets a little darker with deeper shades of yellows, reds, and oranges.

They both have their phones out to take pictures. Every second seems like a new color display. And just like that, the sun disappears from the sky altogether and seems to fall beneath the water. All the clouds in the sky that were white are now burning fiery colors. The horizon has a beautiful reddish-purple afterburn as crepuscular rays shoot into the sky from where the sun has set. Michael stares at the beautiful sunset he's captured on his phone and thinks of sending a picture of it to Andrew, but he decides not to. His fear of being embarrassed by Andrew's rejection stops him.

"That was an amazing first sunset!" Lucy says. She scrolls through her pictures really fast, picks her favorite and posts it to her page on Talk2U. *First epic sunset in Key Largo. #keylargo #floridakeys #vacation.*

It's now almost eight thirty. The sky is losing its colors and turning grayer every second. The no-see-ems are coming out and they're both starting to slap their legs and arms where they're being bitten.

Lucy frowns, "Note to self: bring bug spray tomorrow night." They both get up and grab their wine glasses and the empty wine bottle. They contemplate dinner options as they walk back into the house and agree on something casual and easy: Keys Bite—a favorite from their last visit.

They arrive at the restaurant. It's a seat-yourself kind of place and they choose to sit outside under the big tiki hut. Strands of white lights hang from the thatched roof with several colorful buoys, some paintings of mahi fish, and several rowing oars. They can hear the cars traveling down Route 1, but the noise doesn't bother them. They're on Keys time now—they're laid back and relaxed.

Michael opts for the steak a la Mexicana, while Lucy goes with the fish tacos. After they finish, Lucy looks at Michael with half a grin. "Café con leche?" She says now with a full smile. They order two from the restaurant and get ready to leave when Michael's phone rings. He looks at it. The Caller ID says *BLOCKED*. He turns it around and gives Lucy a curious look.

"Answer it," she says, "could be another two million dollars!" She laughs as she twists her hair up in a ponytail.

He answers without a care in the world, "This is Michael."

"Michael, FBI Special Agent Chris Lopez, we need to talk . . . now!" The deepness of his voice and sharpness of his speech shocks Michael into submission. "We've got your phone's GPS location. Sit still and don't move; we're on our way. We just came over the Key Largo bridge. We'll be there in six minutes." The phone line goes dead.

Michael quickly stands up. He feels as if he's going to lose his stomach. Any feelings of relaxation he had before are gone. He's crippled with fear. His legs get weak, and he grabs hold of the table to steady himself as he slowly sits back down. Scared and unsure, he looks at Lucy, who now has a worried look on her face. "What?" Her eyes beg him to tell her.

He shakes his head and looks at her. In a high mocking voice he singsongs, "Just answer it! Could be another two million dollars!" Panic runs through his mind as one knee begins to rapidly bounce up and down. "Lucy, this is not good. The FBI are on their way, like *now*! Like six minutes away." His glare is sharp. Michael's mind fills with fear. "What the hell did I do now?" Nervously sitting at the table, he contemplates his options. Ditch the cell phone and make a run for it? Maybe call his mother? Then he thinks better of that. She'll just make matters worse.

What only feels like moments later, two speeding dark blue sedans abruptly slow down and turn left into the parking lot of Keys Bite. Four men exit the cars, and two of them stay behind. Two walk toward the outside seating tiki hut, badges in hand, pistols clipped on their waists. There are other diners also eating outside, watching as the armed men walk closer. Michael nervously stands up and the men's eyes land on their target; they know who they want. "Oh shit," is all Michael can mumble as he balls his fists.

One is beefy, with a no-nonsense attitude, and he waves a hand for Michael to come closer. "Come with us." It's a command not an invitation. He looks and points at Lucy still sitting at the table. "You stay there."

He brings Michael over to one of the cars and all four agents gather around Michael under the glowing parking lights. The first agent pulls out a card from his shirt pocket and hands it to Michael, whose hand trembles as he takes it. Michael holds the card with both hands just to steady them as he reads. *US Department of Justice* is written beneath a gold embroidered logo followed by *Federal Bureau of Investigations. Christopher Lopez, Special Agent, Miami Division.* Michael is so scared, he's about to cry.

The agent extends his hand and says, "Agent Chris Lopez." He nods to Michael as they shake hands. Chris then introduces the other three men. "Thank you for taking the time to speak with us." Michael nods as his mind panics, every muscle in his body tenses, and he nervously thinks, *I didn't really take the time; you took my time.* He scans around at the intimidating men.

Chris continues, "Sorry for doing this so late at night, but we really need help, and we believe you may have some answers." Michael swallows hard. His mouth is dry and his heart is pounding as sweat builds in his underarms. A single drop rolls down his back.

Chris looks intensely at Michael. "We need help with a cold case, and we just heard you're traveling with a psychic who has worked with the FBI up in New York. Where can we find her?"

Michael almost faints from relief. His mind goes blank. He blinks his eyes as if to bring himself back then he breathes out a sigh. A smile actually comes across his face, "Oh you mean Madame Pearl." His body starts tingling as his heart starts to decrease its rapid beatings. He quickly looks over at Lucy who is now a ball of nerves, and he throws her a smile. He sees her body move in a more comfortable position, and she nods as she runs her hands over her head, her eyes rolling up toward the ceiling. He sees her lips make a little circle as she slowly blows out air that apparently she's been holding. She gives him a shake of her head, a smile, and a thumbs-up.

Chris continues. "We're really close to solving a twenty-year-old case of a Tallahassee woman last seen in the Florida Keys, and if the psychic can help us, maybe with a confirmation of what we presume to be the truth of where the body is, we can finally close this case and bring some closure to the family."

Michael opens his phone, looks at the business card, and adds the agent's number so he can share Ivy's contact. Michael looks back up at the agent. "I just sent you her contact. I know she's still awake." Michael smiles then says, "But please don't scare the crap out of her like you did to me." Michael shakes his arms and stomps his feet as he moves his body just to release all the fear he's been holding onto.

Chris smiles. "Sorry about startling you." He slaps an open hand on Michael's shoulder, although Chris knows full well that was his intention. "But no worries, we'll take good care of her." He pauses, "And good luck with Whitney. That story is everywhere." All the agents shake Michael's hand and as quickly as the sedans arrived, they take off and are heard rapidly accelerating up the highway, disappearing into the darkness.

Michael shrugs his shoulders as he walks over to Lucy. "Can we go now please? I've had enough for one night." He grabs his café con leche and they leave.

At the house, the bay breeze is gently blowing through the open windows and the blinds are rhythmically tapping the window frames, making for a very coastal and relaxing sound. It's almost ten o'clock and Michael is the first to say he's going to bed.

"Even the caffeine from this café con leche won't keep me up tonight. Whitney Houston, FBI, news reporters—I've had enough. Good night, Lucy." He walks over to her and kisses the top of her head, then enters his room. He flops on the bed, kicks his flip-flops off, and falls asleep.

CHAPTER 26

MICHAEL ABRUPTLY WAKES up, bolting upright in his bed as he inhales a deep breath. It's pitch-black. He's unsure of where he is. He has a moment of panic. His eyes are adjusting to the darkness and scanning around the room, trying to figure out where he is. The breeze comes through the open window, and it moves the blinds. The gentle *clap-clap* of the blinds fully wakes him, and he realizes where he is. Key Largo.

He rubs his face to wake himself up a bit more and slowly releases a long breath. He smiles knowing where he is and lies back down. He looks over at the glowing red digital clock. It reads 3:33. He's now looking up at the spinning ceiling fan and he starts thinking of Whitney.

Look at that. I got your attention.

"You scared the shit out of me."

Just trying to wake you up, that's it.

"Why now? Can't it wait till morning?"

Technically, it is morning, she says with a laugh. She's dressed in her red, white, and blue jumpsuit, the one she wore while singing the National Anthem at the 1991 Super Bowl, complete with the white headband.

Come on, get up; let's go out to the water. There's something I want to show you.

"Now?" He looks at her like she must be kidding.

Well, we can do this now, or I can wake you up every night until you decide to come with me. She folds her arms and pouts. ***You're in charge; you let me know what works best for you.***

"Okay, okay," he groans. "I'm getting up." He realizes he fell asleep with all of his clothes on. He rubs his eyes, yawns, and rolls over as he stands up and stretches his arms over his head. He realizes that he and Whitney are now outside.

That was fast, he thinks to himself. *I don't remember walking out the door.*

They walk toward the water. Whitney takes Michael's hand in hers. As they approach the water, Michael starts thinking about how close they're getting. Really close. He thinks, *Just two more steps and I'll be in the water.* On the third step he tries to stop but Whitney pulls him gently forward and onto the water.

Michael's feet try to find footing but there is none. They are walking on the water. The water gently splashes onto the tops of their feet. The big full moon shines like God left a light on for them. A trail of white light gleams across the water. Millions of stars twinkle in the sky. The two of them silently walk farther out onto the Florida Bay. ***Dreams are very important, Michael. You're gonna remember you had this one a little while ago.***

Without warning, Whitney drops into the water pulling Michael down under with her. At first, he panics. He holds tight to his breath, kicking his legs, trying to bring himself back up. He's fearfully looking up trying to see the surface of the water. But the water is completely dark because of the night. He squirms, trying to get Whitney to release his hand. He feels himself starting to get lightheaded. He lets out some air and watches the bubbles quickly disappear in the vast darkness. He tries one last time to escape Whitney's grip, his eyes begging her to let him go.

Michael feels Whitney's eyes penetrate his as if she's staring into his soul. Suddenly, peace washes over Michael, a peaceful knowing soothing his fear. He realizes now he can breathe fine.

They go down deeper into the water. He sees a golden light. He sees the treasure chest, and his dream from a week ago pops into his mind. He sees all the tropical fish again, the seaweed and the sand and all the shells. He suddenly realizes he's standing right in front of the open treasure chest and its shining golden light. He instinctively extends his hands out in front of him to shield his eyes from its radiance. He tries peeking out of the sides of his eyes, his arms and hands still in front of his face. From the corner of his eye, he sees something move. His eyes quickly try to focus through the blurry bends the water makes as his vision adjusts to what it is that's moving. He sees a green stalk grow and rise out of the golden light. A bud appears and opens into the most beautiful purple-blue iris he's ever seen. He blinks his eyes but is yanked back up on top of the water. He and Whitney are standing on top of the water again, both curiously dry.

A second later, he's back lying in his bed. He quickly sits up again, this time in terror, as he thinks he's all wet. He swiftly pats himself but finds he's completely dry. The glowing red clock now reads 3:34. *How is this even possible?* he thinks. His mind races for clues. *And why that dream again? Am I really awake?* he wonders.

He seems to snap to, as he hears the fan spinning overhead and feels the light breeze coming through the blinds, which gently tap against the windowsill. He can see the full moon shining outside. He looks at the clock again. This time it reads 4:44. He shuts his eyes and rubs his face, thinking he just read the clock wrong. He opens his eyes again and looks at the clock. 4:45. *Is this some kind of game?* He rubs his hands through his hair. He's holding his head, searching his thoughts for answers.

He closes his eyes and once again rubs his face as he lies back down. "I must be going crazy; maybe too much caffeine." His mind jumps from one image to the other, but he quickly slips off back to sleep. He awakens again but this time to the sun shining through the blinds with the thick scent of brewing coffee.

He walks into the kitchen still in last night's shorts. Lucy smiles at him.

He grins back. "Good morning," he says in a sleep-scratchy voice.

Lucy does her best high-pitched impersonation of Debbie Reynolds singing, "Good Morning!" She smiles again at Michael as she pours them both coffee. "Did you get up last night? I thought I heard you walking around."

Michael freezes. "I don't know what happened last night after I fell asleep—well maybe passed out from exhaustion might be more accurate—but I was awakened by Whitney. She took me out to the water, maybe, I think. Or maybe it was just another dream. It was beautiful whatever it was that happened."

With no other logical response, Lucy replies with a "Hmm" and sighs as her body shifts. "I'm gonna eat some cereal. I've already booked us on a snorkeling trip at Pennekamp. We need to be there by eleven. It's nine now. So just relax, eat something, and be ready to leave by ten."

Michael nods. He pours himself some cereal too and takes the bowl and coffee cup out onto the back porch. Some wind chimes make a tinkling sound in the morning breeze. He sits down at the table and notices the nearby minitiki-bar. Hanging on the bar is a clay parrot sign that reads, *It's five o'clock somewhere.* The parrot is swigging a margarita whose contents are seen splashing over the rim. He smiles at the sign and its colorful design.

He falls into a chair and his mind starts wandering to all the places his mother has taken him over the years, all the tropical destinations. But nothing has ever felt like this. Maybe it's because this is a private home. No crowds of tourists, no hotel maids, and no artificial scenery. There's serenity here. He breathes it in. It's something indescribable, a feeling of peace or soul fulfillment. Even if he's doing nothing, he feels like he's done it with purpose.

He hears the mourning doves cooing and sees a few seagulls flying above as he listens to them squawk while they fly out of site. The sun is shining bright and it's warming up. The sky is already a clear blue. A hawk now circles high in the sky above.

Live each moment with purpose, Michael.

Michael snaps out of the trance he was just in. He focuses his vision on a palm tree in the backyard. He's looking at the palm like it's the first time he's ever seen one. He's in total amazement at how the fronds blow in the breeze. It's something so simple yet so beautiful.

You're in the moment right now, Michael. See how simple that is to do? Most people want to keep busy. They keep their minds busy, and they don't allow us in—their angels. Everyone has angels. We share the habits and lessons we learned before we crossed over. That's one reason I was given this opportunity to assist you. Where you're going, baby, well you're gonna need someone like me.

Michael now sees her sitting at the table with him, appearing in the brown lace Vera Wang dress she wore at the 1998 MTV Video Music Awards; she laughs a long deep laugh, throws her head back, and gives a few claps. She points her finger at him. ***That's right baby, someone who has been there before you. Someone who can direct you and then set you free to make your own choices.*** She stands up. ***So, you can either come with me when I ask, or I will show up every single night, waking your ass up, until to decide for yourself to come with me.*** She laughs again as she shakes her head back and forth with attitude, her long curly brown locks springing and bouncing.

Michael's eyes pop and he points. "Wait, that's the dress you matched with Mariah Carey when you both presented for Best

Male Video."

This is the one. She rips off the bottom part of her dress. ***And voila!*** She opens her hand and lets the bottom of her dress drop onto the porch, where it disappears.

"So, what exactly is 'free choice' if I'm gonna be harassed every night, shaken out of a deep sleep to be drowned in the bay?" Michael laughs, remembering what happened earlier that morning.

Whitney also laughs at his comment. ***But you chose to come the first time. That's free choice.*** She winks, blows him a kiss and disappears, leaving brown sparkly lights spiraling around and popping until they all disappear.

Michael looks at his cell phone. No texts from anyone, including Andrew. He switches over to Talk2U and sees thousands of likes and friend requests. He suddenly becomes overwhelmed. He starts to feel anxious; his eyes twitch as if someone is watching him. He quickly scans the fenced-in backyard, searching for movement or a person, but there's nothing. His curiosity gets the best of him, and he feels the need to read what everyone is responding to, but then he stops himself. He takes a deep breath and thinks better about it. He already knows what everyone is gossiping about. The séance. Charles Booream, his mother, and Whitney. He decides he doesn't need to give in to it. He closes the app, grabs his coffee cup—now empty even though he doesn't remember drinking it—and his cereal bowl and walks back inside.

Michael showers and is ready for their snorkeling adventure at Pennekamp. Lucy, already dressed, sits outside the front of the house in the Adirondack chairs just gazing at the water. Michael sits down next to her. She looks at him, smiles, and looks back at the water. Neither of them speaks. They don't have to. They understand exactly what the other is thinking without saying a word.

A few more moments go by, and Lucy puts her hand on

Michael's wrist. "I just love it here," she says. I feel so at ease. I feel like I'm home. It's weird to express how this place seems to have been subconsciously calling to me this whole year. I don't feel this way in New York. I feel alive here. I feel senses that have been dormant are awakening."

Michael nods his head. "I know exactly what you mean. I feel it too. I didn't want to come here, to be honest. I wanted to stay home and find work, be responsible, and do what I thought was the right thing to do. But . . . I guess what's happening is I'm allowing my subconscious to guide me to stop thinking about what the right thing to do is and just trust a process. I'm starting to feel a deep subconscious process that knows better than I do. Something that my soul apparently knew all along. This is one of the many things that Whitney is teaching me. I was just sitting in the backyard, just looking at a palm tree and the beauty of it. That was the only thought in my mind. How weird is that?" Michael shakes his head. "A palm tree filled up my mind." He waves it away as something unexplainable. "Anyway, before we get all esoteric, how about we go snorkeling and meet Jesus!"

Lucy smiles and stands up. She stretches with one leg behind her and her two arms reaching above her head toward the sky and then reverses the position. She repeats this several times. After a few good stretches, she goes back inside for the Jeep keys while Michael grabs a towel and his swimsuit.

Now back in the Jeep and heading north up Overseas Highway, the salty wind whips through the Jeep. Lucy's hair is tied back in a ponytail, but strands of auburn still fly everywhere. Michael loves that he can look right down at the road with the doors off. Just past a red light at mile marker 100, Lucy points to a restaurant on the right.

Yelling a bit over the wind she says, "Key Largo Conch House. Let's try that tonight after snorkeling. Cocktails and dinner before sunset at the house." She pulls strands of hair away from her face. “I read they have a nice porch and a tropical garden patio for dining.”

Michael smiles and nods. Michael points then yells, “Hey! Pull over there at that bank. I want to get some cash at the ATM.”

Lucy slows down and steers the Jeep into a parking space right in front of the bank. Michael unbuckles and jumps out, walks up to the ATM, inserts his card, and presses some buttons. The machine dispenses money with a receipt. He reads the receipt and immediately stops. He looks at Lucy, who’s now absent-mindedly fixing her hair as she looks into the Jeep’s rearview mirror, he darts toward her. He jumps into the Jeep and shoves the ATM receipt in Lucy’s face.

“Look at that!” Michael yells excitedly.

Unsure of what she’s looking for, Lucy quizzically reads the receipt. Then she finally sees it. The balance: $2,000,442.62.

“Oh. My. God! Two million dollars!” Lucy keeps yelling over and over.

Michael’s nervousness alerts him as he realizes she’s yelling, and he quickly looks around the Jeep. But thankfully, nobody else is in the parking lot.

“Shut the front door! I’ve never even seen more than a few thousand dollars in my account! I thought I had something like five hundred bucks—I did not expect to see that!” He puts his hands on his head and his fingers massage his scalp, trying to process seeing his balance. Suddenly, the memories of the glowing treasure chest dream he’s had twice now quickly appear in his mind. He silently gives thanks.

He straightens up. “I know what I have to do.” At Lucy’s puzzled expression, he continues. “I have to send Charles the video of the séance. It’s the right thing to do.” Michael grabs his phone, opens his photos and scrolls to the video. He presses a few buttons and yells, “Sent!” He looks over at Lucy with excited eyes. “Now what do we do?”

Without hesitation Lucy says, "Buy a condo down here. Not a house. Absolutely buy a condo! That's what I say you should do. But first, let's go snorkeling. Maybe meeting Jesus will influence your decision." She smiles as she pushes his shoulder, and he sways to the right.

"Well then, let's go snorkeling and buy a condo!" They high-five.

Lucy puts the Jeep in reverse, turns the vehicle around, and burns a little rubber pulling out of the bank's parking lot. They continue heading up Route 1 toward John Pennekamp.

They arrive and pay for their snorkeling adventure. Soon they're out on the charter boat sailing to the Dry Rocks. The water is calm and crystal blue. The boat stops and drops anchor. A head count is taken. Red and white diver flags float in the water where the divers are. Each person is given a snorkeling jacket, mask, snorkel, and fins. One by one everyone jumps off the boat in search of fish, coral reefs, and some hope for buried treasure. But most of all they want to see Jesus.

Michael and Lucy stay together. The water is like bath water at eighty-eight degrees. It's so comfortable. First they see schools of tropical, colorful fish, thousands of them. The sandy bottom with coral reefs and marine algae is beautiful in itself. They spot a Loggerhead turtle that quickly swims away. A little farther out they see a nurse shark circling at the bottom. Lucy loses her nerve when she sees a barracuda. She lifts her head up to the surface to catch her breath and Michael follows.

Lucy takes her mask off. "Oh my god, that barracuda was about four feet long and I swear I saw its teeth. All I thought about was it attacking me."

"Don't be such a chicken."

As directed by the boat crew, Michael and Lucy look for the boat whenever they rise to the top of the water to make sure they haven't swum too far away. They see the boat and swim closer to it. Michael yells up to one of the tour people and asks where the Jesus statue is. The tour guide points to what seems to be about forty feet away. Michael gives a thumbs-up. They mask up and go back under, kicking their flippers in the direction of the statue.

They see many people snorkeling in the same area, and they know they're getting close. The water is very shallow at about six feet and suddenly, the ocean bottom drops to about twenty feet and that's when they see Jesus. His hands are extended up in the air as if reaching for the sky. It's surreal, a moment in which they wish time would stop. It's mesmerizing and beautiful. Michael releases the air from his snorkeling jacket, enabling him to dive down. The silence underneath the water makes it feel holy.

Michael chokes up a little at the sight of the statue. He tries his best to swim down to it, but there's too much pressure in his ears. He feels enveloped by love and has no cares in the world. He's just floating away while the world goes on spinning without him. The sun is shining down through the water making everything sparkle. He feels his gratitude increase as hundreds of fish swim around him. Michael decides to give touching the statue another try. He takes a really deep breath, releases his snorkel from his mouth and dives straight down underwater. The pressure in his ears is building. He thinks he's not going to make it; he can't swim that deep. The pressure builds but he continues to propel himself toward it. Almost there, he lets out some air. The pressure in his ears is almost unbearable.

Reach! he thinks. *Reach a little further! Contact!* He touches Jesus' right hand. Unable to bear another second, he spins around and starts to swim back up, which seems to take forever. His breath is dwindling, chest tightening. He lets a few more air bubbles out and follows them up. He thinks of Jimmy Buffett's song, "Bubbles Up," as he's swimming and kicking his flippers. He breaks the surface of the water, inhales deeply, and throws his hands up above his head like a preacher on a Sunday morning.

Tears fill his eyes, and he cries from the overwhelming sense of accomplishment.

I knew you could do it.

Michael sees Lucy swimming nearby. She seems calmer than before, probably because there are more snorkelers around her. He sees Lucy stop and float below the surface, just staring at the statue, almost as if she's praying. As he swims closer, she doesn't know he's there. He thinks he sees that her eyes are closed and that she may be meditating. He doesn't go any closer. He gives her a moment to make a memory. He sees Lucy turn her head and her eyes find him.

Lucy swims closer, lifts her head out of the water, and starts crying. "That is so beautiful!" She wipes the salt water off her face. "I feel like I want to go to church now. I felt a love like I never have before. It was magical and beautiful. It changed my life." She's breathing heavily, trying to avoid getting water in her mouth, kicking her fins and spreading her arms back and forth on the surface of the water as the waves keep lapping at her face.

Michael tells her he had the same experience. They decide they've snorkeled enough, and they start slowly kicking back to the boat in silence. They're both trying to burn the memory into their minds. Lucy takes her flippers off in the water, grabs onto the ladder that hangs off the boat, and climbs up to the deck. Michael follows. The crew offers them cups of water and protein bars. Slowly, one by one, all the snorkelers get back on the boat, another head count is done, the anchor is lifted, diver-down flags are collected, and the boat and crew head back to shore.

Back on Pennekamp, Michael and Lucy use the locker rooms to change and decide to tour the visitor's center, which has an aquarium and natural history exhibits. After the aquarium, they walk the natural hammock trails reading all the identifying signs hanging on all the native trees and plants. They finish off their day sitting on the sandy white beach looking out onto the water.

"What an amazing day." Lucy smiles at Michael.

"I couldn't agree more. And, hey, we met Jesus! That in itself makes for a beautiful day."

They sit a little longer in the sunshine before Michael says, "I think that power bar from snorkeling is wearing off. What do you say we go and get some dinner?"

Lucy smiles. "Let's go!"

They pack up their bags and jump in the Jeep. They put the address for the Conch House in Google Maps so they don't pass it. "Holiday Boulevard, what an appropriate name for this street." She makes a left turn into the driveway of Conch House. The rocks in the driveway crunch under the Jeep's tires as she slowly steers into a parking spot. They walk down a brick walkway and follow it around. It opens up to a shady patio under tropical hammocks and flowering orchids. They think the patio is beautiful, but they would rather have a small, intimate table for two on the porch. The hostess greets them and brings them to a table. They sit and reminisce on the day as their drinks and food arrive.

As they finish, Michael grabs the check when it comes and says, "I've got it. After all, I am a millionaire." He smiles and hands his debit card to the server. As they're about to leave Lucy sees a real estate brochure. She hits Michael on the arm, points, and smiles as she grabs one. "This will give you a place to start."

At the house, they pour two glasses of pinot grigio and take the real estate brochure outside to the patio. Lucy opens the brochure and sees that the listings start in the upper keys, the Key Largo area, then the middle keys, which is the Marathon area, and finishes with listings in the lower keys, Key West. She goes back to the front of the brochure where the Key Largo listings are. "One million dollars . . . This one is two point five million; that's too much. Who needs that much house? Then a homeowner would need to hire a person to maintain the property . . . That pool, those fountains, shrubs, and all those garden beds? No thank you. You'll be coming down for a vacation but spend all your time just maintaining the property." She laughs. "That's why you should buy a condo. Condos have HOA fees and all you have to worry about is the interior." She hands the brochure to Michael. "Have a look. See if you like anything."

Michael flips through the whole brochure like Lucy did and he restarts at the beginning. "There are several condo listings, but I'm not particularly drawn to any of them. Maybe we should call a local agent. They'll have a general idea of what to direct us to." He turns the page and sees a business ad: Vanessa J. Chamizo, Realtor. "She speaks Spanish." Michael smiles to himself, and with his best Spanish pronunciation he says, "Hola Vanessa. Not that I speak Spanish, but hey, it helps down here." He reads her website name: *The Keys Are For Me*. "Let's call her."

Michael grabs his phone and realizes that it's the first time since this morning that he's actually opened it. "You know . . . I didn't even miss using this today."

There's a text from Charles.

Thank you! 🙏♡

Your mother gave her permission to use the video. I sent it over to editing. It's airing on TMZ tonight.

Michael's stomach drops. "Holy shit," is all he can get out. He reads the text to Lucy. Her eyes pop open and she puts her hand over her mouth.

Michael says, "Screw it!" His thoughts are not of Charles or TMZ; they move back to the realtor. "What's that number for Vanessa?" He dials but gets her voicemail and leaves a message. He shuts his phone off again. "I'm not even gonna look at Talk2U.

Let's just watch the sunset."

They sit in silence for the next fifteen minutes and it's another spectacular sunset. The colors paint the sky once again every shade of orange, yellow, red, and purple. They sit and watch the little yellow ball sink below the horizon, ending yet another perfect day.

They walk back into the house both thinking the same thing but not saying it.

Michael speaks up. "Should we watch it? At least we'll know what got edited and what was real. You know how Hollywood columnists like to make fake news. And I hope they lead up to the séance correctly and not just make it some ghost story like Whitney Houston is back from the grave."

Lucy pipes in, "I'm sure if your mom has approved, it's gonna be an amazing story. Your mom would never gossip. Now I'm super excited to watch." Lucy jumps on the couch and sits in a lotus position, grabs the remote, and turns the TV on.

"It's eight forty-five!" she yells to Michael. "Pour two glasses of anything and sit your buns down."

There's suspenseful music playing, followed by the station's identification. "BREAKING NEWS! Don't miss tonight at nine. TMZ has the story. Whitney Houston: is she really the guardian angel to the Double D's heir Michael Monroe? A key, a gold chain, a psychic, a film company, a feather storm in New York, and now a séance recorded live in Fort Lauderdale at CBN Studios. You be the judge." The news music cues off.

"OH MY GOD!" Lucy screams. "Did you hear that, Michael? It's gonna be amazing! Oh my god, I bet Whitney set all this up. I bet Whitney somehow convinced your mom to stay with Charles so he didn't fuck this up!" Lucy is punching the sofa cushion out of excitement. "Your mom made sure it wasn't a gossip story. Holy shit, Michael." Lucy is practically jumping up and down in her lotus position on the couch. Michael's hands grow sweaty with nerves, but his face is beaming. He sits down next to Lucy on the couch with their pinot grigios and they wait for what feels like an eternity.

Michael grabs his phone and texts his mother.

We're watching.

He sees that his mother is typing a response.

We just finished it at about 4pm this evening. When we got your video this morning, we canceled everything and went to work. I called that reporter Ed Turgeon. He met us with his photos, and I gave him his story and he gave us ours. It all worked out perfectly. You're gonna love it!

xoxo Mom

The starting music cues. Images of Whitney Houston throughout her career flash across the screen. Then there's a reel from the Beverly Hills Hilton, as media and medical personnel are scattered around the death scene. Yellow caution tape cordons off a room as red and blue lights flash and ricochet off the glass entranceway of the hotel from all the cop cars, fire trucks, and ambulances.

The nightly news anchor comes on. "Greg Salomon here." Dark-haired and brown-eyed, he's wearing a blue suit and a brightly colored tie. He turns and faces another camera. "Tonight's story: Whitney Houston. A global icon. Loved and adored worldwide. She has sold over two hundred million records. She dazzled us on the big screen with movies like *The*

Bodyguard, *Waiting to Exhale*, and *The Preacher's Wife*. She sold out tours in every city she went to. She gave us one of the most beloved versions ever of 'The Star Spangled Banner'. But on that fateful day of February 11, 2012, Whitney passed away at the age of forty-eight."

More images of Whitney flash on the TV. Early album covers and still shots from her concerts and her videos. The camera cuts to Greg again. "Back in 1997, fifteen years before her death, Whitney appeared in Rodgers & Hammerstein's made-for-TV musical film *Cinderella* as the Fairy Godmother,"—Greg flashes a big smile—"and it looks like she just might be at that role again."

Michael sees an image of himself on the screen. "Michael Monroe is the son of billionaire Double D's diamond heiress Olivia Monroe. He was apparently cut off from the family fortune when he was just twenty because his mother felt the family wealth had corrupted him." Images of Olivia flash on the screen of her in expensive outfits at charity events, traveling, and in board meetings. Of course, her famous Double D's are in every photo. Images flash to customers buying diamonds at department stores and more scenes from her diamond ads over the years, but of course the image of her most iconic ad stands still on the screen for several seconds, the one of just the woman's bust and the diamond on her finger.

The news anchor comes back on the screen. "Michael has been living on his own for almost ten years, paycheck to paycheck, without any assistance from his mother. With a degree in culinary arts, Michael has been struggling like the rest of us to pay his rent, pay for car repairs, and find the right job. He's clipped coupons. He's fallen in and out of love with the wrong people."

Now there's a new image of Michael in the top right-hand corner of the screen. "It seems most employers won't hire him because of his name. They feel he won't be dependable. They feel he doesn't need a job and that with just one check written by his mother, all his financial problems could be gone. But Olivia won't help him." An angry image of Olivia with her hand in front of her face pushing reporters back appears on the screen. Images of tabloid newspaper titles appear: *Double D's Son Arrested on Drug Charges.*

Greg's voiceover continues, "Olivia's response to Michael's drug and alcohol abuse was, 'figure it out!' and she gave him an ultimatum as she shoved Michael out of her opulent apartment and closed the door on him."

Greg comes back on the TV screen. "Wow, what a tough mom." He frowns. "Disgusted, discouraged, and filled with rage, we're told Michael was sitting at his home desk chair, looking at an *I Dream of Jeannie* doll and screamed 'What am I doing wrong?' at it." Greg's arms are animated as he plays out for the viewers how Michael may have acted that evening. "He shouted, 'Just give me a sign!' But what happened next was nothing short of a miracle. Apparently, Whitney Houston has shown up to assist him." Greg's facial expressions grow more animated now. "Michael can see and hear her. And she's guiding and assisting him."

Greg takes a deep breath. "We're told it started after his cry for help. As he walked down a New York sidewalk, he passed a key on the ground, and a 'voice' in his head told him to pick up the key. So, he did. Then there was that recent, very odd feather storm in New York City. Apparently, Michael had asked Whitney to not come and go so fast and to give him a sign when she was going to be around so he wouldn't always be startled by her appearing out of nowhere. He said, 'like maybe a feather,' so Whitney gave him this:" The image of the feather storm stays on the screen for a few moments. Greg chuckles at the picture on the screen.

"Now we're told he applied for a waiter's position at a restaurant called Fate, and it just so happened a film crew was filming a movie using a psychic the first day Michael was to start work. Talk about 'Fate,' huh? The psychic was caught on film giving Michael a reading from Whitney. Here's a news clip from the owners of that restaurant confirming something very unusual happened at their restaurant that day . . ." The footage rolls of Madame Ivy and Michael at the restaurant.

"The story went viral. It crashed Talk2U's site and when Charles Booream of CBN got wind of it, he invited all of them down to his studio in Fort Lauderdale and filmed a live séance. Just wait till you see this séance. Prince, Rick James, Michael Jackson, and Whitney all showed up. I don't know what to make of this video. It's poor quality. We've been told during the séance only Michael's phone recorded and here's what happened."

Michael's entire ten-minute séance video plays.

They flashback to Greg again. The TMZ anchor smiles and shrugs. "Maybe nationally renowned psychics John Edwards, Theresa Caputo, or Hollywood medium Tyler Henry can be called in to take a look and analyze the authenticity of the video. Either way, the video is compelling and could really make a person believe that Whitney is guiding Michael. But why Michael?" Greg spins around in his chair as a camera from another angle pans in on him. "Well, that's it for tonight's show. We hope you enjoyed it. We invite you to comment on tonight's show on our Talk2U site or you can email us at studio@TMZ.com. I'm sure we're going to be hearing a lot more about Michael Monroe and Whitney Houston in the future and hopefully we can get Michael on the show . . . and Whitney." He smiles a big, toothy Hollywood smile. "I'm Greg Salomon. From everyone here in the studio, we wish you a good night."

Michael takes a deep breath. He looks over at Lucy. She's speechless too. Then they laugh and start screaming hysterically at the absurdity of their situation. Michael gets up and starts pacing the floor. "I have to text my mom."

Wow, that's all I can say.

Soon three dots appear, indicating Olivia is typing a response.

Did you like how I made myself the villain? My lawyer and marketing team thought of using that angle. Stern, no-nonsense businesswoman. Michael, I love you so much. I'm so proud of you and all I've ever wanted was for you to be independent and able to take care of yourself in case our fortune goes away. I wanted you to have life skills. I've always felt that this was where I failed you as your mother. I'm sorry I slammed the door in your face. I panicked. I've always wished I could take it back and do it over again. I didn't know what else to do. But I think it has finally worked out best for you this way. Call me tomorrow. Love you always.

xoxo Mom

PS—I think Charles did a fine job respecting us.

Michael has a tear rolling down his face as he finishes reading his mother's text. Lucy pries the phone from his hand and reads it. She hugs him tight as he begins to sob. His whole body quivers. He's finally gotten an answer about why his mom never helped him out. He always thought it was because he was making bad choices. But it was really because his mom felt she failed him as a parent and that's what saddens him the most.

Lucy holds him until he calms down. She retrieves a glass of water from the kitchen. "Here, drink," she says, "before Whitney has to dunk you in the bay again." They both laugh and give each other another hug.

"Okay," Lucy sighs, "I'm wiped out. It's been a long day. Jesus and Whitney in one day." She smiles and kisses Michael on the cheek. "You—go to bed now. Good night, my sweet best friend." She puts her hands on his shoulders and lovingly shakes him, then walks into her bedroom and closes the door. Michael can hear her fall onto the bed.

The house is quiet. All he hears are the circling rhythms of the ceiling fans as he sits on the sofa. He walks around the house and shuts off the TV and all the lights. He stops before entering his room, remembering what Whitney told him: if someone will just get quiet enough, they can probably hear God in the breeze. He wonders what he would hear. Would God even show up? Was Whitney trying to tell him something? He thinks about it for a few more seconds then quietly walks out the front door.

It's pitch dark outside with only a few blinking red lights from buoys out in the distance—until the motion sensors flip on with their blinding flood lights. The moon is full. He walks out to the table at the water's edge and sits down. He hears the soft swishing of the water lapping at the shore and breathes in the salty air. The motion sensor flips off and it's dark again. He looks up at the billions of stars that he never sees in New York.

He thinks about the beauty and wonder of the universe. He can see the lights of a jet flying through the night sky. Then he sees a shooting star whiz by, and it fills him with excitement. He looks and finds the Big Dipper and then spots the Little Dipper, too. He realizes that he's never seen the Little Dipper before because of the bright city lights. But here he can see so many stars. He sees a really bright star and assumes it's a planet. Maybe it's Mars. Another thought enters his head: *tomorrow night we should come out here with Lucy's Star Walk app to view and identify all the stars.* He smiles.

The twinkling astral display is beyond his comprehension. His thoughts meander and wonder about all that's up there—and he's sure, almost positive, that there has got to be other life out there besides us. And for just a moment his mind goes quiet, and he doesn't think of anything, just like he did with the palm tree this morning. He just stares at the night sky and at the full moon and its white light reflecting off the water as if it's a path to follow. A light breeze comes out of nowhere. It's soft at first but starts to pick up momentum. The umbrella above the table flaps in the wind and the table trembles. Michael quickly cranks and lowers the umbrella. The wind is persistent. He should go back inside.

The wind now seems to be enveloping him. He feels it all around him. He feels the pressure of the wind on his body almost squeezing him. It feels like a weight. Like a hug. It's moving all around him. And then he hears a voice in his mind, but it comes with a different feeling. It's a different energy; it's strong, powerful, and all-loving. It's the most indescribable love Michael has ever felt. He starts crying from an overload of cognizant senses of the extreme love he feels. His thoughts part, as if to let the voice in.

The wind, that's me. I'm here.

Michael knows the voice isn't Whitney's, but still his soul is shaken. He is astounded by what he's just heard.

Tears roll down his face. He finds himself laughing and crying at once. He starts to doubt himself. He wipes the tears away with both his palms. Love. He feels an indescribable love, the most passionate love, completely unconditional. One that he's never felt before in his life. Maybe he just made it up in his mind. Maybe it's a coincidence. Maybe he somehow felt it somewhere else, and it just lodged in his brain and the memory now has just released at this particular moment. Then he hears the voice he knows.

There's no such thing as a coincidence, Michael.

Michael blinks and snaps back. He seems to be present again. All the feelings are gone. The wind has almost completely stilled. All that's left are his blurry memories of what he's just experienced. Him meeting God, at night, at the Florida Bay, in Key Largo. Did that really happen? Memories he questions, but still, like treasure, he buries them into his mind. Memories he will keep for the rest of his life. His tears stop. The laughter stops too. The absolute bliss is gone. There seems to be nothing left but to be thankful.

What just happened? he thinks. *Could that really have been God? God, was that you?*

There is only silence . . . except for the soft swishing of the water lapping at the shore. Michael decides whoever it was, they aren't coming back tonight. It's time to go back inside. He slowly walks back into the house and crawls into bed.

CHAPTER 27

MICHAEL IS AWAKENED the next morning by the island sound of the blinds hitting the windowsills. He squints and sees sunlight illuminating the edges of the closed blinds. He looks at the digital clock on the nightstand. 8:15. He is in disbelief, thinking about how he finally slept through the entire night without waking up. No trip to the bathroom in the middle of the night and no Whitney waking him up and drowning him. He smiles. He rolls out of bed and lazily walks to his en suite bathroom. Still half asleep and midstream, he hears, ***Good morning!*** from a voice he knows all too well. Today, this sleepy morning, that voice startles him, especially because he is taking a leak.

"Whoa!" is Michael's first reaction. "Again with the bathroom! What are you, some kind of perv?"

Whitney waves her hand. ***I've already told you; I don't see anything. All I see is your sparkling, shining soul.***

"Well, that doesn't take away from the fact that my wiener is hanging out and a lady comes in the bathroom and surprises me! And not just a lady, freaking Whitney Houston!" Michael leans forward to conceal himself.

Well, we can pretend I'm Lily Tomlin and you can be Steve

Martin from the movie All of Me ***and I can ask you, 'Shall I tap?' Would you like that?"*** She roars with laughter.

Michael shouts, "NO! Out!"

He doesn't feel her presence after that, so he knows she's gone, but now he feels bad. "I love you, Whitney. You can come back." Nothing. He flushes, washes his hands, and walks out of the bathroom

"I'm sorry," he says quietly to the empty room.

I know you are, baby. She laughs. ***I'm just getting you ready for your new normal.***

"My new normal?" Michael's forehead scrunches; he doesn't understand her meaning. Then he repeats it to himself as if it's some sort of word puzzle. "My new normal . . ." He shrugs his shoulders as if expecting to catch more of what she's meaning.

Uh-huh, new normal. Get ready, baby. After last night's séance segment, ain't nothing gonna be normal for a while. People gonna be everywhere bothering you all the time. Even when you're peeing. Oh, lord have mercy. She laughs and her voice fades away.

Shock instantly consumes Michael. He has forgotten all about the séance airing last night on TV. "Holy crap." Panic runs through him. He grabs his phone from the charger, and he sees the missed phone calls and texts from Charles, his mom, and several unknown numbers. The last one is a 305 area code, which he knows as South Florida. He opens his door to the living room. No Lucy. He walks into the kitchen. Still no Lucy. Getting a little nervous, he peeps into her bedroom and sees she's not there. Her bed is still unmade, and it gives him some solace; she's around somewhere. He stands there wondering where she could be. His mind is racing and then he realizes his phone is in his hand.

Just text her, you idiot, he thinks. Taking a deep breath, he types a message.

Where are you?

Morning! I'm sitting on the neighbor's dock. Come out.

Michael throws his head back, still in a state of panic. *Why didn't I think to look outside*? He's so emotionally stirred up that he doesn't even think to bring a cup of coffee with him. He just beelines right out of the house to the dock.

As he leaves the front door, he pauses just a brief moment and looks at the palm trees, sandy beach, and the turquoise-blue water as it touches the light-blue sky on the horizon. He instantly thinks of God last night and what happened.

And then his mind begins to panic after he spots Lucy on the dock. She's wearing yellowish-orange yoga pants with a baggy white hoodie. Her auburn hair is in a ponytail. He sits down next to her on the bench.

She gives him a look that says she's know's something is up. "What? Spill it," she says.

"Nothing, I just had the most incredible night's sleep and when I woke, I went to the bathroom, and Whitney pops in while I'm peeing to tell me this will be my new normal. People will be invading my personal space." He pauses. "Then she reminded me that the séance aired last night. Which somehow"—he absentmindedly throws his hands up—"I'd forgotten all about. Until, of course, I unplugged my phone and it had blown up with missed texts and phone calls overnight. I'm scared and anxious. What the hell do I do now?" He props his elbows on his knees, cups his face with his hands, and starts to rock back and forth as he massages his forehead.

"First, call your mom and Charles and make sure everything is okay. Then you do nothing. You do absolutely nothing. You go on. Just go on and live your life."

As he's hunched over massaging his forehead, he sarcastically says, “Well that’s easy for you to say. The world doesn’t want to watch *you* pee.”

Lucy starts laughing and Michael lets out a huff of air, then starts to laugh along with her.

“Oh, Christ, Lucy, what do I do?” He puts his head on Lucy’s shoulder and says, “I need a cup of coffee.”

“Here,” Lucy says, “fill mine up too.” Michael grabs her cup and walks back into the house. He comes back out with the two coffees and a box of chocolate-covered donuts they had purchased at Sandbar Donuts food truck.

“Breakfast of champions,” Michael says as he opens the box. They eat and drink coffee in silence while watching the birds fly over the early morning sunrise with its pastel pinks and blues.

It’s another beautiful morning. A slight salty breeze makes the palm fronds along the coast sway. There are no boats on the water yet, which makes it even more tranquil. They hear a ruffling behind them in the mangroves. Startled, they both turn around to see a green and black striped iguana run across the ground and up a tree. They both start on their second donut before Michael’s phone breaks the silence.

He looks and it’s that unknown 305 area code calling again. He shows his phone to Lucy.

She looks and shrugs. “Answer it. You can always hang up.”

“Remember the last time you said that?” Michael’s eyes make a stern questionable expression reliving the FBI showing up. “Hello, this is Michael.”

“Michael! This is Vanessa Chamizo, the realtor in the Florida Keys,” She says, speaking with a Hispanic accent. “I got your message about seeing a few condos in Key Largo.”

Michael turns the phone to Lucy and says, “It’s the realtor, Vanessa.” He smiles as her mouth makes an O shape. “Okay, yes, Vanessa. How are you?”

“I’m doing well. I’m living the island life.” Michael can hear the smile on her face. "I'm having an open house from ten to one at a condo listing at Treasure Island. It's a bayside condo development that has a community dock for watching the sunset. Might be something you'd like. We can meet there and talk a bit more about what it is you're looking for. But if you have any listings in mind that you would like to see, let me know and I'll probably have enough time for two showings after my open house."

"Oh wow. Awesome. That sounds great. We can meet you at your listing. Check the place out and walk around the grounds for a little while. That sounds perfect." Michael looks at Lucy and she's all smiles.

She stomps her feet on the dock and raises her fisted hands in excitement. "You're gonna buy a condo," she softly sings so Vanessa doesn't hear her before Michael hangs up. Then Lucy ups her game, "You're gonna buy a condo . . . in Key Largo." She's now dancing around the dock. She does a few squats, pliés, and twirls. Michael can't help but laugh. He joins in and the two of them dance together. Michael starts doing the robot dance and marches out on the dock.

Michael stops dancing and sits back down on the bench. "I think it's time to face the music. I'm gonna go back inside and make a few calls."

"I'm gonna stay out here a little while longer and do some yoga. It's so beautiful. Maybe another dolphin will swim by, or maybe a manatee." She smiles at him.

"Well, you enjoy your yoga and I hope you get an aquatic visitor." Michael stands up, walks off the dock and goes back into the house.

He makes another cup of coffee then grabs his phone and goes out on the back deck. Sitting down at the table, he presses the *Call* button next to his mom's name. He doesn't know why, but he has a weird feeling in the pit of his stomach. She answers on the second ring.

"Good morning, darling!" His mom sounds overly chipper. "How'd you sleep?"

"I slept good. I actually slept the whole night through," he says cautiously. Michael thinks about it but chooses to leave out telling his mom about his latest conversation with Whitney that occurred while he was taking a pee. He'll spare her the details—and the mental image.

"That's why I called you and left a message, darling. My publicity team is already on it. They've already created a speech for you." In a very stern voice she says, "Just follow it Michael." She pauses for a moment. "We—well not 'we'—you . . . you need to stand up to the media, Michael," Olivia pauses. "I've been here before, but you haven't, at least not like this. They are gonna come at you like sharks. They will hunt you and attack you. They will do anything to make it look like you're mentally unstable and that this is all a hoax. You will either rise up to them or they will disgrace you and discredit you. I am here for you, and I will do what I can to help you, but this fight is yours Michael." It sounds like his mother is choking up.

"Mom, are you okay?"

"Yes." She catches her breath. "I'm fine." She lets out a sigh.

"Mom . . . Whitney already came to me this morning. She told me to be prepared."

"Michael, you saw what the media did to her. You know how ruthless they can be, and you saw how they beat her down. And when she was down, they kept kicking her." She takes a deep breath. "We need to make sure you're ready for what she endured. This isn't just about you, darling. This is now about Whitney Houston, too. A beloved celebrity who is still loved by millions of people, who's now dead and you're telling the world she's your guardian angel." She pauses. "That's not going to be accepted very easily."

Michael can hear his mother getting up as she talks to him.

He hears her walking and then a high-pitched clink sounds as he presumes a ceramic coffee cup is placed on the granite countertop. He hears her pull the coffee pot out, followed by the sound of coffee pouring. She pushes the coffee pot back into the maker. He hears his mother talking to someone else. "No, really, Isabel, I'm fine. If I need anything, anything at all, I will ask. Thank you." He hears his mother grab the coffee cup and start walking again. "Geesh, these housekeepers of Charles's are a little much." His mother starts laughing. "They don't want me to do anything for myself without them helping. I mean it's a nice gesture, but I can pour my own coffee, thank you."

She sighs as she sits back down again. "But really, Michael, this Whitney guardian angel defies human logic and acceptance. Yes, there are people who believe in spiritual communication, but again, this is *Whitney Houston*. This is not some Aunt Millie from Vermont nobody knows. You've caught worldwide media attention." She fumbles with papers. "They're even talking about you in Japan, Michael. I'm not sure, but have you been out yet today?"

"No, why?" He feels a tingle of stress building in him.

"Yeah, well, so much for that . . . you're on the cover of the *New York Post* and ALL other newspapers today." She says it in a factual tone. Michael gasps. "The *New York Times*, for Christ's sake, the front page has a picture of you, me, and Whitney. We're here on the front page along with someone who's won the New York lottery but hasn't come forward yet." She's silent for a moment. "Anyway," she continues. "We have the *Miami Herald* here aaaand you're on that cover too." Michael is now pacing in little circles in the kitchen. "I guess it's a good thing this séance wasn't filmed in New York." She lets out a nervous laugh. "They would've already been outside your apartment waiting. At least you're a little ahead of them by being down there at Lucy's aunt's house. Listen, no more posting to social media. They already know you're in Key Largo; they just don't know where."

"How do they already know I'm down here?"

"You and Lucy posted sunset pictures to social media, darling. Try to stay put as long as possible. Right now, the paparazzi are probably outside every hotel in Key Largo, waiting for you to surface. Michael, just stay ahead of them for as long as you can." She lets out a long sigh. "On that note, you need to contact Charles. He'll take care of you. He's already lining up media interviews with people he trusts in the industry. They can all do the interviews either via Zoom or over the phone." Michael can hear her voice calming down. "Please, Michael, just do what he says. I'm not worried about me. This story won't affect me or the business at all. If anything, it's free publicity for us. You know how people love a good story. There's no such thing as bad publicity when it doesn't involve you."

"Okay, Mom. I'll call Charles next. You go and relax." He manages to sound calm, but his stomach is a ball of nerves. He's also scratching the sides of his neck; he feels the bumps of hives from nerves.

"Charles is working on setting you up. I'm now just sitting by his pool. Maybe I'll make my way out to the beach and walk along the shore for a while. It's supposed to be beautiful here today. Michael, I love you."

"Go do that, Mom. Find some seashells. I love you, too." Michael hangs up and calls Charles next.

"Michael, my man, how are you?" Charles says, trying to sound casual.

"I saw you called, and I just talked to my mom." Michael cuts to the chase. "What's up? What do I have to do?" Michael's palms are sweaty and he's nervous but he's ready to face this head-on.

"Okay, first things first. I've got a few interviews lined up for you. Everyone, of course, wants you in their studio, but I won't allow that yet. It's part marketing ploy but it's also part protection."

Michael hears Charles pacing around his office—or at least he thinks it's his office. "I've got you four interviews today."

Michael feels yet another heavy ping of disappointment, thinking of the realtor Vanessa and how he is supposed to meet her later. "I'm emailing you all the names and contacts. They're expecting you to call. I asked for their questions and will be emailing them to you. This way you'll be ready to answer. Your mother's publicity team wrote up a speech you'll want to memorize. But basically, it's all going to be up to you. They may ask a question that isn't on the list, but don't answer it. You got that Michael? Don't answer anything else!"

"Okay, got it." Michael starts thinking of what they might ask. "What happens if they want more?"

"More of what?" Charles responds quickly.

"What if they want, I don't know, what if they want another séance?"

"Absolutely not!" Charles seems to not even give the question a thought. "Stick to the questions Michael. These news reporters are trained and sharp and they'll attack like missiles. They'll smile to your face, they'll show empathy, they'll pretend they're listening, and they'll even tell you they understand. What a bunch of bullshit that is. How can they understand this? Anyway, they'll try to gain your trust and then they'll blindside you with a quick sneaky question when your guard is down . . . Don't ever get comfortable! Hear me, Michael . . . stay alert. It's the only way to keep ahead of them."

Michael's stomach is getting queasy and he's rubbing his one palm on his shorts. "Well, you shouldn't have to worry about me getting relaxed. I'm already a ball of nerves and I haven't even done a single interview yet." He scratches his neck and wonders if he's actually getting hives.

"Michael, you'll do fine . . . I'm having media I trust interview you. I've already given them a lot of information. They're going to edit our interviews together. Stay focused and stick to the questions. Got it?"

"Got it."

"Good. And for God's sake, don't tell them where you are!" Charles hangs up.

Michael snaps back to reality. He puts his phone down and realizes how he could've screwed that up.

Michael looks into the room as if he's talking to her. "Whitney, you better show up." He thinks a little harder and this time he says it like he means it. "*Whitney?*" He looks around. Nothing.

Michael takes a deep breath and opens up his email. He reads the message from Charles. It's very short and very specific. Just four names with phone numbers and the name of their studios, and a list of ten questions. Michael looks at the time. It's only a little past nine. If he can rock these out, he'll still have enough time to get to Vanessa's open house. That gives him inspiration.

Another warning pops into his mind; he thinks of how his mother told him not to go out. He has another conscious line of thought: an open house isn't the same thing as going out, right? *Nah.* he tells himself. Nobody knows they're driving a Jeep. They should be fine. He feels a tingle in his solar plexus but shrugs it off. *They'll never know*, he concludes.

He goes back to Charles's list and starts reading all of his approved questions:

How do you know it's really Whitney?
Why did she connect with you?
How has your life changed since she appeared to you?
You're the son of the mega-millionaire Double D's heiress. Why you?

The questions are pretty simple. He looks at the first name on the list. Eva Rojolie. He presses on the attachment and a photo of

Eva pops up. A thirty-ish woman with layered brown hair, brown eyes, and a diamond nose ring. He instantly likes her. He reads she's an anchor with the Miami Fox News.

"Well let's get this ball game started." He presses on the link to her phone number, and it starts ringing. She picks up on the second ring.

In a hurried voice with a thick Cuban accent she says, "This is Eva."

"Yes, hello, Eva. I'm Michael Monroe. I'm a friend of Charles Booream and he gave me your number—"

"Oh my goodness, Michael Monroe!" He hears her excitement. "I was hoping you would call. Wow, how are you? This is an absolute pleasure."

Michael smiles at her question. "I'm doing good; I'm a bit nervous, but whatever." He shrugs as if she can see him. "I'm ready to do this now if that works for you."

"Yes." She pauses and he hears papers shuffling around. "Will Whitney be joining us too?"

"Undoubtedly. I just never know when, until she appears."

"So, she's not with you all the time? She just seems to come and go? Is that what you're saying?"

"Yes, that's about right. I go about my daily routine and when I'm supposed to be doing something that she wants me to do, she'll speak to me or she'll appear . . . God, she used to scare the hell out of me in the beginning. She would just pop in and out and sometimes in the most unusual places." He thinks of her appearing in the bathroom this morning and he laughs to himself.

"So that's it, huh? She just comes and goes."

"Pretty much. It's not planned, like we meet up for lunch every day at noon." Michael laughs. "She's come to me while I've been in the shower. She's woken me up from a night's sleep to take me walking across the Florida Bay." Michael stops himself.

Fuck, fuck, fuck, he thinks. *She's gonna know where I am.*

Stop, Michael, just stop.

Atta boy!

"So, you're here now in Key Largo, correct?"

Fuck! Michael tries to think of a fast answer. *Think you idiot!* ***Keep ahead of her.***

"No. I'm down here in Miami with Charles and my mother." Now he thinks he just threw them all under the bus. But at least he saved Lucy. The images of reporters crowding around Charles's studio and home flash in his mind.

"Your friend, Lucy, she's not with you?"

Michael thinks fast, and he comes up with a white lie. "No, she's by herself now." *Booyah!* he thinks. *She's by herself all right, out there by herself on the dock.* He smiles as he thinks of her out there doing her yoga.

You did good. Charles and your mom can handle themselves.

"I saw a post on Talk2U about you two in the Keys."

"That was a few days ago."

"Oh, okay," Eva says. "Well then let's get to the interview—you ready?"

"Absolutely!"

Eva basically follows the questionnaire. She throws in a couple of fast questions, which Michael proudly averts. He catches on to her quickly and makes sure to just follow the script.

"Well, thank you for calling, Michael. I wish you all the best and I'll certainly be watching this story progress. I'll have this story up online in a few hours. Maybe we can have you in the studio next time."

"Anything is possible."

"Well, it would be great to meet you. And if there's ever anything I can help with, give me a call." Eva ends the call.

He looks at the time. It's a little past nine thirty. One down, three to go. He looks at the second number—Jeremy Richards, KCAL 9 Los Angeles. "LA, huh?" He thinks it may be a little too early to call, but he lets it ring anyway and Jeremy picks up.

That interview goes well, too. Again, he tries asking a few unauthorized questions, but Michael handles him well.

Now he only has two interviews. Michael notices Charles's pattern. He has interviews in Los Angeles, Miami, New York, and Chicago. Charles hit the East Coast twice and then crossed the country.

He looks through the information for his third interview and immediately gets the creeps from the photo of the interviewer, Tim Fortino, WWCW Chicago. Michael thinks that Tim looks slimy and gives himself a quick shake to release the eerie feeling he's getting looking at Tim's photo. With greased-back black hair, he's thick like a quarterback and looks tough, mob tough. Michael gets a bad feeling and decides to wait and go on to the fourth interview, Kari Daniels WTEN New York.

Michael loves Kari. They carry on like two little girls, more than they should. He feels completely at ease, like he's talking with Lucy. Kari asks questions not only about Whitney but about Michael's past employment and what it was like to be raised in wealth and then kicked out and left on his own. Kari tells him she is going to write two stories. The first is about Whitney and the second, which will run in Thursday's edition, will be for readers to get to know Michael better. Michael's interview with Kari finally ends and he puts his phone down. He sighs, stretches, and straightens his back, pushing his chest out while lifting his arms and tightening his back muscles. He closes his eyes and feels the stretch working; he gives himself a little twist, turning side to side. He looks back down and sees that third interview, Tim Fortino, and Michael frowns. He thinks, *I could probably skip it.* He weighs his decision but decides to just go ahead with it.

He presses the phone number. It rings and Michael instantly regrets it as Tim picks up, "Yeah, Bill Lanzi." His thick Italian accent dominates and echoes off Michael's eardrum. Michael hears him chewing on something.

Already skeptical and caught off guard, he coughs softly to clear his throat, "Um, yes, I'm Michael Monroe. I thought this would be Tim Fortino." Michael already dislikes Bill more than Tim.

"Nah, Tim had to leave." He chews a little more into the phone. "What can I help ya wit?"

"I was told to call about an interview covering the Whitney Houston guardian angel segment." Michael gets disgusted and just wants to hang up. "You know what? I'll just call Tim back later."

Michael goes to hang up the phone and he hears Bill yell into it. "Nah, Tim, he ain't gonna be comin' back anytime soon."

Michael rolls his eyes sarcastically and thinks, *Why? Did you already dispose of the body?*

"Yer the one who claims to be talkin' to that dead Whitney Houston?" Michael hears Bill laugh. "What she sayin' to ya, I will always love you?" He laughs a little louder. "Hang on a sec, will ya?"

Michael hears the *thunk* of the phone being put down, followed by heavy footsteps in the background. It's bringing an image to Michael's mind of a bald, sweaty, fat man. Michael hears Bill's hushed voice talking to someone else there in the room, "Why do I always get all the crazies?" Michael hears a loud shuffling of papers, then more footsteps and a swoosh of air as Bill sits back down in the chair. "Aaaaahh. Okay, I got the notes." Michael hears the wheels of Bill's chair squeak and creak as he presumably slides it toward the desk. "Okay, so what would ya say to da people who think yer crazy?" Michael doesn't have an answer ready when Bill fires off another question. "I've done some homework on ya, been arrested before for drugs. How do we know ya ain't on them again, like this is some kind of psychedelic trip yer on." Michael can hear Bill dramatically moving around in his chair.

Michael becomes outraged. "Yeah man, this is crazy shit I'm on; it's got me talking to Whitney Houston." His inner being rages like hot lava as his mind starts racing thinking how to convince people he isn't crazy. He's being insulted and humiliated with personal attacks by this man who wants nothing more than to disgrace him.

"I betcha yer mom thinks you're batshit crazy too!" Bill laughs. "What's next, ya gonna be talkin' to aliens?" It sounds like Bill takes a bite out of something. "What's wrong, kid," he says, slurping as he chews. "Cat got yer tongue?" He laughs again. "How about Whitney; what's she got ta say 'bout all this? You know what, kid, forget it, this story is bullshit! Just another rich kid on drugs looking for attention." The phone line goes dead.

Michael can't stop the anger. He's never been so disrespected and ridiculed; suddenly he realizes, as his mind works through the different scenarios, what kind of story this man was going to write. It won't be positive, to say the least. How can he tell Charles and his mom he screwed up an interview? Now Michael has both hands on his forehead as he rocks back and forth, wishing he'd never called. "Why did I call?" he keeps asking himself over and over. "What do I do now?" His pits are sweaty, and his shirt is sticking to him. He rubs his palms on his shorts, disgusted with himself.

He catches a glimpse of something moving; he hopes it's Whitney. He gets a little happier when he sees Lucy standing in the sliding glass doorway of the back porch. She's wearing a droopy oversized white linen sun hat with really big, thick, round black Jackie O sunglasses. Michael cheerfully smiles as he stares at her. She's in a formfitting silky yellow dress that clings to all her curves and flatters her toned body. Her outfit finishes with white sandals. She looks really *rich*. Michael wonders why she's dressed like that. "Are you ready to go look at your first condo showing, Mr. Monroe?" A big smile appears on her face, and she walks out onto the deck. "Do you like the hat?" She pulls down on the sides of the hat like a model and purses her lips. "The hat and sunglasses are my aunt's. She's got great taste." She twirls around.

Oh, Michael thinks. *It's to impress Vanessa.*

"Get dressed. We'll throw sunglasses and a hat on you, too. Nobody will ever recognize us." Now Michael understands the outfit. "Now let's go buy you a condo!" She does a little cha-cha dance.

Michael walks into his room, still smoldering about that last interview, and angrily mutters to himself as he showers. Then he puts on his favorite pair of blue LL Bean shorts, a three-button light-blue polo shirt, and his black flip-flops. He quickly runs gel through his hair. He notices that he's already gotten some sun. His face is lightly tanned as he looks at himself in the mirror. He smiles. He feels confident, which is rare for him.

I like your boat shoes better.

Michael snaps back to attention. "Oh, there you are! Where were you when that reporter was insulting me?" He feels the anger again.

Don't let him take away your joy. You can choose to be angry, or you can choose to be happy. Either way, it's your choice.

Michael hesitates, thinking about what Whitney just said. He smiles and says, "I choose to be happy." He looks down at his brown boat shoes by the bed. "Hmm, you think?" He shrugs his shoulders. "Okay, boat shoes it is." Michael changes his shoes and walks out of his bedroom to meet Lucy, who's sitting like a queen in her hat and sunglasses in the enclosed sunroom, staring out at the water.

A slight breeze is gently moving the palms. The bay is very calm. "I truly believe I could never get sick of this view," she says.

He sits down next to her on the white leather loveseat, puts his arm around her shoulders, and says, "Well then let's go buy our own Key Largo bayside waterfront condo."

Unbeknownst to Michael, Whitney is there, but this time she's with the late R&B sensation Aaliyah. They're standing in front of Michael and Lucy. Aaliyah's long, straight dark hair swoops over her sunglasses. She takes the sunglasses off, hangs them on the front of her black sleeveless shirt, and taps Whitney with her elbow.

"Did the fool really think he'd be able to outrun the paparazzi . . . in flip flops?" She lets out a soft, shy laugh, shaking her head with a disapproving "tsk."

"Aaliyah, baby girl, I don't understand half the things that run through that boy's head. I tell you, his thoughts are more messed up than a feather in a windstorm." They both laugh and disappear into the ether.

CHAPTER 28

LUCY DRIVES THE white Jeep north up Route 1. Michael gazes at all the buildings and storefronts they're passing. There are many restaurants and marinas selling boats. Michael yells over to Lucy, "They sell boats down here like New York sells cars."

Michael types in the address of the listing: 326 Starfish Lane. Lucy puts her left blinker on and waits for a lone white van to pass. Lucy then accelerates and Michael's phone falls out of his hands and drops on the passenger floor.

"Dammit!" he yells and bends down, but his seatbelt keeps him erect. He unclicks the seatbelt and leans forward to pick it up.

"Shit . . . stay down, Michael." She presses her hand on Michael's head.

"Owwwww!" Michael yells out and tries pushing up from Lucy's hand.

"A news van just flew by," Lucy says, shooting him a look. "I'm protecting you."

"Oh," he sulks. He rolls his head back and forth for effect. It gets him no sympathy from Lucy.

"We're a half mile away." Michael reads the driving instructions to Lucy. "A quarter mile up on the right . . . And turn right here onto Summer Drive." Michael points as Lucy turns onto the street. "Turn left on Windy Avenue. This will bring us to Starfish Lane and it's right . . . there!" *The Keys Are For Me* open-house sign tells them they're in the right place.

Lucy parks the Jeep and shuts the motor off. They sit there for a few moments observing the surroundings. People are whizzing around on golf carts, and they can see the pool area, which is full. There are several more groups of people wandering about.

Michael looks at Lucy. "Are you thinking what I'm thinking?"

Lucy nods her head.

"It's really busy," Michael says. "It's like a little tropical outdoor shopping mall, too many people and too many units."

Lucy nods again. "But it's pretty and nicely landscaped."

They get out of the Jeep and walk up the stairs to the unit. The kitchen is dated, with all-white laminate countertops. It probably hasn't been updated since the early nineties. They pluck a sales sheet from the kitchen counter.

Waterfront condo. Enjoy sunset every night right from your own condo.

1,200 sq. ft. 2BR/2B. Seller motivated.

It lists all the appliances, tiled floors, carpeted bedrooms, and ample closet space. It has a garage for a car and space for water toys. HOA fees and taxes are included, and it comes with a deeded boat slip. A woman comes around the corner and smiles at them.

"Hola, I'm Vanessa Chamizo." Her accent is strong, but her voice is clear. "Welcome to Treasure Island." She stops and looks at Michael. Her smile quickly fades as she turns her head to look into the other room almost in a panic. Her quick movements make her sunglasses fall off her head. She bends over to pick them up and puts them back on the top of her brown hair.

Michael smiles back at her. "Hi, Vanessa. I'm Michael Monroe." They shake hands. "And this is my friend, Lucy Calery." Lucy shakes her hand.

Vanessa stands there smiling until something clicks in her mind and her face changes to worry. Her eyes widen as if she's feeling some sudden anxiety. Without saying a word, she reaches around both of them and abruptly opens the kitchen pantry door, shoving them inside. They both stumble backward and fall over mop buckets and brooms, dust pans, a garbage can, and a vacuum. Michael and Lucy land in a heap with a clatter, letting out a few grunts and moans as they look up at Vanessa from the floor.

"Don't say a word!" Vanessa whispers, as she puts her hands into a prayer pose and then a finger over her lips and quickly closes the slatted closet door on them. She whispers through the slats in the door. "Hang tight and please don't move. Please trust me. I'll be right back." Michael hears Vanessa say, "Mierda, what do I do now?" as her footsteps leave the kitchen. There's light trickling through the louvered door so it's not completely dark inside the pantry. Michael and Lucy stare at each other, completely unsure of what to think, but they stay still on the floor. Moments later they hear footsteps and voices coming closer to the kitchen.

"Yes, well thank you for coming," Vanessa says. "Don't be afraid to shoot me any questions you might have. The estate is very motivated and open to offers."

The other people ask a few more questions and Vanessa is very quick with her answers.

"Yes, yes I see, I understand." Vanessa seems to be losing her patience now. "Well okay, have a great day, thanks for coming by. Goodbye now."

Vanessa closes the door. Michael hears her talking to herself. "Goodbye. Go now. Go. Shoo. Bye-bye. Get out!"

Her footsteps bring her to the pantry again. She turns the knob and opens the door. With a big smile on her face she says, "Hello," with welcoming open wide arms. She doesn't see Michael and Lucy until she realizes they're not standing, and her eyes scroll downward. She stares at Michael and Lucy, still squished together on the floor, arms and legs on top of each other, with a fallen mop and broom on top of them. At a loss for words, they both have bewildered looks on their faces.

"Oh. My. God." Vanessa starts laughing. "Here, let me help you up. I am so sorry." Vanessa reaches for Lucy's hand and pulls her up while Michael gets up on his own. All three of them stand in the kitchen as Michael and Lucy dust themselves off.

"You're Michael, the Whitney Houston Michael. Double D's Michael. The same Michael all over the news and everyone, even my last clients, them,"—she points outside through the window of the couple walking away—"the ones who were just here are talking about you. When I recognized you and put two and two together, I may have panicked a little." She pinches her two fingers together as if to signal a smidge.

Lucy says, "Well, I say while we're here, let's look at this condo." She grabs Michael, and they tour each of the bedrooms and take a quick look into each bathroom. They spend the most time in the family room, which has a sliding glass door and balcony overlooking the natural mangroves and the Florida Bay. They all sit down in the family room. Michael and Lucy plop on the sofa, and Vanessa takes the armchair. None of them say anything for a few moments. They all just stare out at the sunny day through the sliding glass door, mesmerized by the sailboat outside on the bay.

Michael breaks the silence. "I wish I was out there on that boat with nobody chasing me or me having to give interviews. I wanna just enjoy the Florida Keys. I'm supposed to be buying a condo, not hiding from people."

Vanessa asks, "What do you think about the condo?"

"It's nice, but it's not the one for me," Michael says. "The grounds are nice, this view is nice, but I have to say I've—*we've*—been a little spoiled by Lucy's aunt's house. Ground level, secluded, and waterfront. And I mean"—Michael spreads his arms as wide as they can go—"waterfront. Nothing but water. That's what I want. Unobstructed views of the sunset every night."

"I'll tell you what," Vanessa looks at both Michael and Lucy. "I have a realtor friend who has an open house today in Playa Sunset a few miles down. It's a gated townhouse community. It's a seventeen-acre property with only forty units and its waterfront."

"Well, what are we waiting for?" Michael stands up from the sofa. "I'm ready to see Sunset . . . "

"Playa. Playa Sunset." Vanessa smiles. "*Playa* means 'beach' in Spanish. Sunset beach."

"It sounds absolutely amazing," Lucy chirps. "I'm ready to go."

"Okay," Vanessa says. "Let me wrap up here. I need to close all the blinds, shut off the lights, and turn the thermostat up." She gets up from her armchair.

They wait in the kitchen while Vanessa tidies up the condo.

Walking outside in the warm sunshine, Michael and Lucy help Vanessa put all her materials in a silver Mercedes. "Probably best to just follow me," Vanessa says. "We're only going about three miles down the road."

Michael and Lucy jump in their Jeep and they head south down Route 1. Michael points at Rock Harbor Club and yells over the wind of the open Jeep. "There are some nice listings in there; we should have Vanessa show us some of them."

On the left is a big green-painted souvenir shop named Shell World. They whiz by it and now on the right is a cute little gem of a restaurant called Harriette's. A banner is hanging that reads, *Serving breakfast and lunch, seven days a week.* It's painted yellow and has blue trim. Michael smiles as he thinks the colors are very cute and "Keysy." Before they know it, Harriette's is a blur too. Michael admires all the varieties of palm trees and lush tropical greenery, but his thoughts are quickly interrupted when

Lucy slows down behind Vanessa at the entrance to Playa Sunset.

Vanessa stops at the main gate and punches in the gate code. The hydraulic gate opens slowly. Vanessa pulls in and turns right. Lucy follows but stops when they see a beautiful water fountain splashing water at the entrance with lots of lush tropical trees and flowering shrubs that are all nicely landscaped. They pass a few units on their left and see the tennis courts on their right. Vanessa pulls into a double parking space between two buildings. Lucy swings in next to her.

"Welcome to Playa Sunset." Vanessa smiles but all they can see is her brown hair, big sunglasses, and white teeth. "So what do you think of the grounds so far?" She's wearing a turquoise-blue and black short-sleeved shirt. The turquoise in her blouse is actually made up of little sea turtles outlined in black, and she's wearing white pants that fall just above her ankles with gold-colored sandals.

Michael smiles as he looks at the little white beach stones that are between the two buildings. "It's beautiful so far. I loved that big beautiful fountain at the entrance."

"Come on then," Vanessa invites them with a wave of her hand. "Let's take a walk around the property. Oh, and by the way"—Vanessa points to the corner building—"that's the unit right there. 9A." Michael smiles. He loves it already. They walk along a paved road, passing the entrance gate with the fountain as Michael takes a picture. He notices his phone is full of more voicemails, missed calls, and posts from Talk2U.

They continue following the blacktop as they walk past flowering bougainvilleas, air plants growing off trees, and gorgeous orchids, which bloom in shades of purple and white. A short walk away, at the end of the road they see a building with a carport and wide-open blue behind it.

Vanessa says, "There's the water on the other side of that building." They walk past a few more units as Vanessa points out the lovely pool and community clubhouse. There are so many tropical plants and varieties of palm trees that Michael feels like they're walking through a Costa Rican rainforest jungle. After about a two-minute walk in the baking sun, they see a white sandy beach with a few tables scattered around. As they approach the waterfront buildings, they see the Florida Bay. Michael and Lucy stop dead in their tracks.

They see numerous tall palm trees swaying against the blue sky and a boat dock with several boats. They walk to the end of the sandy beach and look into the shallow, clear-blue water of the bay. They see a crab run sideways across the bottom. There's a tiki hut out on the boat dock.

"Can we go out there?" Lucy asks.

"Of course." Vanessa gestures around her. "It's community property."

Michael points to the posted yellow sign that reads, *CAUTION, crocodiles in area.* He hesitates. Lucy looks around apprehensively.

"Yes . . . Playa Sunset has their very own mascot," Vanessa says with a laugh. "You're in the Keys and you're on the water. You have to expect these things. Plus, they truly don't want to eat you. That's just a Hollywood thing. Believe it or not, they're really more afraid of you." She points back and forth from Michael to Lucy. "They swim away from adults. Little dogs"—she shrugs her shoulders—"well, those you'll have to watch after." Michael and Lucy just look at each other. "I've been told there's a crocodile that lays eggs here in this moat every year. Crocs are very territorial. They come back to the same place each year. It's crocodile mating season right now. It starts in late April and goes into August. They're really peaceful creatures and fun to look at . . . from a distance," she laughs.

They continue walking now that Vanessa has calmed their fear of crocodiles a bit and walk out onto the wooden dock to the tiki hut. Under the tiki is an ice machine and a bar. Inside a few colorful buoys hang as decorations. There's a white plastic six-foot table and matching chairs underneath a spinning ceiling fan. They all sit down under the tiki hut in the shade and let out a collective sigh.

"This is amazing." Michael smiles at Lucy. The tiki hut has mangroves on one side, but it looks right out as far as the eye can see at the Florida Bay. There's nothing but sky and water. They hear the soft splashing of the water against the coral rocks.

Lucy notices a familiar site, a white house on the shore off to the left. "I can see that house from my aunt's house! Michael, this is so amazing! This will be the same exact sunset we've been looking at." Lucy has tears welling up in her eyes as she puts her hands in a prayer position. Michael just closes his eyes to absorb it all.

Lucy says, "It's so quiet, just like at my aunt's house. Nobody's around."

"Yes, it is," Vanessa responds. "Only seven units are owner-occupied. The other thirty-three units are part-time vacation homes."

As an older, curvy, and well-endowed woman, who's very tan and wrapped in an orange sarong, comes walking out on the dock, she spots them and yells over.

"Yoo-hoo . . . " She gives them a big smile and wave. "Hello, I'm Rosemarie." She has a thick Long Island accent. She rubs suntan lotion on herself and proceeds to lie face down on a beach chair. Apparently, judging by the color of her skin, she enjoys lying there.

"Are you both ready to see the condo now?" Vanessa laughs. "Or do you just want to stay out here and buy the dock rights?"

They walk a white-pebbled trail through a shady walkway under the natural habitat of the hardwood hammocks along the moat. They pass a few more *CAUTION* signs for crocodiles and see several iguanas and geckos scurrying along the ground or climbing up trees. They walk past the pool, which has a hot tub. Several little wooden bridges cross over the moat. The moat has little islands with narrow wooden planks you can cross over. The islands have tall patches of grass scattered with little trees. This makes the property's natural scenery adorable and remote, like something out of Gilligan's Island.

They make their way back behind a row of lanais until they get to the corner unit. Vanessa says, "This is the one." She points up. "There's a second-floor bedroom balcony over this lanai and as you can see, this unit is ground level. You can just walk right out off the back lanai. We'll go around to the front to give you a proper entrance." Vanessa starts listing the condo's features. "This unit is fifteen hundred square feet, two bedrooms, and two and a half baths . . . "

She opens the front door and the cool air from the air conditioner hits them as they both sigh. The cool air is a relief from the hot, humid outside air. Michael and Lucy enter first into a small foyer area with a beautiful dark hardwood staircase leading upstairs. To the left there's a half bathroom, tastefully decorated with a black granite countertop vanity. The floors on the first floor are made of Mexican terra-cotta tile.

"Same tiles as in my aunt's house," Lucy says. "I love it already."

The L-shaped galley kitchen has the same black granite countertop as the half bathroom. All the cabinets are light wood. The kitchen is fully equipped and ends with a sliding glass door that leads out to a small lanai, which has views of the tennis courts.

"All the dinnerware, furniture, and artwork are included," Vanessa mentions. "This unit is being sold fully furnished." She spreads her arms wide. "A true turn-key condo."

They leave the kitchen and walk into an open-concept large room with high ceilings. It has sliding glass doors on the side wall that Vanessa mentions is one of the perks of an end unit because it lets in extra sunlight. The sliding glass doors are next to a nautical dining room table with six chairs.

"This table is teak," Vanessa says. She tries to pick it up and grunts because the table is too heavy and doesn't move. "It's made from refurbished sailboats." The tabletop is highly glossed with smooth slats of white and blue wood. There's a cute island-themed chandelier hanging over the table. The walls are painted a soft yellow but between the tan Mexican floor tiles and dark wood plantation shutters with matching doors, the condo has a strong Spanish feel to it. After the dining table is a large dark wood TV cabinet with a sixty-five-inch flat-screen TV. There's a coffee-colored sectional sofa and two end chairs, a few end tables with lamps, and a large tropical-leaf-blade ceiling fan and light.

The artwork is very traditional, with lots of blue water scenes, green and brown palm trees, flowers, and images of turtles and other sea life. A large blue-green rug is spread out near the sofa. There's a second set of floor-to-ceiling fifteen-foot sliding glass doors, which open to the lanai. When fully opened, it makes the large room and lanai one gigantic space.

The back lanai overlooks the natural tropical hammocks, the moat, and the moat's islands. Both Michael and Lucy gasp at the tranquility of the landscape.

"This. Is. Amazing." Michael smiles and folds his hands over his heart. He looks at Lucy and she too is amazed by the beauty. As the three of them are standing in the lanai, the listing agent who's having the open house enters.

"Hello, I'm Lisa Feliciano." She smiles graciously and shakes Michael and Lucy's hands. Lisa has dark curly hair and stands about five foot three. She's very bubbly and personable. "This unit came on the market and went right under contract, but then the buyer's financing fell through and it was just relisted. This listing won't last long! I'll be here if you have any questions." She walks away and gives them their space.

"Let's go see the upstairs, shall we?" Vanessa closes the sliding glass doors to keep the heat out. She leads the way with a sway of her arm. They walk back through the main room and to the front door and start climbing the stairs, about fifteen of them.

They hit a landing and can either go left down a hallway to the spare bedroom or climb three more stairs and enter the master bedroom.

"This is the stairway to heaven," Lucy says.

The upstairs also has a tropical island feel to it. The dark hardwood floors, white walls and French doors with white curtains opening up to the master bedroom against the dark hardwood plantation shutters make it look like something from South America.

"Wow," is all Michael can say. The master bedroom is large, with fourteen-foot ceilings and its own tropical ceiling fan. There's a king-size bed with a light-blue comforter and white throw pillows. A dark wood dresser with a matching mirror is against one wall. Keeping with the Spanish theme, a dark wooden desk and a black rolling office chair sit on top of an ornate red and blue area rug.

They walk over to the sliding glass door, open it, and walk out on the balcony. Outside again, the sunshine is hot and humid but feels good on their skin after walking through the air-conditioned house. They step over to the railing and look down over the palms and the gently flowing moat.

"Just beautiful!" Michael breathes in the warm, salty air and looks at Lucy as she admires all the tropical foliage. Back inside, they enter the en suite master bathroom.

Leaving the master bedroom, they check out the guest bedroom, which is equally charming.

"I absolutely love it!" Michael says, grinning ear to ear. "I love the whole condo. I love the grounds, I love the waterfront, I love the moat. I love it all!" He pauses. "I even love the mascot crocodile." They all laugh.

"It's amazing," Lucy says. She pauses to find the right words. "I never thought a unit that wasn't waterfront would be able to compare to my aunt's house, but this . . . this is incredible . . . This is as if you put an order in to God and said, 'find me the perfect Key Largo condo,' and voilà . . . you get this!"

"Technically speaking," Vanessa says, "you have the moat, which is filled with water from the bay, so you are"—she uses her fingers for air quotations—"waterfront." She smiles.

"I don't need to see any more. This is magical and perfect. The same sunset view as your aunt's house. The grounds, the moat, the dock and tiki hut, sandy beach, tennis courts, pool, hot tub, and the serenity." Michael tears up but holds it back. "I absolutely love it and I couldn't ask for more." Edwin McCain's song by that name jumps into his mind.

That's a great song. Always been a favorite of mine.

Michael breathes in the serenity of Whitney being around. *Did you do this?* He thinks his response.

Maybe, a little guilty.

"Write it up, Vanessa. Full offer—six hundred thousand. I'll pay in cash."

"I'll send you all the papers through DocuSign." She steps closer to Michael. "I can recommend some home inspectors, too, so you can have the place checked out before you buy."

"Perfect." Michael's phone buzzes in his pocket, but he ignores it. He doesn't want to let go of the lovely, relaxing feeling he has from walking through this dream condo.

Vanessa speaks again. "I know this little bar called Pirate's Booty. It's about two miles from here. We can go there and have a celebratory sangria."

Michael and Lucy both smile at the invitation.

"Sure! We'll follow you in the Jeep," Lucy says.

They find Lisa downstairs and let her know they're taking the condo and to expect the documents and Lisa is very pleased. She congratulates them and says, "Can I have a picture?"

Michael raises a questionable brow.

"It's gonna be fun to tell friends I met you."

"Oh, okay." Now Michael understands. "But please don't say we're in the keys or even when this picture was taken or that I'm buying a condo. Please!"

"Deal." They all huddle together and smile as Lisa takes a selfie of the four of them.

Vanessa, Michael, Lisa, and Lucy leave and get into their cars. Vanessa lowers her window down and yells, "Just follow me!" Lucy and Michael snap on their seatbelts and pull out behind Vanessa.

Driving south down Route 1, Vanessa puts her blinker on. They follow her onto a side street and drive to the end where they see a brown tavern with a big neon sign that reads *Pirate's Booty*. The bar sits right on the water and has an amazing sandy beach view. There are lots of colorful nautical decorations around the building—skull-and-crossbones flags, anchors, lobster traps, and even a few cannons. There are open treasure chests that are designed to be used as benches for guests.

Lucy sees the treasure chest benches and squeals, "Oh, look how cute!"

Michael's smile says everything. There are a few people sitting around the patio having drinks; some are on their cell phones.

Vanessa smiles and points. "It looks like if we sit out here on the treasure chests, we'll be all right."

"Yeah," says Michael, "but I would love to be on the water. Look at that view!"

"Too many people out there," Lucy says. "Let's stay here. Don't forget, you just bought that view!" She smiles and rubs Michael's back between his shoulder blades.

They all sit down and put their cell phones on the table. Michael pulls his wallet out of his back pocket and places it on the table too.

A waitress comes over to their table and chit-chats with Vanessa. Vanessa then orders four white sangrias.

The waitress leaves and Lucy asks, "Four sangrias?"

"Yes, I texted my husband, Eddy. He's coming over by boat and is going to join us. He should be here any minute. You don't mind, do you?"

"Oh, no, not at all," Michael waves his hand and smiles.

Vanessa leans back to see around the building just over the dock and sees her husband's boat heading their way. "Here he comes." She points to the white boat.

Suddenly, they hear someone scream, "It's Michael Monroe!"

CHAPTER 29

A CROWD OF people start moving toward their table and Vanessa's immediate reaction is to jump up and start running.

"RUN! FOLLOW ME!" Vanessa grabs everyone's cell phones and Michael's wallet and throws it all in her purse; she then throws her purse to the waitress who took their order. "Hold this for me, Meeka. I'll be back!"

She takes off around the back of the building. Michael is confused, thinking they should be running toward their vehicles. Vanessa runs as fast as she can out onto the dock. Lucy and Michael are right behind her, and the excited crowds of people are right behind them, closing in.

The end of the dock is getting closer. Lucy yells out, "The dock is ending. We're stuck! Where do we go now?"

Vanessa is franticly waving her arms at her husband, Eddy. Then she yells, "JUMP!" and with a big splash, she dives into the water.

"What about the crocodiles?" Michael screams as he flies through the air and splashes into the water. Then Lucy is last to dive in. They both start swimming toward Vanessa.

The white boat pulls up close and stops. Vanessa's husband,

Eddy, is a native of Key Largo and he's what locals call a "Conch." He's of Cuban descent and a contractor by trade but is a fisherman at heart. He quickly throws an anchor and drops the ladder. Vanessa reaches the boat first, grabs hold of the ladder, and pulls herself aboard. Michael reaches and climbs up, then Lucy. Eddy pulls the anchor up while Vanessa grabs the ladder.

"Sit down and hold on!" Eddy orders as he slams the boat throttle down, guns it, and makes a really sharp turn that creates a huge, white bubbly wake with lots of waves in the no-wake zone as other boaters scream at Eddy to slow down as the boat speeds out of the marina. Michael looks back at the dock and the crowds of people they leave behind.

Vanessa pulls her wet hair back. "Mierda. I lost my sunglasses." She glances at Michael and Lucy, who sit looking shocked in their soaking-wet clothes, then looks down at herself. She notices there's a piece of seaweed on her shirt, so she pinches it with two fingers and flings it away. The boat is charging ahead at about thirty miles per hour.

"I'm glad I left my aunt's hat in the Jeep!" Lucy yells above the sound of the roaring motor and wind. She looks at Michael and yells, "This is gonna be an epic memory!" Michael and Lucy hug and Vanessa scoots over to join in.

Eddy takes them through back channels that look like tunnels as they sail unnoticed through the thick mangroves.

"I'm so sorry! This is my fault." Vanessa looks like she wants to cry. "I never should have asked you two out for sangrias. So stupid!" She reaches under a seat cushion and grabs three dry towels. She hands one to Michael and Lucy. They all dry off as best they can and then wrap the towels tightly around themselves.

Michael yells over the sounds of the boat motor and wind, "Stop it! I wouldn't have wanted it any other way! That was amazing! And now we get a boat ride. I feel like Bond. James Bond. Who could ask for anything more? What a day!" His smile is beaming and this time he rubs Lucy's back. "This is what a vacation should be: spontaneous, exciting, and unpredictable. Not just hiding in some condo."

Eddy finally steers the boat down a canal and docks alongside a white house on stilts. He and Vanessa jump off and safely tie the boat to cleats then help Michael and Lucy climb off.

Vanessa runs into the house and comes out with more towels. She hands them to Michael and Lucy. "Come on, we'll drive you back to your Jeep. Things should be okay again. Plus, I need to get my purse and your things. As a realtor my phone is my lifeline!"

Michael thinks of his phone and panic creeps in when he thinks about who might have posted their great boat getaway. His mother has probably called sixty times. Now a little anticipation crawls into his stomach.

The four of them squish into Eddy's blue MINI Cooper. He drives to the road that Pirate's Booty is on and parks a good distance away. Eddy and Vanessa get out and walk down to the bar. As they enter, they hear the conversations of people talking about what just conspired.

Meeka, the waitress, recognizes Vanessa and her husband. Without saying anything, she grabs Vanessa's purse, hands it to Eddy, and they both leave. Nobody seems to notice a thing.

They quickly walk back to the MINI Cooper. He swings the purse to Vanessa's side of the car as he slides into the driver's seat. Vanessa fishes out their keys, cell phones, and Michael's wallet. Eddy starts the car and pulls right up to the Jeep. Michael and Lucy jump out and quickly get into the Jeep. Vanessa gets to her car only to see a crowd of people running toward them again, cell phones in hand. Eddy quickly reverses his car and blocks the road with his Cooper. It makes the crowd hesitate just enough to allow Lucy to jam the Jeep into reverse, spitting gravel and dirt from under the tires as they bolt back up the road and out to the highway.

Michael and Lucy arrive back at her aunt's house. Lucy turns the Jeep around and backs it up in the driveway and they just sit in the Jeep looking out at the water, still all wet, hair clinging to their faces, neither of them saying a word. After a few minutes Lucy takes a deep breath. "Okay, I'm zenned again. Let's go in, get some dry clothes and a lot of wine, and enjoy the sunset."

"Amen to that. What a day. What time is it now, anyway?" He shakes his phone, and it lights up with the date and time. 6:43 p.m. "Sunset is about an hour and a half away." Michael squeaks as he slides off the Jeep's seat all wet.

With two full glasses of pinot grigio and a plate of cheese and crackers, they set up at the table near the water's edge again. It's one more amazing Florida Keys sunset. A few cormorants fly and dive into the water in front of the glowing orange sun. Tonight there are more clouds than the previous nights. The sun's colors are illuminating the clouds with thousands of prisms. Every second, the sky changes. Clouds drift, the sun lowers, and several pelicans glide, wings extended, across the water's surface. They sit watching the world spin as the salty water splashes at the coral shore.

"How about we drive down to Key West tomorrow?" Lucy throws out the question.

"That sounds perfect to me. It gets us out of Key Largo. I'm sure they'll be searching for us but we won't be here, ha!" Michael's memory serves him well as he envisions going over the bridges with the tropical blue water and all the boats anchored closely together at the sandbars. "I love that drive. I can't imagine anyone trailing behind us . . . Maybe news vans, but we'll spot them."

"I say we just order a pizza from Tower of Pizza tonight and have it delivered." Lucy pauses and looks right at Michael. "Hey, you need to look for those documents from Vanessa." As if reading from a mental list, she continues. "And have you heard anything from your mom and Charles?"

"My phone has been completely blowing up all day. Last time I looked there were over two hundred missed calls and texts and more than four million hits on Talk2U. I don't even know where to start." He waves his hand and sinks lower into his Adirondack chair. "As far as the phone messages, unless it's someone I know"—He uses his finger to swipe through the air repeatedly—"I'll just delete, delete, delete." He rubs his fingers on his forehead to hide his exhaustion. "I'll let Charles tell me who to contact. I don't need every news station calling me. Like, how did they get my number, anyway?"

She gives Michael a sad look and a loving pat on the head. "Sorry, pal. They just figure things like that out." She pauses and then asks, "Just cheese pizza or do you want toppings? I'm calling now."

"How about veggie with pepperoni?" He smiles.

"Veggie with pepperoni?" Lucy smirks at Michael. "What are you one of those flexitarians who can't make up their mind?" She recites the pizza order into the phone, gives them the address, hangs up, then screams, "SHIT! I just gave them the address."

Michael quickly thinks and decides. "I'll hide in the laundry room off the kitchen. They will never see me or go back there."

"Yeah, but all of us were splattered on Talk2U today running down the dock. People know we're here in the keys." She pauses. "Come on, sunset is over; let's go back inside." Lucy slaps at her ankles. "Plus no-see-ums are driving me crazy."

"Hey, I got it," Michael excitedly turns to Lucy. "Why don't we just leave the money under a rock on this chair for the pizza delivery person. They'll see it. We'll leave a note to leave the pizza here."

One hour later, Michael and Lucy are eating their pizza while sipping pinot grigio.

He throws one hand in the air and says, "I'm done! No more pizza for me." He falls back onto the couch. "You know what?

We should watch the video of us running for our lives down the dock. I bet it's hysterical. Come on, open up your phone. I don't want to deal with mine quite yet."

Lucy grabs her phone and taps on Talk2U. It's the first image on her page. She gasps, "Wow!" They see a still image of the three of them running on the dock. The view count: 421 million. The caption reads, *Michael Monroe in Key Largo.*

Lucy taps the play button on the sixty-second video. Apparently, the person taking the video was also running, as the video jumps up and down and goes in and out of focus.

As Vanessa, Michael, and Lucy are all running around the building, Whitney's name is on everyone's lips. They approach the long dock. The video continues and they spot the white boat coming in and Vanessa throwing her arms up in desperation. They see a crowd of people chasing them down the dock. Then they see Vanessa throw herself off the dock, followed by Michael and Lucy. They all swim up to Eddy's boat and haul themselves up the ladder. Anchor up, ladder up, and the boat blasts off, leaving a wavy, white, foamy trail. The video stops.

Both Michael and Lucy are speechless. They both slowly turn to look at each other.

Michael says, "I thought that was gonna be hysterical, but it was the complete opposite. I was scared for myself watching that video."

"I don't know what would have happened if Vanessa hadn't done what she did."

Michael instantly thinks of Whitney and how she had to live like that for thirty years, constantly on the run from the media.

Aren't you glad I had you wear your Sperry's today?

"Whitney's here." Michael tries to explain to Lucy what's going on in his mind. He goes into deeper detail.

"Well, I'm happy you're at least listening to Whitney. I don't know, Michael. You said your mom had guilt she didn't raise you correctly. Maybe there's some truth to that." Lucy puts her hands up like she's defending herself. "Not that I'm blaming your mom for anything. She's a beautiful, caring woman. But maybe she was correct when she said she didn't do you justice. Maybe she meant that she didn't teach you life skills or offer you proper decision-making skills. Maybe." Lucy pauses. "But did you ever think that maybe you need to listen to yourself? Maybe you've been struggling because you haven't trusted your own instincts. But look at you now." She grabs him by the shoulders and looks into his hazel eyes. "In less than a week, you've made a complete change. You have two million dollars. You're buying a condo in Key Largo. Did you ever think this could happen? If someone would have told you your future three weeks ago, what would you have said?"

"Absolutely not!" He adamantly shakes his head back and forth.

"With Whitney guiding you, you are unstoppable."

Whitney appears to Michael in a low-cut purple sequined gown. He thinks she might be angry, but she smiles.

I really do like this friend of yours. She's a keeper. But I will say one thing, baby—she points to herself then to Michael—***you and me, we ain't done yet.***

Whitney spins, raises her right hand above her head and snaps her fingers. Purple sparkles shimmer and they fade away after she disappears.

Lucy retires early to get a fresh start for the drive to Key West in the morning while Michael tackles his phone messages. He's scanning area codes. 530, delete. 820, delete. 254, delete. 845, delete. He sees his mother has called numerous times. Charles called like ten times. His anxiety builds as he scrolls, then he stops. He sees Andrew called. He looks at the time of the call. Three thirty.

He thinks that was probably right about the time when they were jumping off the dock. He looks at the time; it's currently ten o'clock. He opts to send him a text.

Hey there! It's been a crazy day. I just saw you called. It's late but I at least wanted to send a response. Going to bed very soon. Heading to Key West tomorrow. 🌴 ☺

Michael continues scanning and deleting phone calls when Andrew responds.

I tied up all my loose ends. I'm free to go.

I can be in the Keys in an hour and a half. 😍 🌴

Michael's heart starts to race. He responds.

I'll wait up.

CHAPTER 30

AFTER TEXTING WITH Andrew, Michael calls his mom.

"Darling, are you okay? I've been so worried. Neither you nor Lucy have responded to our calls. What's going on?"

He explains the day's adventures to her. "I bought a condo, Mom!" he blurts out. "It's beautiful."

"You bought a *condo*?" He hears the excitement in her voice. "Well, that certainly was quite the day. I just laid by the pool and read a Lauren Groff novel."

"Andrew is on his way. We're all going to Key West tomorrow."

"Ooh-la-la," Olivia says. "I do like him very much." He hears his mother take the phone away from her face to speak to Charles, and then she says, "That settles it. We're coming to the Keys, too!"

She pulls the phone away again. When she comes back, she says, "Charles has the company's helicopter. We'll fly into the Key West airport."

Michael laughs. "You do love to make an entrance. Mom, I'm so happy!"

"We can be there by eleven." She pauses. "Happiness is all I've ever wished for you, Michael. Happiness and love. I love you, sweetie."

"I love you too, Mom." Michael chokes and holds back tears. For the first time, he doesn't feel like a disappointment.

Let those feelings go, baby. They don't serve you anymore.

As they hang up, he hears Whitney's voice again. ***I love you too, Michael. Sleep well. I will always be here for you.***

Michael cocks an eyebrow. Whitney usually says, "I am always here with you." He shrugs it off.

Michael's lying in bed when he sees headlights and hears a car's motor and the sound of stones crunching beneath tires. The headlights go off and he hears the car door slam. He quickly jumps up and runs out of the bedroom to the front door. The outdoor motion sensor light flips on and he sees Andrew standing there with a smile and a small gym bag hanging from his beefy shoulder.

"Hey, man!" His beautiful blue eyes and smile shine under the porch light.

Lucy appears out of nowhere.

"What's going on out here?" As she steps out onto the porch. "Oh. My. God . . . Andrew!" She runs down the three steps to the driveway and gives him a big hug even before Michael has the chance.

All of a sudden, they hear another car door slam and a high-pitched voice say, "Hey cuties, I hear there's gonna be a party, and we're going to Key West!"

Christie is looking as adorable as ever, with her bouncy blond hair, pink spaghetti strapped top, and little white go-go shorts.

She grunts as she struggles to roll her suitcase over the stones, practically dragging it along. "This stupid thing is so heavy," she says with a pout. Andrew looks at her as if to say, "You're kidding me, right?" He reaches down, grabs her suitcase with ease, and walks up the three steps to Michael, who is still standing on the porch. He sets Christie's suitcase down on the porch, gives Michael a big hug and kisses him softly right on the lips. He holds Michael's face in his hands, looks right into his hazel eyes, and says, "I've missed you."

"Oooh!" says Lucy.

Michael, taken completely off guard by Andrew's greeting, melts, and any inhibitions he has are gone. Right off the tip of his tongue, he says, "I've missed you too," and he goes in for another small kiss.

Christie interferes. "Are we just gonna stand out here and watch you two love birds kissy-kissy all night long, or are we gonna go inside? Mama needs a drink!" The group laughs. Andrew picks up Christie's suitcase and they all walk inside. Lucy shows Andrew to the third bedroom where Christie will sleep, as Andrew drops her suitcase off.

Walking to the kitchen, Lucy says, "All we have left is white wine."

"I don't care if it's green," Christie says. "Just fill the glass."

Lucy smiles and pours four glasses. "To Key West!" They raise their drinks in unison and clink the glasses together.

Christie takes a sip and announces, "Okay, I'm coming around again. Mama's got her juice." She giggles like a little girl.

Lucy, who only poured herself a quarter of a glass, drinks it down and says, "Okay, this has been fun, but we're leaving tomorrow at six a.m. I suggest everyone drink up and go to bed." She turns and starts walking to her bedroom. "Good night," she says as she waves a hand in the air. She stops, smiles, and turns around to face everyone again. "I'm so excited both of you are here," she says before disappearing behind her bedroom door.

"Well, I had a doozie of a day at the studio," Christie says. "I swear thousands of people are still calling, wanting another séance! The drive was so relaxing and this wine"—she raises her glass—"this wine is gonna put me right to sleep." She turns and heads for her bedroom. "Good night, boys." She runs back and gives Andrew a hug and Michael a kiss on the cheek.

Andrew complains, "Hey, what about me?"

Christie gives him a kiss on his cheek too, then she turns around and closes the door to her room.

Andrew looks at Michael and smiles. "Well, that just leaves us two. Where am I sleeping?"

"Where do you think you're sleeping?" Michael says with a smile.

"I was hoping that, but it wasn't expected."

They walk into Michael's room. Andrew puts his bag down. He looks at the two separate twin beds.

"Here, let's just push these together. I think there's a full-sized blanket in the closet we can use," Michael says. They push the beds together and spread out the full-sized comforter. "There."

Andrew sits down on the bed and starts kicking off his sneakers. He pulls his shirt up over his head and throws it on the ground. He stands up, opens the clasp of his belt, unbuttons and unzips his pants, pushes them down, and steps out of them. He's standing in white Calvin Klein boxer briefs, looking like a young Mark Walberg back when he called himself Marky-Mark. Andrew has a strong, lean body. Michael glances again at his five oriental tattoos running down his rib cage and his colorful tattoo sleeve.

Andrew looks right at Michael with a smirk and says in his deep voice, "I'm a proper lady. This is all you're gonna get tonight. Now get in bed and let's go to sleep."

Michael follows orders. He undresses, shuts the light off, gets under the comforter, and lies on his side with his back toward Andrew.

Andrew rolls over to him, pushes himself right up against Michael's back and puts a hand around his waist. He props himself up on his arm and gives Michael a kiss on the lips. “Good night, baby.”

“Good night.” Michael thinks of Thomas Rhett’s song, “Die A Happy Man” and smiles at its truthful lyrics.

CHAPTER 31

AT FIVE O'CLOCK Lucy is the first awake. She turns the coffee maker on and fumbles around the kitchen for quick, easy breakfast foods to eat before they leave. She spots a chocolate-covered donut and quickly enjoys it with her coffee. The plan is to stop at Midway Café in Islamorada for breakfast on the road.

Surprisingly, Andrew is up next. He walks into the kitchen with just gray joggers on. "I thought I heard someone rattling around in here."

"I'm sorry to wake you." She sees Andrew and smiles bashfully. Lucy makes a comment, "Not much left to the imagination in those gray joggers you got on there, Michael is one lucky guy!" She nods her head toward his crotch and laughs.

"Wasn't expecting anyone to be in here." He waves his hand and reaches for a coffee cup that she put on the counter. He takes a sip and sighs. "I'll go wake up Sleeping Beauty."

Lucy quickly asks, "Which one?" They both laugh.

"Touché. I guess both." He walks out of the kitchen and into Christie's room first.

Lucy hears a long "Wwwhhhhyyyyyy?" coming from the other room. Moments later, Christie is standing in the kitchen.

Lucy is surprised by how attractive she is, even fresh out of bed. Christie too has on gray jogging pants and yet a different pink tank top. Her blond hair is tied up in a scrunchie.

"Coffee?" Lucy asks.

"Pleeeeease!"

Andrew wanders back into Michael's bedroom, sits on Michael's side of the bed, bends down, and gently kisses him awake.

"Wow, I could get used to this," Michael says as he stretches his arms above his head, his eyes barely open. He quickly grabs Andrew around the waist and pulls him back in bed alongside him.

Andrew wiggles and starts to complain. "Ouch!"

Michael stops immediately. "You okay?"

"Yeah," Andrew says smiling. "Something was poking me." He looks with flirty eyes and a smile as Michael blushes. "Come on, put that thing away and get up." He presses his hand on Michael's head and shakes it a little in a playful way. "You don't want to make Lucy mad." Andrew pauses and looks at Michael as if he's about to ask him a question. But instead he just shakes his head and stands up.

"Hey," Michael pulls him back down, "What happened? What's up?"

Andrew gets a little serious, looks at Michael and says, "How can someone like you be single?" He pauses and looks away to avoid eye contact. "Your mom is the Double D's lady; she's known throughout the world." He lifts his hands and shrugs his shoulders. "You must have men throwing themselves at you."

"Andrew," Michael looks right at him. "I feel the same way about you. I mean look at you." He waves his hands up and down at Andrew's handsome face and muscular body. "I think to myself, 'How can this guy be single?' But even worse," Michael now points to himself, "I think, 'How can he really like *this*?'"

Andrew gets even more serious, and he lies back down next to

Michael and gently kisses him on the lips. "I really like you." He smiles a beautiful smile and stares at Michael with his beautiful blue eyes. Andrew then quickly jumps right up and makes the air in the room playful again. "Come on, get up. I'll make your coffee. How do you like it?"

"Light and sweet, just like you." Michael smiles as Andrew leaves the room.

Everyone showers and Lucy tells them her plan to stop at Midway for a fast breakfast. They pile into the Jeep right at six thirty. The two girls are in front, and the boys are in the back. They arrive at Midway minutes before it opens, which gives them a moment to think of a place to have lunch when they arrive in Key West.

"I've always liked Pepe's," Andrew suggests. "Especially eating outside under their enclosed porch. It's a nice rustic old place with lots of Key West charm."

Christie googles it really fast. "Oh, honey, that looks like a great place! Oooh, look at all the kitties!"

The *OPEN* sign inside Midway turns on, and only Andrew and Christie go in. They order egg sandwiches for all four of them and more coffee for the road.

Back in the Jeep, they take off, but Lucy quickly pulls over to the right shoulder near a bridge across from a marina called Bud N' Mary's. She shuts the motor off. "Let's watch the sunrise." The slowly rising sun is a glowing orange ball as it rises up from below the fiery horizon. A few minutes later, all the colors fade away, leaving the sun looking like a white sphere, while enhancing all the white clouds in the sky.

Andrew comments, "Did you see the sun change colors? It's called scattering. I've read that when the sun is low, either at sunrise or sunset, it changes colors from an orange to the white we're seeing now. The earth's atmosphere scatters the blue light. This changes the color of the sun at both sunrise and sunset. Pretty neat, huh?"

Lucy starts the motor back up and yells out, "Eighty miles to go! Let's make a stop at Bahia Honda. It's a gorgeous beach. I love walking up that bridge that just ends. I believe that's where they filmed that scene in the Arnold Schwarzenegger movie *True Lies* with Jamie Lee Curtis."

The wind is blowing Lucy's hair all over. She looks in the rearview mirror at Andrew and asks, "Do you come to the Keys a lot? You mentioned your tattoo being inspired by the Keys."

He yells over the wind, "Yes and no." He shakes his head. "I love the Keys. Problem is, they're very expensive to live on unless you share with a roommate. I would love to have a property down here at some point. It's a dream of mine."

Lucy doesn't say anything and just smiles at Michael in the rearview mirror. He blushes and smiles back. Andrew doesn't notice.

They're climbing another bridge and there's nothing but turquoise water that meets the bright blue sky. Scattered palm trees on islands make for the most beautiful landscape.

"Here we are! Mile marker fifty-nine, the start of Marathon." She throws a hand in the air with a "Whoop-whoop!"

Andrew looks at Michael and bumps him with his shoulder. He smiles at him as he slides his hand under Michael's hand and entwines their fingers. He gives Michael's hand a couple of quick squeezes. He smiles again. Michael smiles and squeezes back.

Lucy yells out, "Mile marker forty-seven. There's a restaurant on the left, Sunset Grill, that I've seen all over social media. Looks like a great place for dinner and sunset. It's right at the beginning of Seven Mile Bridge." She pauses, "I've also read that this is one of the longest bridges in the world." They're all taking in the beautiful sites of boundless magnificent blue water as they cruise over the bridge. The newly renovated old highway is on their right, now a walking and biking path. They look down at Pigeon Key and just after it, they see there's a gap in the old highway so people can't drive vehicles on it. They hit mile marker 44 and start the climb of the hump in the bridge that brings the bridge up to sixty-five feet above the water, allowing bigger boats and ships to sail under. This creates more excitement for the drive, being higher above the water and able to see even more sky and water in all its breathtaking beauty.

Christie yells out, "Sky, wind, water, four new friends, and a Jeep—makes for a great selfie." She stands up in the Jeep, holds the camera high and snaps a picture of the four of them just as they're cresting and starting to descend.

Christie is still busy taking pictures as Lucy spies on the boys in the back. They seem to be in their own little world. Smiling, quietly talking, and getting to know each other a little better.

Soon, Lucy slows down and starts to turn left. "We're here. She pays at the Bahia Honda park booth and parks the Jeep near the visitor's center. "It's eight thirty now; how about we meet back here at the Jeep in an hour?"

They all roam about the park together. It's still early, so not many people are there yet. Lucy is wearing her big hat and sunglasses, while Michael has his baseball cap pulled right down to his sunglasses. They start walking up the pedestrian bridge until they are met with a steel railing not permitting them to go any further, but it still makes a great spot for photo ops. Right below them are the white sandy beaches, the different shades of water from sandy clear to an emerald green and then turquoise blue. The grounds are spotted with green mangroves and lots of palm trees. On either side they look, they can see the bubbly champagne shores. The sun is rising higher in the sky and the heat and humidity are also turning up—it feels about eighty-five degrees. They swing back around and walk through the very small butterfly garden and take a little walk around the white sandy beaches.

With the bridge in the background, standing on the sandy white beach with the palm trees, turquoise water, and blue sky makes for an amazing picture. Lucy gathers everyone together for a group photo and sets the ten-second timer on her phone camera. She runs back in place and the camera snaps a brilliant picture of the four of them all smiling frozen in one space of time. Lucy looks at the photo. She's got her hand on her head, holding her hat from blowing away in the breeze. Michael is beaming, with Andrew standing slightly behind him, smirking with his colorful tattooed arm around Michael's shoulder. And Christie is just being fabulous Christie next to Andrew.

Hopping back into the Jeep, they continue heading south. Andrew yells from the back with one hand in the air, "This is the last bridge we cross before Key West!" They all high-five.

Seeing the colorful welcome sign that welcomes them to Key West, Lucy turns right at Roosevelt Boulevard. She finally finds a parking lot between Duval and Caroline. She puts the Jeep in park, shuts off the motor, and yells out, "Key West, baby!" She gets out of the Jeep and stretches. It's sunny and beautiful. The temperature, now approaching eighty-eight degrees, is forecasted to climb into the nineties by midday. The other three get out groaning and stretching their arms high into the air.

Christie has the energy of a cheerleader. "I want a picture at the southernmost buoy and the Mile Marker Zero sign!" She smiles and does her best cheerleader "Rah" as she throws both her arms in the air and kicks her leg up.

"Okay, first stop, Mile Marker Zero," Andrew says with a macho smile. Then, in a confident voice, he points. "This way." They walk down Caroline Street for a few minutes and make a left onto Whitehead. Eventually they get to Fleming and see the green mile marker sign.

Christie starts skipping and twirling like a ballerina. She's just an excited, happy lady who runs to stand next to the sign. She tosses her phone to Andrew so he can snap some pictures of her. She calls everyone over to join her and Andrew flips the screen around to snap a selfie of all of them.

They continue down Whitehead, walking past Hemingway's House and there in sight is the big red and black southernmost buoy. Christie is bouncing and bobbing like the Energizer Bunny. There's a small line for photos, so they have to wait behind a few other people. As they're standing, they hear a noise that sounds like a low-flying plane.

It gets louder and they hear the *chuf-chuf-chuf-chuf-chuf* of a propeller. They notice everyone looking up in the sky. That's when they see the big white CBN helicopter flying over them. Everyone around them is pointing up at the helicopter. Michael smiles and starts waving. He yells to Andrew and Christie that that's his mom and Charles. Lucy and Christie are jumping up and down, waving their arms. Andrew, who remains calm, coolly puts one arm up in the air and gives a big wave. Michael pulls out his phone and texts his mother.

We're below you. Waving from the buoy.

The chopper spins around and gets a little lower. *Chuf-chuf-chuf-chuf-chuf.* Olivia texts back.

I see you- xoxo!

They can just make out Olivia waving to them before the chopper speeds off and heads toward the airport.

They finally get their turn at the buoy. Christie gets her solo picture and Andrew takes another selfie of the group when they notice they aren't alone anymore. Hundreds of people are now surrounding them and hundreds more are seen running toward them at the buoy. People are getting right up next to Michael and taking selfies. They're pulling and shoving at him to get their turn for a picture. A large crowd of people are swiftly approaching, pushing others to get closer. The scene is getting out of control fast. High-pitched soprano screams of Michael's name are heard as well as low baritone voices from every direction. Andrew won't let Michael go. Christie holds on to Lucy, and Lucy has her arm locked with Michael. The four of them are swaying, losing their balance but they stay standing as the crowds aggressively push at them. The scene has now become an explosive mob. Thousands of tourists have gathered for the chance to meet Michael Monroe.

The crowd just keeps getting thicker and more out of control, so nobody registers that the CBN helicopter has returned until its shadow is above the crowd and the wind from the blades has everyone backing up as it quickly descends and abruptly lands in the middle of the crowd. Two large muscular men in black uniforms, sunglasses, and baseball caps explode out of the helicopter and grab Michael and the other three, pushing them quickly into the chopper. Within seconds they lift off the ground, getting higher and higher, as Michael looks down and sees thousands of people surrounding a little red buoy that gets smaller and smaller until it's out of site.

The chopper drops them off at a helipad in Truman Annex, where Charles has a condo. On Olivia's suggestion, the six of them agree to take the short walk for lunch at Blue Heaven. After what just happened at the buoy, Michael feels hesitant to go out anywhere but agrees only if the two security men go with them. The security men change into civilian clothes so they don't stand out as much and they leave with Michael and his group while

Olivia and Charles stay behind to address a few last-minute phone calls and emails.

Not having been followed, they arrive and enter through the big blue iron gates of Blue Heaven. They decide to sit outside at two small round tables that they pull together. Michael sees a big floppy straw hat coming through the restaurant and heading toward him. He smiles, knowing it's his mother. She's wearing a teal silk sleeveless shirt, long flowing white skirt, and sparkly sandals and holds a Gucci floral clutch in one hand.

Olivia is jaw-dropping. She looks like she walked right out of *Vogue*. She pulls her hat off and Michael notices she has a new haircut. It's short on the sides and in the back with long bangs hanging toward her right front. Her hair is dyed a stunning silver pink. She runs her fingers through her hair, puffing it up a bit.

"Ta-daaaa!" she says and strikes a pose. Her thirty-karat Double D's are positioned on a gold chain front and center.

Charles comes around her in his Burberry shorts, button-down white linen shirt, and tan leather loafers with a big bulky gold-and-diamond watch on his wrist. He's right beside her proudly smiling, raising a pointed finger, as if inviting everyone to check out this magnificent woman.

Michael walks over to her and gives her a big hug. They embrace for a moment.

She looks at Michael and says, "You're the love of my life."

Michael tears up but manages to smile.

"I love you too, Mom. I love the hair."

Olivia kisses Lucy on the cheek, then Christie, but she stops and stares at Andrew. Her eyes are now squinted, which only accentuates her light beige eye shadow. Judging from the slight frown on her face, she's formulating a critique.

Michael watches Andrew as his body gets a little tense anticipating what Olivia will say. The scent of Olivia's Coco Chanel floats through the air. Olivia lifts her big straw hat and shoves it on Andrew's head. "There . . . that's what was missing." Andrew smiles and sighs as his body relaxes.

Olivia says to him, "You get a kiss too, darling." She adjusts the floppy hat so it sits a little sideways on his head and she kisses him on the cheek. Charles and Olivia sit down and ask the servers for two more chairs. The group looks a little confused until they see Ivy and Ester walk through the restaurant.

Michael jumps up. "Madame Pearl!" He gives her a big hug and hugs Ester, too.

"Your mom told us they were taking the helicopter down here to see you. We've never been on a helicopter or seen Key West, so we said, 'What the heck?'" She giggles. "Here we are. But I'm not doing a séance!" She glares and points her finger at Charles and smiles. "But you're not going to believe this." She grabs her phone from her purse, taps it a few times, and turns the phone around to show everyone an article in the *Miami Herald*. The headline reads: "Psychic Cracks Cold Case Murder." She brightly smiles as Michael quickly reads the article.

"So the FBI found you. I kind of knew they would. They scared the shit out of me that night."

"I bet they did! Well, this old psychic's antenna can still do the job."

The restaurant is getting busier when they realize that all the security men are standing on high alert as people are noticing them, snapping pictures and making videos.

They all get up and start to leave, and several people stop them for pictures. Some just want Michael; some want just Olivia or Olivia and Michael while others are happy with the whole group. They agree to a few photos.

The security men finally break them free from the crowd and they leave. Michael, Lucy, Andrew, and Christie start to walk away but Olivia yells to them, "We've got the limo, come ride with us." Michael shakes his head. *Of course you have a limo,* he thinks.

Ester speaks up, "I think we—Ivy and I—would just like to walk around on our own. Get a feel for this crazy coral rock of an island. What's the slogan here? *Key West, where the weird go pro.*" She laughs at the statement.

Lucy responds, "Okay ladies, go have a great afternoon. But remember to be back at Mallory Square for the Sunset Celebration."

Christie chimes in. "I really just wanted to see the buoy and the mile marker sign. I'm happy anywhere else we go." As she finishes, she throws her arms up in the air and twirls like a ballerina again.

The group has tried to be inconspicuous, but it's hard when they are flanked by two beefy security men, and everyone recognizes Olivia, Charles, and Michael.

As they're walking down the sidewalk, people yell out "Yo, Michael! Where's Whitney?" Or they offer high-fives. Most, of course, want their picture with him, but the security guards keep most back. Michael walks hand in hand with Andrew.

They stop at Bourbon Street Bar, a gay bar. Michael and the girls take stools at the bar while Andrew, Charles, and the meaty security men stand behind them.

The bartender notices them and says, "Holy Mother Mary! I need a picture." He grabs his phone and snaps one of the group. He quickly serves them.

Charles is getting lots of attention—gay men just adore older wealthy men. A drag queen comes up to him. She's about four inches taller than Charles; her big, blond wig makes her almost a foot taller. She's dressed in a shiny hot pink sequined gown, with eye makeup to her hairline and overdrawn pink lips.

She touches Olivia's arm and says in her deep, scratchy Harvey Fierstein baritone voice, "Oh honey, when you're done with him, send him my way. I just love my men handsome, distinguished, and rich!" She blows Charles a kiss and "accidentally" slides her hand over his rear as he clenches. But Charles shrugs it off; he's accustomed to gay men flirting with him.

Charles boldly yells, "Yeah, well, I'm keeping that ring from your finger that went up my ass," he shouts with a smile.

The drag queen struts away with a little extra swish in her walk laughing a deep belly laugh and yells back over her shoulder. "It's all yours, honey!" She blows him a kiss.

Next, they stop inside Jimmy Buffet's Margaritaville. They all buy a few trinkets. Olivia spots a fedora that's the same color as the sand on South Beach with a black ribbon around it. She puts it on Charles and says, "I love it."

They leave and continue down Duval, passing several bars, tattoo parlors, and lots of souvenir shops. They enter several art galleries; Olivia purchases a painting and makes arrangements for it to be shipped back to New York, while Michael buys one for his new condo. They pass a couple of restaurants with outside dining and musicians playing reggae steel drum music before they come to Sloppy Joe's. They stop for frozen strawberry daiquiris. It's like a storm of people wherever they go—voices scream for pictures from every direction as the bodyguards keep pushing them away.

Lucy looks at her phone. "It's almost six and Mallory Square is going to get packed. I think we should head over now. I want to be in the front row for sunset."

Charles chimes in. "Good idea—time to get out of here. They'll have food and drink vendors there. There's also that restaurant right by the square where we can sit in peace and wait."

Lucy smiles as she looks at Charles in his new Cuban-influenced fedora. "That hat looks great on you."

Olivia smiles at Charles and says, "Yes, he wears the hat rather well."

He smiles at her and gives her a soft, fast kiss on the lips.

"*Ooohhh,*" Michael and Lucy poke fun at Olivia and Charles

kissing.

They're now strolling through a narrow cobblestone alleyway, passing several open-air bars with circulating ceiling fans, hearing the acoustic hum of the excited vacationing visitors echoing from bars singing along to Kenny Chesney songs. The alleyway brings them to the steel-arched entrance sign of the famous nightly sunset celebration and arts festival known as Mallory Square.

As they enter the mystique of the brick promenade, locals and tourists are already milling around, going in and out of the novelty island tiki shacks, purchasing T-shirts, balloons, and other touristy trinkets. The aromatic scents of the Cuban cigar kiosk catch Charles's attention. The Cuban merchant is rolling an herbal and spicy-scented cigar—tobacco with flavors of black cherry, cloves, and coffee—and the scent carries through the air. Charles buys a dozen.

They see a street performer set up with several people already crowding them. Past the planters of swaying palms, they realize the person at the table is Ivy, reading tarot cards. She nods and gives them a smile.

Michael's excited for her. "They're gonna get a good reading. We should go over when she's finishing up and boast a little for her. We can get her more attention and customers."

Christie chimes in. "I wanna have my tarot cards read!"

Andrew smiles, nudges her a little and says, "Well, go up there and be next in line before the crowds get here."

Olivia cuts in and says, "It would be wonderful to hear what she has to say about you, darling. I think you should do it." She gives Christie an approving nod.

"Well, if she's anything like she was back at the studio

when my father showed up, she is gonna give you one heck of a reading." Charles smiles and also prompts her to go do it.

Michael yells out, "I dare you!"

Christie takes all of them up on it and she walks over to Ivy and stands in line.

Michael walks away from the pack and steps closer to the water. He's feeling somber and just melancholy that he hasn't heard from Whitney all day. And like running into a thick brick wall, the truth hits him hard. She's gone.

Michael instantly stops. The truth freezes him in place. He can't even think to put one foot in front of the other and just walk.

He's devastated, but he realizes that she's done her work. She helped fix his life. He's made money, he's found Andrew, he's even bought his very own condo in Key Largo. Joey, the owner of Fate called and left a message, saying there's a job waiting for him back in New York when he gets home. And now he knows he'll figure out a way to make his dream of owning a restaurant happen one day because he believes he will.

He thinks about all that has happened in such a short amount of time. Still frozen in place, he lifts his head and smiles up at the sky as if looking, begging for Whitney. He grasps the key she helped him find and remembers his ten years of confusion, dysfunction, and chaos that has exponentially changed so quickly.

He thinks of how messy his life was just two weeks ago and sends a silent plea to Whitney. *Please, Whitney, come back. I can't keep doing this without you.* He cups both his hands together in a mercy offering and tries to hold back tears, but they come anyway. His body trembles and his shoulders droop.

Andrew walks up behind him and puts his arms around his waist. He holds Michael and gives him a big squeeze. "Hey, man, you okay?" Michael doesn't answer. He just sobs.

Michael, with tears rolling down his face, slowly turns his head to look at Andrew with his heartbroken, bloodshot eyes. He looks deep into Andrew's blue eyes and gives him a soft kiss on the side of his lips and says, "Yeah, I'm good, but she's gone. Whitney's gone." He starts inhaling and exhaling really fast, catching his breath. There's silence for a few moments as they just stand and stare at the water. "And I"—he coughs at an itch in the back of his throat—"well, I miss her already . . . I'm happy—I'm truly grateful—but I'm really sad and I wish I could've said goodbye."

More tears roll down Michael's face, but now he now starts to laugh. Michael's body shakes as he cries and laughs at the same time. Andrew just squeezes him tighter, but his loving embrace only makes Michael quiver more.

As the rest of them see Andrew and Michael, they decide to give them some space. There's an instinctual sense of understanding about what's happening. Whitney has fulfilled her mission. They wait a few minutes before they all walk up to Michael and Andrew. Olivia doesn't say anything; she just hugs Michael.

"Michael, darling, if I could take away all your pain, I would. What has you so upset?"

"Mom, I'm really sad, but yet I'm also crying because I'm happy." More tears roll down his face. "Whitney is, well . . . gone. She's done." He inhales a deep breath. "But I don't think she would want me or us to grieve." He takes several deep breaths and blows them out with force. "She would want us to celebrate. And dammit, we're in Key West and it's almost sunset and that's what we're gonna do!"

The group squeezes into a tight huddle. They hug, cry, and laugh as Michael lifts his right hand high up into the falling sunset display and says, "Here's to Whitney and Key West!"

Charles adds, "Now let's get some drinks before we all shrivel up."

Crowds of people are now flowing onto the pier for the sunset celebration as the nightly street performers are already performing their acts. There are tightrope walkers, jugglers throwing fire, dogs leaping through obstacles, and even sword swallowers. Each performer stands inside a circle as bystanders gather around to watch and throw gratuities in the performer's tip cups.

Charles comes back with sangrias for everyone. Lucy pulls out her phone and captures a picture of the toast as the sun begins to set.

Soon, groups of people notice Michael and start clamoring for a picture with him. The crowd is becoming anxious and aggressive, all cramming around Michael for a picture or a video. The beefy security men have their arms up keeping people at a distance. Michael hears the screams of his name being yelled in every direction. The two security men are no match for so many people as they close in around him. Michael starts to feel dizzy, almost faint from all the commotion and the screaming. Someone comes up from behind Michael, grabs hold of his waist, and starts pushing him away from Andrew and the security men.

Michael quickly vanishes from view as he's swallowed deep into the thick crowd. Fear overcomes him as he's pushed through walls of people. He can't look back to see who's pushing him for fear of tripping or falling to the ground and being trampled by the crazed crowd. He's being pushed faster and further past the blurs of all the faces. But still people are trying to grab at him. Cameras flash everywhere like throbbing strobe lights. The flashing lights only disorient him even more as he goes deeper into the crowd.

CHAPTER 32

ANDREW, LUCY, AND Christie keep pushing as they shove through the crowds to find Michael. Charles grabs Olivia's hand and he confidently leads her through. But nobody can see Michael. He's vanished.

The three of them are all screaming his name but having no luck fighting through the crowds. Charles spots Andrew and is able to make his way over with Olivia. The security men have also lost sight of Michael. Olivia is distraught. She's screaming Michael's name. Dozens of street performers are still performing, which only makes the crowds worse and even thicker.

Hundreds of tiki torches are burning and it feels like a Mardi Gras carnival. There are belly dancers shaking their beaded outfits and snapping their finger cymbals, clowns carrying balloons, ballerinas spinning and jesters twirling sparklers. Men juggle flames and swords are skillfully swallowed. Dogs climb up ladders and cats jump through hoops doing tricks.

The sun is minutes away from touching the water when Andrew finally spots Michael. He screams, "MICHAEL!!" but Michael doesn't seem to see or hear him. They all push through the crowds to get to him. They finally get close enough to Michael but yet they still can't get near him. The aggressive crowd is belligerent and eager to get what they want. And their sights are set on Michael.

Andrew sees that it was Ester who grabbed Michael and pushed him away. It seems like she's pushing Michael into the center of a circle of people that are gathering around him snapping pictures.

As the crowd screams his name, millions of tiny, sparkling lights appear and circle around Michael. They're brighter than the sun and blinding. The lights flicker, sparkle, and shimmer as they're swirling. The lights begin to congeal and form a translucent orb. The orb begins to loosely form a shape. A blurred figure starts to appear, constantly moving, solid yet transparent.

Andrew finally breaks through the crowd, along with the security men. Lucy and Christie are next, followed by Charles and Olivia. They complete a circle around Michael.

The sparkling lights swirling around Michael finally stop moving. They just seem to be floating in place in front of him, shimmering, when Whitney appears. The crowd gasps and grows completely silent.

"I've come to say my goodbye." She stares at Michael with immense love. "May I have this dance before the sun sets? I wanna dance with somebody," she pauses, adding a loving smile "and with somebody who loves me." She fully materializes, smiling widely. She holds her hand up as she motions with a sway of her arm and golden sparks of light flash around her. As she moves, thousands of sparkling lights follow her.

She wraps her arm around Michael's shoulder. The glittering lights sparkle and swirl, blur and fade, yet come back with solid brilliant color. The lights continuously follow her movements as she and Michael slowly waltz in the middle of what feels like thousands of people.

Whitney looks at Michael and says, "You never needed me baby."

They keep spinning and twirling.

“How can you say that? You changed my life.”

"I didn’t do anything."

The glowing orange sun is now starting to meet the ocean.

“You gave me everything I didn’t have.” Tears start streaming down his cheeks.

"No, Michael, I didn’t." Whitney stops dancing for a moment. "You, baby, you are the one who acted. You manifested your dreams through your desires, thoughts, and emotions. I did nothing but cheer you on."

“You made me love myself.” He pulls her tighter as they dance. “I would not be here right now if it weren’t for you.”

"Ummm, yes, you would." She laughs.

“It’s not possible for me to be here without you.”

"Anything is possible, Michael! You met Him at the water two nights ago, and He told you as he hugged you in his arms, He said, ‘I am always with you.’ That’s how everything is possible."

“So that was real?”

"More real than you can ever imagine. All those dreams you had—the treasure chest, Vince Lombardi, your dad with the sword. That sword dream was the day you started leaving the old you behind."

Michael looks at her, confused. “How is that possible? In that dream, my dad was trying to kill me. I was so scared.”

"Michael, look at me." She stares directly into his hazel eyes, red-rimmed and puffy from crying. "Your father was not fighting against you." She looks even deeper into his hazel blur. "He was fighting for you. The swings of his sword slashed your old thoughts. All your negative thinking, your demons, and old habits all had to go so new thoughts would be free to shine through."

Michael breaks down sobbing. “My father!” He grabs onto

Whitney with all of his might and cries into her. His tears make her sparkling lights explode. They sear and hiss, vaporizing into clouds of smoke. His tears seem to start dissolving Whitney. The sun is now just a sliver of yellow above the water.

"Michael, your father is so proud of you. He loves you no matter who you are or who you love or whether you're rich or poor. Learn to let go." She stops dancing and looks into his eyes one last time. "That goes for me too. It's my time, baby. But our friend, Madame Pearl. Well, she has one last gift for you, from me."

As the last of the sunlight disappears below the water, so does Whitney, but Michael can still hear her. Her big, bold, beautiful voice seems to echo across the ocean. ***Oh, and Michael . . . I will always love you.***

"Whitney!" Michael shouts. "Noooo! Don't go!" Michael spins in the center of the circle by himself. His arms are open wide, and he stares up in to the sky, searching for any sign of Whitney. He grabs for her, wanting one last laugh, one more anything, but nothing comes. The crowd begins to scream and cheer.

His spinning slows as he becomes aware again of the thousands of people gathered around. Still disoriented, he finally focuses on his mother, Lucy, and Andrew.

He feels a tug on his sleeve and turns to find Ester beside him. "Would you like to hear Whitney's last message?" she asks.

Yes, please, yes! Michael nods, allowing Ester and the security men to lead him out of the circle as he wipes away his tears.

The sun has now set, but the beautiful streaks of tied-dyed oranges and reds reflect off the water. Darkness is coming. The crowds are starting to depart. Ester leads Michael to Ivy's table and gestures for him to sit. Michael's mother and friends follow protectively and anxiously surround them.

"First," Ivy says and then pauses. "Thank you all for coming into my life." Michael sees tears welling in her eyes. "These last few days—well, they have been nothing short of a miracle. I have been very blessed to be able to come along on this journey." She collects herself and looks at Michael. "Dearest Michael, Whitney has one last little trick up her sleeve."

Olivia swats at Madame Pearl with her Gucci clutch. "I can't take it anymore! Just spit it out!" She catches the arm of a passing server. "We'll take eight of those key lime margaritas!"

Charles buys and they make a quick toast. The cups slosh together, and they take a swig.

"Okay, Madame Pearl," Olivia says. "No more nonsense. Just tell us."

She points to Michael's pocket. "There's a ticket in your wallet—a lottery ticket." She takes a folded copy of the *New York Post* from her lap and lays it on the table. She points to the headline: "Unclaimed Winning Lottery Ticket for Seven Million Dollars Sold in Manhattan." She looks up at Michael. "And you've been holding it this whole time."

Michael's face grows hot, and he feels faint. Forgetting he's holding the drink, he throws his arms in the air and it splashes everywhere.

He hollers, "Oh, my god, yes!" He grabs and hugs Andrew and kisses him hard on the lips over and over. He turns to hug his mom as they all come in for a group hug. Finally, he spreads his arms wide open and looks up into the night sky. He yells out, "Thank you, Whitney, thank you for everything! I will always love you!"

Michael hears in his mind, ***I didn't do anything,*** with her big, roaring laugh. ***Michael, my love, how will I know that you'll always love me?***

Michael screams back to the nighttime sky, "Because I get so emotional, Whitney!"

CHAPTER 33

NINE MONTHS LATER, Michael looks around his restaurant. After purchasing Fate a few months earlier, he has transformed it into exactly what Michael had dreamed of. He created it according to the inspiration from his vision board, which still hangs above his desk at home.

Advertisements have been taken out in the *New York Times* and other local papers, thanks to Lucy.

All the employees have agreed to stay on and continue their employment with Michael. And they were all given bonuses while the restaurant was being transformed. He even gave them raises when they returned to work.

Plus there's Michael's newfound reporter friend Kari Daniels from WTEN New York. She's the one he had liked so much from dealing with the séance interviews. The news team has agreed to have him come on the show for a live interview, and the news station has agreed they will be airing live on the first day his restaurant, Hello, Dolly, formally opens, which is next week.

The unpredictable young server Jane, who always showed up late, has been replaced by a handsome new server named Andrew.

Olivia couldn't possibly be seen in any of her old clothes for her new job as hostess, so she went shopping.

And lastly, the trailer has been released for a new upcoming cold-case thriller, *Whatever Happened to Betty Jane?* It's hitting theaters in three weeks.

I've got some good saints out there—that's right—
that pray for me constantly.
You've gotta have that!

—Whitney Elizabeth Houston

ACKNOWLEDGMENTS

HOW DO I put all of this into words—the thank yous? I'll start at the beginning with Whitney Elizabeth Houston. Without you there is no book or title or guardian angel in beautiful sequined gowns appearing and disappearing. Thank you, Whitney, for sharing your gift and your life with us.

Thanks also go to my family, who supported this project when it was just another crazy idea of mine.

And, of course, I must thank my husband, Greg, who always encourages me to follow my dreams.

The first person to cross my path after I started writing was Weston Middleton. Thank you for offering me guidance and telling me "First things first—hire a good copyright lawyer."

That brings me to Paul Rapp, Esq. Thank you for all of your legal research and telling me it was okay to move forward with *How Will I Know* using Whitney Houston as a guardian angel.

Kelly Weaver, my soul survivor, you kept saying, "Come on, Whitney." Thank you for encouraging me to keep moving forward.

Then along came Mandy Miller, a lawyer, editor, runner, and lover of the Florida Keys. She was the first to look at my manuscript and say, "It's a great idea but you really need to hire an editor. Your first chapter is all wrong and here's how to fix it." Thank you for that.

Robin Catalino, you took my mess of a manuscript, under the advice of Mandy Miller, and reconstruction began. I am forever grateful.

Rejection after rejection followed until Koehler Books said, "We want your manuscript. We like the idea, and we see promise, but it still needs significant tightening—an aggressive line-by-line scrubbing. Oh, and the format is a mess as well." (These are the actual words!) They ended by telling me my book needed heavy lifting to polish it up to professional standards.

Suzanne Bradshaw, thank you for the cover design.

Becky Hilliker—my editor—you have a gift! What you did to this manuscript is incredible. You made my words pop, and my thoughts come to life. You got into my mind, asked yourself *Where is he going with this?* and then you went for it! You understood me and my crazy dyslexic mind.

Thank you, Becky! Xoxo.

To everyone else who will come after this book is published, thank you.

Patricia Wood, thank you for your kindness and friendship.

This book is based on true life events. Realism-Fiction. And I'll give you some hints. My father did sell precious metals (gold, silver) and diamonds when I was young. Olivia is based on my Grandmother Booream, who always loved to dress up and wear big, bulky jewelry. Lucy is my bestie, Traci. All the dreams in this book were mine over the years—the car on the ocean and the treasure chest, my dad swinging the swords, Vince Lombardi saying, "That's your problem—you don't believe you can have all of this," God at the water with the wind—that's all me. It really did happen. And lastly, in November 2012, a voice popped into my mind. *Write a book, call it* How Will I Know *and use Whitney Houston as a guardian angel.* Thank you, Whitney.

When I completed the book and got stuck and couldn't go any further, you told me, "You know what to do." And you were right. I hope I have honored you.

Love, Marc.

Printed in the USA
CPSIA information can be obtained
at www.ICGtesting.com
JSHW080027280324
59998JS00005B/16

9 798888 242742